For The Love of Grace

Andy Blackman

Clink
Street

London | New York

Published by Clink Street Publishing 2016

Copyright © 2016

First edition.

ISBN - Paperback: 978-1-911110-53-8

ISBN - eBook: 978-1-911110-54-5

Dedicated To:
The Wolf Pack
(Encouragement comes in many ways)

Acknowledgements

This book of course is a work of fiction, the places are real, but that is where the similarities ends, everything else came from me, apart from a little help from the internet, which in this day and age is our friend, it came from me is a strange statement to write, for I know I am not special, I was born in a council house went to a comprehensive school, was never a gifted child and did not achieved anything of note before I left school at 16, but since I left school my education started, I have heard the phrase "school days are the best days of your life", well I am sure who ever said that never went to my school, and it was only after I left school my education started. Which bring me onto my book, I have always been an avid book reader, I can remember at work one day during lunchtime thinking of the awful book I had just finished the previous evening, when the thought popped into my head why not write one yourself, this idea I thought stupid, me a common man writing a book, surely authors are people that have been to university and have a degree in literature and understand writing techniques, I am just a normal man, then a vision popped into my head of an old teacher, I had not thought of for well over forty years, and clearly as the sun was shining I remembered what he told us one day in class, he said "the only thing holding you back from achieving great things is yourself". As these word filled my mind all doubt left me and I knew I would try and write a book.

As you may have seen the book is dedicated to the Wolf Pack, which no doubt some will wonder and think it was a strange dedication, well let me explain and all will become clear. I used to share an office with four other people, all different jobs all different personalities, and not a lot in common apart from all having a sense of humour who enjoyed banter, if one of us said something funny or daft them the others would make fun of them for ages until the next incident and it was someone else's turn, I of course had my fare share of being on the end of the others banter, one day we decided we were like a Wolf Pack always turning on the weakest member, and the name stuck. And in the early stages of writing the book, they were all in their individual ways invaluable for inspiration and guidance. Sadly as in all thing it was not to last, and we were disbanded and our old office taken over and we were scattered throughout the building, but for a period of time we were the Wolf Pack, who were the Wolf Pack, I know it will give them a great sense of enjoyment to see their names in print so, Thank you the Wolf Pack, Ann Marriott, Richard Hackett, Matthew Harvey and James O'hara, once again as I said in my dedication "encouragement comes in many ways".

So here it is my first book, I hope you enjoyed reading it as much as I enjoyed writing it, I set out to write the book to see if I could, but like a child I have nurtured it until it became the book it is today, and I must admit I am proud of my creation. The characters are traits of people I have know, but not based on any one individual, the plot I hope you enjoyed and even that changed throughout the writing process, but the central theme remains the same and John Lennon said it best "all you need is Love".

Once again thank you for reading.

Andy Blackman

The Return

As the wheels finally touched down at Heathrow International Airport, Flight BA12 from Washington was starting to become alive. The weather was clear for a mid-October morning. As the plane taxied to the arrival point, people on the plane started to move and collect their belongings; slowly Tom opened his eyes, but did not move. It always amazed him that people rushed to exit an aircraft – not like they were going anywhere fast, then rushing off to the baggage collection point where nine times out of ten the bags would never appear before the passengers. It was a tradition all over the world, and Tom had been to most airports around the world; never were the bags out before the passengers. But, he guessed, people live in hope – it was what sometimes drove them.

Eventually a tap on the shoulder brought him awake, not that he had been asleep. He had sensed her the moment she had leaned over. The fragrance of her perfume was exotic. He opened his eyes and smiled; she smiled back and asked if he was ready to depart the aircraft, very polite, very British.

Gathering his belongings, he slowly left the aircraft. Tom followed the signs for the exit and baggage re-claim area.

Not rushing, he slowly made his way to the baggage re-claim area, and smiled to himself – the bags were not coming off. So he walked to the far side of the area, leaned against the wall, and waited. Watching people hustle for position along the carousel waiting for their bags to come off always made Tom smile.

Eventually they started to arrive and the line became less cluttered, so eventually after spotting his case go past twice, he timed his pace to arrive just as his bag was level, and in one swift moment he had retrieved it and was off even before the person next to him had a chance to glance at him.

The next part was the hardest. He was now entering the 'Twilight Zone' as he called it – customs – this was the only area he had no control over. It was simple: he would either be allowed to enter or be arrested. If the right person was on duty and was awake and diligent then this could go hard.

He waited in line and when beckoned forward, moved towards the glass booth with the waiting customs official.

The customs official looked at the American passport, glanced at him and asked, "Reason for your visit?"

Tom replied, "Business." With another glance at the passport, the customs official stamped the passport then handed it back and said, "Welcome to the UK." Tom smiled and moved through the exit into obscurity once again.

Being back in London was a strange experience. Even at this early hour it was busy, but he loved the hustle and bustle of urban life; no one really paying any notice, just rushing off to where they need to be, which of course suited him. He liked to be the grey man. Everyone saw him, but didn't really notice him: perfect.

Tom queued at the taxi rank waiting for a taxi. At this time of morning there were plenty to accommodate the waiting arrivals. Once in the taxi Tom told the driver his destination; he had not chosen the hotel but knew who had, and he had chosen well. By now he was sure the security services would have been alerted by his arrival.

The taxi driver kept up a running commentary all the way to the hotel. This made Tom smile, as London cabbies are unique throughout the world for being experts on every subject from football to politics; they always had an opinion on every subject.

Once he paid the cabbie and watched it disappear down the road, he turned and walked up the steps into the hotel; not before giving the local area a once-over scan. Tomorrow he would give the area a proper going over.

Walking through the lobby to the reception desk, he was not surprised that the place was busy and full of bustle. Scanning as he went, once at the reception desk he smiled at the pretty girl behind the desk who gave a radiant smile back and asked if she could be of assistance. Tom told her he had a reservation and gave her his name, which she quickly found on the computer, and turning to her rear, pulled a key from a pigeon hole and placed it on the counter in front of him.

Tom scooped up the key and turned to leave when the receptionist called him back and told him she had a message for him; as she passed the folded hotel headed paper over to him, Tom nodded and place it in his jacket pocket, not seeming at all surprised he had a note.

The receptionist glanced once more towards Tom's receding back, before turning quickly to the next guest, letting all thought of Tom fade into a distant memory.

At the lift Tom quickly stepped in and pressed fourteen; before the doors had time to close, he was joined by an elderly couple who wanted twelve. They remained in silence at the lift ascended to floor twelve. When the doors opened they both stepped out onto floor twelve, the doors quickly closed again and the lift ascended to the fourteenth floor. Stepping from the lift, Tom looked at his watch. He had timed the ascent from the ground to fourteenth floor, even with the stop on twelve, and it still only took four minutes, which was pretty good in his book.

He slowly stepped out of the lift and glanced left and right, taking in all his surroundings. To the left was the stairs and fire exit, and four rooms; to the right, six rooms. He slowly walked to his room, listening for anything out of the ordinary. Once at his room he placed the key in the lock and turned the key, waited a second before opening the door; this was always an uncontrolled situation as beyond the door was unknown. He slowly pushed open the door and noticed the automatic light came on, which was always a good sign that the room was empty.

He walked into the room and placed his suitcase on the bed, and stood scanning the interior of the room.

After five minutes he walked over to the bathroom and carried out the same procedure; he then walked over to the window and stared out on a London waking up. To a casual observer his actions might have seemed strange and bizarre, but for someone like Tom Sharapova it was an everyday occurrence.

In a small room in a large nondescript building, not more than twenty miles from where Tom was staring out at London, sat a bored man, eyes closed, leaning back in his hard plastic chair with his feet on the desk trying hard not to fall into a deep sleep. These night duties were a pain but at least this was the last of a seven day stint for him, and he was not due back on nights for another four weeks. This week had been pretty mundane; as the night register with only four entries could attest, it had been another quiet night. Not that he expected it to be any different. After all, he was part of MI5 UK's Internal Terrorist Assessment Teams, and the night desk was only manned by one person. Staring at the large clock on the wall, it was now six thirty am. Thirty minutes until the day staff took over and he could go and spend a few hours with the wife and kids before they left for work and school respectively; then shower and bed, and then looking forward to a nice long relaxing weekend with the family.

The ringing phone brought his eyes open and his chair back to the floor with a bump. He gave a quick yawn and a rub of his eyes before picking up the phone and listening. There was no point in saying anything, as not many had this number and those that did were not in the habit of waiting for pleasantries. It was his counterpart at MI6. As he listened he wrote, his eyes growing wider and wider as he did. After three minutes he slowly replaced the receiver and realised his day was about to become a nightmare.

Quickly taking a folder marked 'Operation Procedure', he turned to section four – Operation Titan – and after scanning the single sheet of paper, he started to make phone calls in the order on the list. After the calls were connected, which mostly only took one or two rings, he only said one word, "Titan," before hanging up and moving down the list. Before ten minutes were up he had rung all the names on the list. He then re-wrote all the MI6 desk agent had said to him, word for word; this would form part of the forthcoming department brief.

The conference was called for eight am, which was highly unusual for MI5, as normally the day did not start until nine am for most departments in the agency. Six men sat around the long oblong teak table, staring at the Director of MI5, who sat at the head of the table. The director turned to the duty night agent and nodded; he read his report word-for-word as dictated to him by MI6, and his subsequent actions he had taken. Once he had finished his report, it brought a murmur from the assembled group.

A man on the left of the director asked, "Can we be sure it's him?"

Another commented, "We can only hope it's a false alarm," which started everyone talking at once.

"Gentleman," said the director, lightly slapping the table. "Let's not get ahead of ourselves, first we need to confirm or deny he actually entered the UK. What time did he supposedly arrive?" the director asked, turning to the man seated on the right.

"Flight BA12 from Washington into Heathrow, landing at five am, came through customs at five forty-five am with an American passport. It did not get flagged until some twenty minutes later after the picture scan of the flight's passports were processed and matched against the database.

"Once it got flagged MI6 rang the night desk, at six thirty am," to which the duty desk agent nodded in confirmation.

"Gentlemen, first let's make it our priority to make sure he is actually here, let's try and do this as quietly as possible. We do not want to spook anyone at this early stage. Let's keep it in house until we have a positive ID, then we can go outside the department if we need to, we don't want a panic only to find out it was a case of mis-identification, like last year's fiasco. Stanton," the director said.

"Yes, Director," replied Stanton.

"Get every available agent on the streets, for any credible intelligence. Also let's check all the Heathrow CCTV to see if we can trace his steps, also check the taxi rank, he might have used a regular taxi."

"Will get on it straight away," said Stanton, making notes as the director spoke.

"Let's reconvene at twelve noon for an update. Gentlemen, anything I have missed?" As the director scanned the room, all six heads were nodding. The director stood, and said, "Good, let's get to work."

At twelve noon, five men were sitting around the oblong teak desk; the night agent was no longer part of the assessment team. They all sat in the same positions as before. There was a quiet buzz around the room as talking was kept to a whisper. The only exception was the director, who at this stage was missing. Eventually after five minutes, the director walked in followed by another man, who went and sat directly opposite at the bottom of the table. "Gentlemen, you all know my counterpart in MI6, I thought it was prudent at this stage to include his department." As all five heads turned he nodded; they all knew who he was, if not by personal contact then by reputation.

The Director turned to the left and said, "Stephen, the floor is yours."

The man called Stephen cleared his throat and said, "We can confirm it is him: Tom Sharapova is definitely in the UK," which caused a storm around the table. Eventually the room quietened, and Stephen went on to give a brief overview of what they knew of Tom Sharapova:

Name: Tom Sharapova
Born: Unknown
Place: Unknown
Education: Suspected of an IQ above genius.
Can speak up to 10 languages, 8 fluently.
Expert in all weapons, proficient in all forms of martial arts.
Started successful haulage business in Odessa with Sebastian Sharapova.
Sebastian Sharapova killed by suspected rival Russian mafia.
Turned chief enforcer for Vladimir Sharapova, boss of the Ukraine/Odessa Mafia.
Hunted down and killed all suspected of Sebastian Sharapova killing.
Left Russia – early 80s – reason not known
Suspected of becoming successful freelance assassin. World agency sources have credited him with over 200 assassinations.
Last sighting before UK: Washington DC.

"Not a lot to go on," said the director, "carry on, Stephen."

"OK, this is what we can confirm so far. Arrived on Flight BA12 from Washington into Heathrow, landing at five am, came through customs at five forty five am, took a taxi from the Heathrow taxi rank, taxi dropped him off at the Dorchester Hotel, central London." This brought a murmur from around the table. The director said, "We need to find out why he has decided to come to the UK. Can all you department heads put this as a top priority. This man is dangerous and does not take small jobs. His reputation is too good for that, so why is he here?"

"Perhaps a holiday," someone said, which brought several smiles around the table.

"No, people like Tom Sharapova do not take holidays. He is here for a reason and I want to know why," said the director. "How many agents we got on him?"

"Seven agents," came a reply from the left,

"Good. I want an hourly update on his movements." This

brought a nod from the left. "Have we covered the hotel room and hotel phones yet, and is the hotel co-operating?"

"As soon as he left his room this morning we were in and the place is now wired. As for the hotel, they are being co-operative so far."

"Good," said the director.

"OK gentlemen, that's about it for now, let's convene in four hours, and hopefully we can have something concrete to go on." This brought a murmur from around the table. "Thank you gentlemen, that will be all," and they all stood to leave apart from the MI6 director, who remained seated.

The Director of MI5 looked at the MI6 director and said, "Well Laurence, what is your uptake on this?"

"I am not sure," said Laurence, "it's obvious he is here for something big, he is taking a big risk coming to the UK."

"What do our American cousins have to say on the matter? After all, he did fly in from Washington," asked the MI5 director.

"Not a lot, being very quiet. Having lunch tomorrow with my CIA counterpart in London, hopefully he will be able to shed some light on the proceedings."

"Good," replied the MI5 director.

"Lunch, Julie?" said the Director of MI6, standing up.

"Why not?" said the Director of MI5, looking at her watch.

Grace

Tom let his mind wander back to the last time he was in London, and tried to remember how long it had been. Over thirty years; Tom was just a boy when he left, born and bred in the slums of the east end of London in the early 1950s, where sixty per cent of children born never made it to adulthood, and those that did were mentally and sometime physically scarred for life. Only a small few like him managed to survival it all and prosper, but that was the rub, the reason Tom had prospered was due to his upbringing; that was the irony of it all, which made him smile again.

Tom tried to picture those dark days, but although some images were vivid and easily recalled others were clouded in darkness as if his mind refused to bring them out, which Tom guessed was the brain's way of telling him some things are best left forgotten.

Tom's most vivid memory was of his mother, who up until Tom was fourteen was his universe, his one constant in the harsh environment Tom was living in; his mother loved him without reservation even when Tom was bad. His mother was always defending him, like a lioness defending her cubs; she was his world.

Tom had never known his father. Tom had asked his mother once about him but she shook her head with a sad look on her face, and told him, "He died in the war, but he would have loved you as much as I do," which was enough for Tom and he never asked again.

Tom also knew he was better off than most of the kids in his street. He only had his mother to scold him, whereas some had drunken fathers and older siblings to hide from. Tom always knew that his mother's house was his sanctuary.

Tom was not particularly tall for his age, nor well built; then again, most kids in the area looked like they were skin and bones. No one looked exceptional, just all dressed in hand-me-downs or clothes bought with 'room to grown in', but one thing that Tom did have was a razor sharp mind. Nowadays Tom would have been called gifted, but back then you kept traits like that hidden, for fear of being singled out or noticed.

Tom had the ability that once something was seen or learnt, it was never forgotten, and his powers of recall were amazing. Nowadays they called it a photographic memory.

When Tom was very young, his mother used to sit and tell him stories before Tom fell asleep and Tom would dream of far-away kingdoms, always lost in a world full of wondrous things. Tom recalled the exact moment he saw printed words for the first time: his mother had asked him to go into the cupboard in the kitchen and fetch her a bar of soap. It was on the second shelf so Tom realised a chair would be needed to reach such a height, so dragging a chair over and climbing up Tom peeked over the shelf lip searching for the soap. It was hard to miss the large block of pink smelling stuff; as he reached, he noticed the items on the shelf were all resting on something covered in blank ink. As Tom tugged at the paper all the shelf items moved as well, and before he knew it he was sitting on the kitchen floor with various items scattered about him. In his hand he was clutching what he later learned was a sheet of newspaper.

His mother came in to see what all the noise was, but far from being cross, she looked into his face and realised Tom wanted to understand what he had found, so from that night on instead of make believe stories his mother would teach him words from the printed page.

That, Tom realised, was the defining moment of his child-hood. He had moved from a curious mind to a mind hungry for knowledge.

It was not long after that his mother realised that she was unable to keep up with his constant demand for fresh knowl-edge, so she decided to send Tom to the local school thinking that this would satisfy his thirst for knowledge.

No one in particular was close to Tom, as up to now, his mother was all he needed in companionship. So come the first day of school, Tom had woken early with a belly full of but-terflies, apprehensive yet excited. Tom hardly noticed eating his breakfast, or leaving the house clutching his mother's hand. This was more for her than him; Tom would have rather skipped ahead, eager to arrive.

The sight of the big black iron gates of the school grounds made him feel less excited but the butterflies were still dancing about.

The air was filled with the sound of laughter and children's shrieking voices. What seemed to him like every kid in the neighbourhood and more were there; the noise was deafening and quite intimidating, but still Tom was not going to let any-thing lessen the experience of this day. His mother nodded to a few others standing around, and as Tom looked up he was not sure if the smile on her face was of pride for him, or for her, but she squeezed his hand tightly all the same.

A loud bell sounded. Most of the kids stopped what they were doing and turned slowly and walked towards two large doors with the words "School Entrance" over the lintel. There were only a few kids who had not moved; most were with a grown up and stood unsure what to do next. Once all the kids had entered through the large school doors, there standing alone was a tall lady dressed in a black gown, holding a large clipboard.

She then, in a loud chip voice, started to call out names. One by one when kids heard their names they began to move toward her. On hearing his name, Tom let go of his mother's hand but felt her still holding on. Puzzled, Tom looked up to see her mouth the words, "Be good," before letting go.

Tom then moved to the group forming around the tall lady with the clipboard.

Eventually there were fifteen other kids standing around, looking upwards toward the tall lady dressed in black. "Welcome to North Compton School. I am Miss Gull, the Headmistress of North Compton School. 1 run the school with a strict disciplinary regime. You had better get to know the school rules quickly, or retribution will follow on swift wings." Most kids looked puzzled by this, but some understood the threatening warning from the Headmistress.

Miss Gull turned and not even looking back, said, "Follow me," and all fifteen kids moved as one, following her to what some had decided was walking into Hell. Miss Gull led them down a bleak grey corridor lit by powerful bright lights, with shut doors spaced at intervals along its length. As she walked, Miss Gull kept up a running commentary of dos and don'ts, never once looking back to see if she was still being followed.

Abruptly she stopped at the last door on the left, and turning to face the children she informed them that this was their class room – R5, and every morning and afternoon when the bell sounded in the playground they were to move directly to this room for registration, ready for the day's lessons. "Any questions?" she asked, looking around, glaring at the faces and daring them to ask one.

She sharply rapped on the closed door which promptly opened as if by magic, like it had been waiting with expectation for the knock. There stood a tall thin man, also dressed in a black gown.

Miss Gull informed all that this was Mr Douglas and he was here to educate and enlighten them, and pass on all his worldly knowledge – to which she gave a short giggle, as if only she understood the joke, quickly returning to the sour face to deliver the next introduction of Mr Douglas's responsibilities and duties towards them.

She informed them Mr Douglas was their form tutor and he was in all things the final law in school procedure and discipline, apart from a visit to her office, which she made sound like a trip to the dentist was more appealing. With this, she gave Mr Douglas a sharp nod of the head before abruptly turning on her heels and marching back down the brightly lit corridor. As she went she shouted, "All yours, Mr Douglas."

They all stood staring back down the corridor at the retreating form of Miss Gull, feeling that somehow they have escaped a terrible fate, being left behind and not following her. After what seemed like an eternity, Mr Douglas loudly cleared his throat and in a loud voice said, "Enter and find a desk."

Tom quickly found a desk and sat down, not really bothering to see who was sitting where. Eventually the noise from desks and chairs being scraped stopped, and silence once again descended on room R5.

Mr Douglas introduced himself again and explained that he had been teaching for years so he has seen every prank and dodge in the book; he was here to teach and he was not bothered if the class were not here to learn, he was going to teach come hell or high water.

Although dressed in old ill-fitting clothes over his skeleton body, his voice when he spoke was crisp and clear, with a strong power that held the listener captivated by every word.

While he was telling the class this, he was writing his name on the big blackboard at the front of the class room, which was laid out in three rows of wooden desks across the class room going backwards, making fifteen desks in all.

This was the first time Tom realised that not only could words be read, they could be written as well; he was annoyed at himself for not making the connection sooner and could feel himself going red. Looking around the class, he noticed no one was looking in his direction. All were concentrating on the big blackboard at the front and the words Mr Douglas was writing.

After spelling his name on the board Mr Douglas sat at his

desk and took out a folder, which he informed them was the class register. He stated he would take the register twice a day, once in the morning and once after lunch, when they were to stand up and shout, "Present," when their name was called. So starting at the letter A, he called each child by name. He glanced up as each child stood and spoke.

Mr Douglas then informed them that, if missing from any register call, the next time he saw them they were to have a note from a responsible adult stating why they had missed the register call. If they did not produce a note then a, "Quick visit to the head would be in order," he said, looking about. Most of the children were thinking, *perhaps that's one to avoid*.

He then asked for them to look about and make sure that the desk they were sitting in was always the same, which would assist him to get to know their names when lessons were being taught.

Tom noticed he was on the left hand row of desks second in, so no one to the left, but as he looked right, he looked into the smiling face of a girl. This was the first time a girl had ever smiled at him apart from his mother, so as he tried to smile back he felt his face redden, which caused the girl to giggle and as she did others looked to see what the fuss was about. Before anyone could comment, Mr Douglas had slapped the desk with his hand and shouted, "Eyes front," which saved Tom from further embarrassment.

The rest of the day went quickly and Tom soon found himself walking towards the exit, being pushed and shoved by others rushing to get out of the school before they changed their minds and shut the doors.

Tom had been given instructions by his mother not to loiter on the way home and to hurry, or she would come looking for him, so leaving the school gates with the masses Tom headed down Brick Lane towards home. Halfway down Brick Lane, Tom heard a small voice behind him say his name. As Tom turned, he saw it was the girl from class still smiling and saying, "Tom is your name – right?"

"Yes," Tom said, and then realised that he had not bothered to learn her name, but she hid this fact and said, "I am Sally, we can walk together if you like."

Not daring to speak, Tom nodded his head and fell in step as they walked together down Brick Lane. At the bottom they both stopped; Tom was going left and Sally was going right. Sally smiled once again and said, "See ya tomorrow," as she skipped off in the opposite direction. All Tom could think was that he had seen an angel, and let out his first decent breath of the walk home.

The next day Tom was up early and raring to go, even his mother noticed how eager he was. "You're keen," she said.

"Oh am I?" said Tom, going red, which made her laugh.

"Do you want me to walk you to school again today?" said his mother. Tom stopped what he was doing and was trying so hard to think of an excuse why his mother should not walk him to school that he made the answer come out in a single high pitched squeak, which made her laugh even louder. "OK, OK," she said, "I know when I am not wanted." Still laughing, she kissed him on top of the head and said, "Have a nice day, and be good." Tom smiled as he left the house.

Tom ran to the top of his street. Still out of breath, he noticed Sally coming from the opposite direction; when Sally was near, Tom waved and said, "Hi how you doing?"

Sally smiled and said, "Good thanks, you?"

"Yup, fine," said Tom. As they walked to school Tom asked Sally about her family. Sally explained her father and her older brother worked at the docks, her mother stayed at home to look after her younger sister, and she had been pushed off to school. Tom got the impression Sally was not as enthusiastic about school as he was.

Sally then asked about Tom's family. Tom said, "Only me and mother." Sally tried to ask about Tom's parents, but realised Tom did not want to talk about it, so she let it drop and changed the subject.

"So what you think of Mr Douglas?" asked Sally.

"I think he is brilliant," said Tom.

Sally looked at Tom. "I can see you are going to be Mr Douglas's star pupil," said Sally, laughing. Tom looked embarrassed, so Sally linked arms and said, "Don't worry, I won't tell anyone," which made them both laugh.

At the school gates, the pandemonium from the previous day was just as intense. Both Tom and Sally stood on the fringes of the running and shouting children, and waited for the bell. As the bell sounded, Tom and Sally joined the throng entering the school doors. Every door in the well-lit corridor was standing open, and children entered left and right, along the corridor.

Tom and Sally entered R5 and noticed Mr Douglas was not present yet, so both sat at their respective desks and chatted. Eventually Mr Douglas entered and said, "Quiet." Every child sat up and stared to the front expectantly. Mr Douglas took the register, and was amazed that all of them had returned for a second day; normally at least one would have dropped out with some imaginary illness.

Mr Douglas said, "First we need to get some administration out of the way." Mr Douglas placed a pile of red books and a pile of paper on the front desk of each of the rows, and said, "Take one of each and pass them back." After each child had a red book and a piece of paper, Mr Douglas said, "This book is for homework and the paper is your timetable. At times I will give you a topic and when next time you attend class, you will present your work in this red book." He held one up. "Any questions?" asked Mr Douglas, scanning the room. "Notice on your timetable it will show by blocks of timings what subject you are going to be covering during the lesson period. Any questions?" asked Mr Douglas again. "Good, then if you all look at your timetable you will notice we are going to start a double period of Mathematics," which brought a groan from the class.

At the end of the week, the whole class had a book on each subject, plus a book to write in for each; these could be left in class or taken home, the choice, Mr Douglas said, "Was up to you," but if a child lost a book, then as he put it, "Your parents will be duty bound to replace the lost book."

Tom loved school; well, not school exactly, but the lessons. Mr Douglas made every lesson seem exciting and enjoyable, from maths to history. Tom absorbed everything.

The only lesson they took outside their own class room was Physical Education or PE. This was done separately from the girls, so twice a week the boys would go one way and the girls the other, never to meet until after the PE lesson.

The PE teacher was Mr Grimes, an ex-soldier, who still thought he was fighting the Germans, and every lesson told them how lucky there were to be born in this modern age, but never gave any quarter to anyone; most lessons were done outside come rain or shine, winter or summer, football or cross country or some sadistic game invented by Mr Grim – this was what all the boys called him behind his back.

His favourite saying was 'A fit body is a fit mind', but it was hard to reconcile this on a cold November morning being lashed with rain. Even though Tom enjoyed all sports and excelled in most, to him his favourite was cross country, as it allowed his mind to wander free.

The only drawback from the all-boys sessions was it sorted out the pecking order of strength and the natural bullies. One in particular was Bert Cross. He was bigger than most boys, and liked to show it; not very bright or athletic, he just drifted through school making everyone else's life a misery. Once he had his target in his sights there was no let up until the torture had run its course and he became bored and had moved onto the next victim.

This particular day Mr Grim had decided to teach the boys some self-defence, to sharpen up the reflexes. To most it was torture but to Tom it was pure knowledge. Mr Grim was explaining that even the smallest can defeat the biggest if they know what they are doing; to this end, he threw one of the smallest kids in the class over his shoulder, landing firmly winded on the grass. Mr Grim stood there grinning as if he had thrown Goliath himself. Mr Grim then told the boys to pair up, and practise.

Bert Cross made a bee-line for Tom. Tom then realised that he was the next victim of the Bert Cross torture school; the thought quickly passed thought his mind, but Tom heard a small voice say, "Remember the training, even the smallest can defeat the biggest with the right attitude and technique."

As Bert Cross came lumbering over, Tom open his legs and squatted down, ready for the on-slaught. Tom's mind quickly cleared and his breathing slowed. Tom felt as calm then as he had ever been in his life, considering he was probably about to take the biggest beating of his life. Tom vowed he would not go down without a fight; Tom would stand or be conquered.

Bert Cross came with a smile that said it all, and as he out-stretched his arms to embrace his prey, Bert lunged and found nothing but fresh air. Tom had side-stepped him and now stood at Bert's side; Tom grabbed Bert's wrist and as instructed, pushed his thumb into the fleshy part of the hand between thumb and finger, and gave a sharp twist upwards. Bert gave a sharp cry of pain, which made everyone stop and stare.

Bert could not understand or comprehend the actions that had taken place; what should have been an enjoyable beating had turned into a painful experience.

As Bert sagged to his knees he was aware of the pain in his arm, and as he struggled to be free the pain was amplified, so he realised staying still was the best option. Next he felt a breath on his neck as Tom whispered in his ear. "Leave me alone or next time I will break your arm."

Bert slowly felt the pressure on his hand subside, and look-ing up into the clear green eyes of Tom, Bert had no doubt that the whispered threat would be carried out, so he took the threat seriously.

Mr Grim had come over to see what the commotion was, and reading the situation correctly, defused the situation with a few words to the group.

After that day Bert Cross never came near or even tried to engage Tom again.

The years of schooling passed quickly after that day. Tom did not experience any major incidents. Tom was top in all lessons, and participated in all the sporting teams. The only constant in all the years was Sally, who was his only true friend and companion. One day Sally said, "See Tom, told you you would be Mr Douglas's star pupil," as she had prophesied all those years ago.

It was during the last year of school that he first noticed others taking an interest in Sally. To him she was the same as the first day they met, but recently Sally had changed in ways Tom could not quite fathom or understand. Sally was becoming distant, and most days was not around to walk home from school.

Tom decided to ask his mother about this change of events, so over tea one night Tom broached the subject with her. His mother smiled and said, "My poor Tom. So eventually, life has caught you up." She was silent for a minute, then looking Tom directly in the eyes, his mother said to Tom, "Listen carefully and I will try and explain it all to you, I think you are now old enough to understand."

She then went on to enlighten Tom on the differences between men and women, and in graphic details the 'birds and the bees'. After an hour Tom was becoming quite embarrassed over the things his mother was saying; Tom had never heard her speak so plainly to him before and a lot of it was becoming a revelation.

Obviously the boys at school who were in the know, especially when they were in the changing room, would pass on their wisdom to all who listened, although most of it left more questions than answers; but no one thought of asking anything about it, as to do so would of course make you look stupid and have the ridicule of your peers, so everyone nodded as if to say, "Knew that," without actually understanding.

Later that night, lying in bed, Tom pondered all that his mother had told him about the differences between men and women. Although at the time he was ready for the floor to open up and swallow him, Tom digested it all and slowly he now understood Sally's pre-occupation with other things. Tom sighed and realised it would never been the same again between them. He hoped they of course would always remain best friends, but each had a path to follow where sometimes the other could not follow, and this made his eyes water. Tom could not remember the last time he had felt this sad or so ready to cry. He turned his face to the wall and fell into a deep troubled sleep.

The next day, his mother was her normal happy self when Tom came down to breakfast, rattling on about Mrs Brown at No. 10 whose front step had not been cleaned for days, and perhaps something was amiss.

Scandal in the street was what kept his mother and her friends going, as long it was happening to someone else and not on their door step.

She was going on and not really taking much notice of Tom as he prepared for school; he was relieved, really, that she had made it so easy and not uncomfortable after last nights 'chat'. For that he would always be grateful.

Just before Tom left for school, he gave her a hug and a kiss. She put him at arm's length and said, "What was that for?" and Tom replied, "Just for being you, mater," which was his pet name for her, to which she smiled and said, "Be off with you and be good," kissing him once more on the cheek.

She watched him stride up the street with his bag slung over his shoulders, and her eyes watered. What a wonderful young man he had become, he was her world. She was surprised by the hug, which also alerted her to the fact that he was now a head taller than she was; so different from that little bundle of screaming arms and legs that was left with her all those years ago. As she thought back to those times, not once did she regret taking in the lad, although technically he was nothing to do with her.

Grace's mind drifted back to days gone by; she tried hard to forget some memories, some more painful than others, and over the years some had faded to distant random images, and even now were hard to recall. Others were always there, in vivid colour over the years; sometimes suppressed but never forgotten.

It was 1942 and the country was at war and finally getting mobilised, everyone doing their bit for the war effort. Life for her was pretty good; she was working as a nurse in a hospital up west.

Grace was on a general ward in the hospital, mostly civilians rather than military, but recently the injuries were just as bad, especially since the bombing had intensified. She had volunteered the first few months of the war after her parents' house had been hit by a stray bomb, killing both her parents instantly; she had been away at the pictures with a friend, otherwise she would have been there, so she took this as a sign that her calling was just.

Grace first met her friend Julie when she first arrived at the hospital as a student nurse; they were to share a room together in the hospital grounds. Julie could not have been more different from Grace; she was an East End lass born and bred, and as Julie used to rib her about being 'Grace by name and Grace by nature'. Julie came from an upper class family somewhere from the shires, and as far as Grace could make out was unjustly treated by her parents, who refused to fund her social lifestyle during a war, so in rebellion she applied and got into the hospital as a student nurse to the annoyance of her parents.

Although work was hard and tiring they sometimes had a day off, which normally meant they ended up in the local pub; Julie was never alone for long and Grace always secretly admired her friend's openness and ability to entice men to her side. Grace on the other hand was always quite shy around men, but when she first saw Tom Backer enter the pub – well, technically this was incorrect as she had known him since childhood but had lost contact over the years – he came over and said, "Hi." Julie nudged her in the ribs as an invite to go for it.

Tom asked, "Do I know you?"

"Maybe," said Grace.

"You are Jim and Doris Chapman's daughter."

"Correct," said Grace.

"Sorry to hear about your parents," said Tom.

"Thank you," said Grace. "How's your parents doing?"

"Dad died last year, heart attack, mum still lives in Durant Street off Brick Lane," said Tom.

"Oh, I know it," said Grace.

"Can I buy you a drink?" said Tom, smiling.

Grace smiled back and said, "Lovely, gin and lime please."

Grace and Tom met whenever they could, but due to Grace's heavy work roster, it was not as often as they would have liked. When they were together, they would spend every precious second alone in each other's company. After a few months, Tom told her he was being posted away to a training camp in Dorset. The thought of not having Tom in her life was hard to conceive until he took her hand and went down on one knee and proposed; it seemed he was having the same feelings as Grace. They hastily managed to arrange the wedding in two weeks, with a helping hand from all at the hospital.

The wedding was at the local church; it was a small affair, only attended by family and close friends. Grace wore her nurse's uniform and Tom his army uniform. The reception was held in the local pub they had first met in. Afterwards, Tom surprised Grace with three wonderful days in Brighton for a honeymoon.

After Tom left, two weeks later Grace found out she was pregnant. Grace would visit her mother-in-law whenever she could and always was amazed at how the scenery about the district changed with each visit; every time a new bomb crater would appear where a house once stood.

After six months, due to her size, the hospital decided to

give her leave of absence and the obvious place was her mother-in-law's, which of course was OK for a visit, but to live in was not filling Grace with hope.

Before Grace departed, she made Julie promise that she would come and visit her whenever she could.

It was a complete surprise to Grace how quickly she settled into the day to day routine of life with her mother-in-law, and was grateful by her attitude and kindness towards her. After all, she had taken her precious Tom away from her, and Grace knew that Tom and his mother had a close bond, and she secretly hoped that she could have the same relationship with her child.

Although letters from Tom were far and few between, she wrote to him every week about the progress of their child, every kick and bump, wanting him to be involved; she knew in her heart that if he could have been there with her he would have been. Sometimes Grace would curse the 'bloody war' for stopping her happiness, but Tom's letters were full of love for them both and hope for the future, and how much he was looking forward to becoming a dad.

After eight months, life was looking up. Julie visited as promised once a week, with the gossip of the hospital and tales of her new beau. It was after one of Julie's weekly visits – Julie had left at around four wanting to get back to the hospital before it got dark; London was still not a safe place to be, especially after dark. Worse now, as there were no lights to guide you.

Grace decided to go upstairs and tackle the box room, which was going to be the nursery. Grace had decided on yellow, but actually getting yellow paint during wartime was a quest in itself. No one had yellow paint; black, brown and green seemed to be the favourite colours of the day. Until Grace found a little paint shop up west, when after a hard negation and an emotional burst of tears, the owner felt pity towards her in her current situation and came forth with two tins of sunflower yellow, which of course Grace had to haggle over; after all there was a war on.

It was while Grace was sitting in the dying daylight pondering what it would look like once it was all finished; in her mind's eye, she could picture the nursery all finished. She sat smiling to herself. From a distance Grace heard the sirens going off and glancing out of the window was surprised as it was not yet dark. Grace had not even closed the blackout curtains; then again most people waited until the last dregs of light faded into night before closing their blackout curtains, not wanting to be deprived of any daylight.

Grace went downstairs as quickly as she could in her condition, calling for her mother-in-law as she went. "Gloria, you there Gloria," shouted Grace. Grace looked in all the rooms and was surprised her mother in law was not about. Grace wondered where she could be; Grace tried to remember if Gloria had told her if she was going out today, but just lately Grace's memory was getting worse, but she put this down to the baby. Grace grabbed her torch and as quickly as she could went down to the Anderson shelter, built halfway down the garden between two mounds of earth.

The sirens were getting louder and the ack-ack guns started to fire. Grace was starting to get scared as the drone of aircraft overhead filled the sky. Just as Grace was squeezing through the entrance of the Anderson shelter, bombs started to land. Grace sat on the small bench that stretched across the shelter, and closed her eyes. Not really a sufferer of enclosed spaces, even she was finding it hard to breathe.

Grace tried to control her breathing as taught by the midwife and think of happy thoughts. She thought of the baby and the first time Tom would see her; Grace was convinced her child was going to be a girl. And then a thought struck her: Tom or Grace had not even considered names, she must remember to write tomorrow and ask him his preferences, as Grace had her own choices but something that monumental should really be a joint effort. This made Grace smile and she felt a lot calmer. Grace hoped Gloria was safe, wherever she was.

Bombs started to land, some close enough to make the shelter shake and dust to swirl around. All of a sudden there was a great thud as though the earth were being ripped open and Grace was knocked forward and hit her head on the shelter door.

Grace slowly came round, not really understanding what had happened; apart from she knew it was now morning. Grace could make out shafts of sun light streaming above her, and muffled voices. Grace tried to cry, but the cry caught in her throat and she felt a sharp pain in her side and legs. Grace then worried about her baby; all she knew was she could not move and was in pain.

Eventually the sunlight grew wider and wider, and hands reached down towards her. Grace cried out in pain, before once more blacking out.

When Grace awoke she was in a well-lit room. Grace tried to speak but no words would come; as she tried to sit, a strong hand pushed her back down. It was a few seconds before she focused on a familiar face – that of her ward matron. Grace then realised she was in her own hospital.

The matron took a cup of water and slowly allowed Grace to drink her fill. Once Grace laid back down she felt better; and then Grace realised she could not feel anything from the chest down.

Grace felt tears weld into her eyes as she understood the baby was gone. This pain bit deep into her heart, and finally Grace sobbed openly for her loss.

The matron left for a few minutes and was followed back in by a tall doctor in a white coat whom Grace recognised; at least Grace was going to be told bad news by someone she knew.

The doctor sat on Grace's bed and took her hand; he started by telling Grace how extremely lucky to be alive she was. Grace smiled. She did not feel lucky. The doctor said, "Although you don't believe it now, in time you will do, Grace." The doctor then went on to explain that there had been a direct hit on the opposite house and the adjoining garden; this had caused a gas explosion which ripped the house opposite to bits, and the Anderson shelter she was in to lift and flip. Grace had landed upside down with a pile of dirt and rubble on top of her.

The doctor said, "I am sorry, we could not save the baby." Grace had gone into premature labour but the size of the baby and the shock was too much for the baby. Grace asked what the baby was, and the doctor said it had been a girl, just as Grace had predicted. Grace had also sustained a broken leg and a broken ankle; the ankle was still a concern, said the doctor.

The doctor also told Grace about her mother in law. She apparently was in the house opposite visiting, so when the siren went off they decided to go under the stairs, but the whole house had been take out by the direct hit and subsequence gas explosion.

The doctor said that the miracle was her own house was un-touched, apart from a few broken windowpanes and a hole where the garden used to be; as most of the explosion was focused the other way, the house had got off pretty light all things considering. The doctor patted Grace's hand and said, "I am very sorry for your double loss. We will leave you to it, and pop back later to see how you are getting on." Then the doctor and Matron left.

Grace, lying in bed, felt strange, as she was undecided who she felt worse for, the child or her mother-in-law; but Grace knew the grieving process was a long slow process. Then Grace thought, how many times had she stood with a grieving relative saying those exact words? Grace now knew that the words were both pointless and empty, as she closed her eyes and cried again.

Eventually after a few days Julie came to see Grace, and as soon as they looked each other in the eyes they both burst into tears and clung to each other for comfort, neither letting go or having the courage to speak first.

After a few weeks, Grace was allowed home. Returning to the house was not as bad as Grace imagined; some kind soul had replaced her broken windows, and the garden had been levelled, but it was strange looking from the kitchen window straight up to the next road, through a hole where the house opposite should have been. As Grace sat and stared out of the windows, she kept half expecting to hear her mother-in-law Gloria come in.

Grace started a letter to Tom three times. Eventually she finally explained the double blow they had both endured; Grace tried to sound positive, as she knew Tom would feel the loss as much as she was.

The next day Grace was sitting in the kitchen when she heard the front door open, and Tom's voice shout her name. Grace could not believe Tom was here, and shouted back, "In the kitchen, my darling." Tom came in the kitchen and saw Grace with her leg and ankle in plaster, and the two crutches beside her. Tom knelt down in from of her, placed his arms around her and started to cry. Grace started to cry as well, and said, "I am so sorry, I could not save our child."

Tom looked into her eyes and cupped her face and said, "My darling, you have nothing to feel guilty about, none of it was your fault." Grace held Tom tight and they both let their grief wash over them, until the day turned to night.

Next day Grace asked Tom how long he had.

"A week's pass," replied Tom, as it was special circumstances.

"How did you know? I only wrote to you the other day," asked Grace.

"Mum had me as her next of kin, but they were not able to contact me until yesterday as I was away at a remote training camp; but when I came back, I was summoned to the office and they told me about mum and you," replied Tom. Grace felt guilty that the only reason Tom was here was because of a terrible tragedy, but she could not help but feel relieved.

A few days later Tom and Grace buried his mother in the same grave as Tom's father. The baby was buried next to Tom's parents, and after some heart searching they decided on Ruth as her name so she could have a gravestone which read:

Ruth Gloria Backer
Loving daughter of Grace and Tom Backer
Taken before her time, now with the angels

Grace and Tom spent the next few days trying to remain normal and trying not to think about Tom's imminent departure, but each day, as it became closer, their moods darkened. On the day of Tom's departure, Tom asked Grace if they could say goodbye at the house, as he was worried the trip to the train station would become an ordeal for her with her crutches as she was still not fully mobile. Grace hugged Tom, and kissed him deeply. "What was that for?" asked Tom.

"For being the most wonderful and considerate husband in the world," said Grace, Tom smiled and took Grace in his arms and carried her back upstairs.

Grace stood on the doorstep and watched Tom walk up the street; at the top, Tom stopped and turned, took off his cap and waved back towards Grace. Tom was silhouetted in the dying sun that was still just above the horizon, so Grace's last view was of her Tom bathed in glorious sunlight.

Every few days Julie would pop in and help where she could, before dashing out to meet her latest beau – not really elaborating, always conscious of Grace's situation. For this Grace was always thankful; that was one of Julie's special qualities.

Once the plaster came off, every day Grace would go for a walk, sometimes with Julie and sometimes alone. when she was alone, Grace would walk up to the church yard and sit with Ruth. Slowly at first, but after months of walking Grace was feeling stronger and fitter; she had been doing the exercises given to her by the hospital, and of course Julie was always on hand to make sure Grace stuck to the regimen, never overdoing it or rushed it.

Grace finally felt ready to return to work. She would always have a slight limp from the shattered leg and ankle, but in time it would fade to be hardly recognisable.

The first week back was not as bad as Grace thought it would be. Although busy, it helped her for a time to forget about her personal problems. Grace volunteered for nights, as for her, it was the worst time; keeping busy during the darkness was far better than lying in an empty bed unable to sleep. At least after a productive night, sleep became easier when you are exhausted.

One evening Grace was sitting at her nurses' station when the emergency bell sounded, which meant an ambulance was inbound with casualties. Grace knew it was not bomb victims, as there had been no air raid sirens. Waiting at the loading bay, Grace saw the ambulance in the distance. As it pulled up, two attendants with a trolley rushed to the ambulance and opened the back doors.

There on the ambulance trolley was a young man covered in blood. The two attendants took the young man from the ambulance and took him to the emergency room. The ambulance men briefed Grace on the young man's injuries, before she followed the trolley.

The two men placed the young man on the emergency room table and left. Grace started to check the young man when a doctor entered the room, and said, "So what we got, nurse?"

"Two stab wounds to the chest, and a slash to the right side of the face," said Grace.

The doctor leaned over and said, "Nasty." Grace and the doctor cut away the shirt, and the doctor said, "You sort the face; I will deal with the stab wounds."

Grace leaned over the young man and smiled. "I need to clean the wound, this might hurt a bit," said Grace. The young man said something but Grace did not understand the language he was speaking, so she held up the cloth to her face and pointed at his; the young man nodded as if he understood. Grace washed the slash and realised it needed stitches.

Grace said, "Doctor, this slash on the face requires stitches."

The doctor looked up and said, "I am sure your needle work is far neater than mine nurse, so you carry on." Grace gave the young man a local anaesthetic, and began to stitch up his face. The young man stared intensely at Grace as she worked. Once Grace had finished, she stood back and admired her work; the stitching was from just below the right side of the temple tracing a line down to the chin, just missing the eye socket, Grace thought the young man had been lucky – a little bit to the left and he would have lost his eye.

Next day Grace went to the ward to see how the young man was doing. Above his bed, the sign said 'Ivor Sharapova – Russian Sailor'. Grace smiled as she approached the young man, who was sitting up in bed. As he saw Grace approach, he held up his hand and he tried to smile but could only manage a lopsided grin. Grace put a hand on her chest and said, "Grace." The young man smiled and said, "Ivor," as he placed a hand on his chest.

For the next few weeks, whenever Grace got the chance she would visit Ivor, bring him books, and teach him English; he also tried to teach her some Russian. Grace loved visiting Ivor. He told her all about life in Russia, and she told him about Tom. Ivor told her one day he would be captain of his own ship.

"I love the sea," Ivor said, "and could never imagine living on land." His tales used to make Grace laugh and together they would sit for hours, laughing at each other's stories.

Grace had been really busy the previous day and did not have time to visit Ivor, so when she went to the ward she was surprised to see Ivor's bed empty. She asked the ward sister what happened to Ivor, pointing at the empty bed. The ward sister said, "Ivor left yesterday, he has a ship today leaving for Russia." As Grace was turning, the ward sister said, "Oh yes, sorry, nearly forgot he left you this. Asked one of the porters to write it as he translated it." She passed Grace a white envelope with the words 'Nurse Grace' on the front.

Grace went to the nurse's rest room, where she knew she would get some privacy, sat down and opened the letter:

My dear Nurse Grace

I am sorry we did not get to say good bye, but perhaps that was for the best.

The Doctor and the Russian Embassy Official came today, and said I am well enough to return to sea.

My ship sails tomorrow back to my home land of mother Russia. I am pleased to be finally going home, the only regret I have is I will miss you and our time together, which I will always cherish in my heart.

I want you to know, that over the weeks, you have shown me a side to human nature that is lacking in my home land that is compassion and understanding for a stranger in unfamiliar land, without your friendship, I think my stay would have been not so happy.

If you ever need my assistance or help in the future, please contact me. I will always be ready to help someone I class as a true friend.

Yours with love

Ivor Sharapova

After reading the letter, Grace had tears in her eyes, she closed her eyes and prayed for the young sailor who she had befriended. "Get home safely, Ivor," she whispered.

One day Grace was sitting in the nurses' lounge after a busy tiring day, with her eyes closed, when Julie popped her head in the door to see who was about. Spotting Grace was alone, she came in and sat next to her and linked arms. Julie rested her head on Grace's shoulder and whispered, "I have a problem," then went onto explain she was six weeks late, and did not know what to do; Grace kissed her forehead and said together they would work it out.

Over the following months, Julie did not show that she was obviously pregnant. They discussed her returning home to her parents, which although was most properly the correct thing to do, Julie said she could not live with her parents disappointment; although never said, it was always present in their eyes and manner, and this she could not bear.

As for the father, that was a nonstarter; he was an RAF pilot married with kids. Julie said they had met in a underground station during a bombing raid, and afterwards went for a drink onto a full-blown affair which petered out after a few months. Julie was unsure if he wanted to know at all, and was sure that support would be less than forthcoming.

So they decided Julie would resign from the hospital on some pretext of her having to return home, and Julie would move in with Grace until the baby was born, then decide what to do next for the best.

It was a bright sunny morning. Recently Grace was having trouble sleeping; vivid events flashed through her mind, leaving her soaking in sweat and feeling exhausted. Of course, the hospital councillor said that this would happen after such an ordeal Grace had endured, so as sleep was so troubling Grace had decided to wake with the daylight and busy herself during the day.

Grace was sipping her second cup of tea of the day when she heard a loud knock at the door, then Julie's voice shouted, "I'll get it." After a time, Grace wondered who Julie could be speaking to, so curiosity getting the better of her, Grace decided to go and look.

As Grace opened the kitchen door, standing white-faced was Julie holding a brown envelope crumpled in her hands; her eyes were full of tears and at once Grace knew, and collapsed on the floor.

Grace woke with Julie looking down at her with her big green eyes full of tears, not speaking. Julie raised Grace up and sat her in a chair and handed the envelope to her. Grace's hands were shaking as she sat opposite her, both staring at the envelope addressed to Mrs G Backer.

They both sat in silence; the only indication that the world was still moving was the tick of the hall grandfather clock and the passing of the odd car in the street. Eventually Grace let out a sigh, and said, "Well, better get it over with," and lifted the brown envelope and ripped the top off.

Grace read the short telegram; finally, after staring at the letter what seemed like an eternity, Grace passed it to Julie. Julie read the telegram, which informed Grace that Tom had been killed in the Far East whilst fighting the Japanese. Grace then slowly rose and walked out of the room, closing the door quietly behind her. Julie decided to leave her friend to her grief; she would be here if Grace needed to talk, apart from that she would try and keep their world revolving.

The next few months Grace ran on autopilot. The world seemed void of all colour. Nothing could excite her or break her deep black mood, apart from the fact she was quietly conscious of Julie's growing waist line. Julie tried on many occasions to engage Grace with normal mundane everyday things, but Grace sometimes was in another place, that Julie could not visit.

Grace would never forget the night Julie gave birth; it had been raining for days, a constant heavy downpour that eventually gets into the very fabric of your existence, where nothing can keep you dry apart from staying indoors. The thunder had just started when on cue, Julie gave out a cry of her own, and it seemed every time there was a rumble of thunder and flash of lightning, Julie would reply with her own cry. As the lightning flashed over, it made the lights dim and flicker, and eventually go out. Grace lit some candles which gave the room a gothic appearance, which added to the drama. After hours of labour during the violent thunderstorm, Julie gave birth to a bouncy nine pound baby boy.

Once everything was tidied up, Julie fell into a deep sleep and Grace lay the sleeping baby next to her, and while all was quiet, went and fell into a deep and exhausting sleep of her own; the first she had had for many months.

Grace heard the crying from far away, as if she was in a tunnel and the cry was coming from the other end. Slowly her senses returned to her and although her eyes were still closed, she could make out it was day outside, but all she could hear was the crying baby which now was becoming all-encompassing.

Slowly Grace opened her eyes and realised she was still fully dressed on her bed, her first thoughts was of the crying baby and Julie, and it annoyed her that the baby's mother not two feet away from him was unable to comfort the poor thing.

Grace moved towards the door and saw the room Julie had been in had the door wide open. Grace went across the landing and looked in; the unmade bed was empty and next to it was the crying baby.

Grace went and picked up the crying baby and cooed softly to it, and whispered, "Wonder where your mummy can be." The baby responded to her voice and stared at her with big green eyes.

Taking the baby, Grace went downstairs calling Julie's name as she went. Strange; she was not downstairs either. Grace was having difficulty processing all the information going on, as she was still feeling the effects from her deep sleep. Grace sat in a kitchen chair pondering on what could have happened to Julie, when she noticed the white envelope propped against the sugar bowl.

Slowly taking up the envelope, she noticed Julie's neat handwriting on the envelope with just one word: 'Grace'.

Still with the baby in her arms, she slid her finger under the lip and extracted the single piece of folded paper. Opening the paper up, Grace read the following:

My Darling Grace
I am not sure how to start this letter as it is the hardest thing
I have ever done in my life, over the months you have been my
rock, your life has been so full of misery and sometimes you
have nearly broke my heart as I always felt inadequate to help
you, but you have had the strength and endurance that I could
never have to always carry on, you have always placed me first
which I will always love you for, I ask this one last thing of you
please bring up my Son as you would your own, you will make
a far better mother than I could ever be, since the first moment
I saw the baby I knew I had no maternal instinct, that I know
you will have. Please do not hate me but I know I could never be
as strong as you and bring up a child on my own, I know I am
taking the coward's way out, but I know I am giving my Son the
most precious gift of all, knowing he will be raised by the most
remarkable woman I have ever known.
*   Always Julie*

Grace slowly placed the letter on the table and with her eyes full of tears, held the baby close to her breast and sobbed.

Grace decided to call the baby Tom, and afterwards found that registering the baby was easy. After all, the country was just recovering after the war, so official paperwork was not rigorously checked; she was after all another women found pregnant giving birth to an unplanned child in an over-stretched system, where not too many questions are asked.

Slowly, Grace brought herself back to the present as she watched him walk up the road; those fourteen years had flown past for both of them.

Grace was sitting in the kitchen, eyes closed with the sun shining on her face, her mind drifting to days gone past, recalling memories and moments from them. Her last fourteen years of existence had been the bringing up of the boy. He was her world, her very reason to rise each day and meet the new dawn with hope. She had had offers from men admirers, especially working at a hospital – one doctor was very keen – but still Grace kept her distance and stayed dedicated to her Tom, and never once had she wavered from the duty that her best friend had asked of her. She did wonder from time to time what ever happened to Julie, in fourteen years not even a letter or a card; it was like she had vanished off the face of the earth.

Slowly some parts of her past had finally been put to rest. Tom, her husband, she found out had been killed in a Japanese prisoner of war camp while working on the Burma railway. She had received a visit from his old regiment after the war, and they had presented her with his medals; also they gave her back all of his effects and some of her letters, which she placed with his and kept safe upstairs in a suitcase.

Grace was feeling pleased as punch and sat sipping a cup of tea and smiling, Tom had been awarded a place at the local grammar school; Mr Douglas had put Tom forward for the exam and Tom had excelled in all subjects. Even the unemotional Miss Gull was impressed by Tom's academic record, and made Grace feel even prouder when she said, "This is a first for North Compton School, to have a student go on to further education and excel. I am sure we will in future hear great things of Tom Backer."

A sharp knock on the door brought Grace out of her daydream; looking at the clock on the mantelpiece, she thought Tom would be home soon for his tea, better get on. Feeling her age, she went to answer the door. As she opened the door she was confronted by two tall policemen. Grace was not surprised; after all this was the East End of London, and something was always going on.

"Mrs Backer," said one of the policeman.

"Yes, can I help?" said Grace, not thinking for one moment he was actually here for her.

"Is your Tom in?" asked the policeman.

"No," said Grace, "he should be on his way home after school. Why, what's this all about?" Grace started to have a deep foreboding in the pit of her stomach.

"There has been an incident," said the policeman.

"What kind of an incident?" said Grace, feeling her blood beginning to rise.

"Sorry Mrs Backer, I am not at liberty to answer that question."

Pompous ass, thought Grace. "Well, who can?" she said, starting to get a really uneasy feeling.

"Can I come in and look around?" said the policeman.

"Why?" said Grace.

"We need to find your Son. There has been a murder," said the other policeman.

Grace staggered back against the door frame as the policemen pushed past her, and proceeded to search the house, after a time returning to Grace who had not moved since they had entered.

The policeman said, "If he shows up, it will be in his and your best interest if he comes voluntarily to the local police station," to which Grace just nodded. Closing the door, she stumbled into the kitchen and sat heavily onto a chair. Her heart was racing and Grace could feel sweat beginning to appear on her neck, she was confused. How could her Tom be involved in a murder? They must have it wrong. Perhaps he saw one taking place, and was a witness.

She was still trying to make sense of it all when another knock at the door brought her thought back to the present.

Grace staggered to the door thinking it was Tom, not even realising he would never knock, but Grace had become distraught and desperate for news. Grace opened the door on her friend from across the street, Doris. By the look on her face, Grace knew the news was not good; without talking, Grace turned and walked back into the kitchen with Doris following in her wake.

Grace sat down and Doris sat next to her. Taking Grace's hands in hers Doris slowly explained the events to Grace. Apparently Sally Newton had been found murdered, and the police were treating Tom as the chief suspect. Grace had a thousand questions go off in her head at once.

Grace looked at Doris and said, "Tell me all you know."

Doris went on to explain that apparently Tom and Sally were seen after school earlier, at the top of Brick Lane in a heated argument. Sally pushed Tom away, Tom grabbed her arm but she broke free and ran towards the old derelict factory on Morton Street off Brick Lane. Tom was seen following her, and that was the last time anyone had seen either of them.

Apparently Sally was supposed to be home by four to baby sit, so her mother could go to work. After she failed to arrive home, her mother went to the school to find her. The school raised the alarm to the police, who after a search found her body in the derelict factory on Morton Street. That was when people began pointing the finger at Tom; after all, everyone knew they were best friends, and they were seen arguing, so when the police finally spotted Tom on the way to the school, they approached him and he ran off, so they were looking for him now.

After gleaning every piece of fact and gossip from Doris, Grace thanked her and stood up and walked towards the door. Doris realised her presence was no longer required and followed her out.

Once alone back in the kitchen, Grace sat and placed her head in her hands and closed her eyes. Grace thought about her poor boy, alone and afraid; what would he do? Tom would go somewhere if not here, somewhere he felt safe. Grace opened her eyes and smiled, she knew just the place Tom would go.

But before meeting Tom, Grace had an errand to run, and hoped the man who could help her was still in the country. Going to the paper, she turned to the listings, found what she was looking for and quickly left.

Grace went as fast as her feet could carry her to the docks. At the gate, she asked for the Harbour Master's Office; after being shown the way, Grace hurried towards his office. At the office Grace knocked and entered, the harbour master looked up and smiled. Grace said, "Excuse me, I know you are busy, but I am looking for a ship."

"Come to the right place," said the harbour master, smiling.

Grace smiled after realising what she had said. "Sorry, I am looking for the Red Star from Odessa, Russia, don't suppose it is still here?"

The Harbour Master said, "Let me check the register, and see."

"Thank you," said Grace.

After a few minutes, the harbour master said, "Yes here it is, Red Star, not due out until morning tide at six am tomorrow. Anything else?"

"Yes, can you tell me what pier the ship is at," asked Grace.

The harbour master looked down again and then said, "Pier eleven." Looking back up, Grace had already left.

Grace found her way to pier eleven. Staring up at the huge bulk of the Red Star, she saw a figure and waved. Captain Ivor Sharapova ran down the gang plank, towards Grace. "My dear Nurse Grace, what a pleasant surprise, after all these years." They hugged and Ivor kissed Grace on each cheek. "How did you find me?" asked Ivor.

"It's been a little game of mine over the years, to check the shipping listing to see if a certain young Russian sailor ever became a ship's captain."

This made Ivor roar with laughter. "How is the family?" asked Ivor.

"That's why I am here, Ivor. I need your help," said Grace.

"Ask anything Nurse Grace, you know you can count on me."

After Grace explained the problem to Ivor, they hugged and kissed again, and Grace departed to meet Tom.

Grace waited until it was dark. She had not been idle in the preceding hours; Grace knew she would get the truth from Tom, she still knew when he was lying to her. It was a sixth sense Grace had with Tom, not that Tom bothered to lie; their relationship was built on love and respect for each other so even when in trouble, Tom always owned up to her. Grace had packed a small suitcase for Tom, placed all the money she had available into a brown envelope and slipped it into her coat pocket.

Grace turned on the front room light and closed the curtain and turned on the radio, giving the appearance of someone being at home. Grace hoped no one would come calling while she slipped out.

Grace went into the kitchen and turned out the light. As she stood looking out of the window, she was thankful the moon was full and was casting good light. Grace stood for about ten minutes to see if she could spot any movement; she smiled, as the reason she was going to be able to slip away so easily was the house opposite that had caused her so much pain was still not built but remained a large hole between the other two houses. All she had to do was walk up the garden, climb the fence and walk into the next street before anyone was aware Grace had left the house.

Grace quickly opened the back door and slipped out over the garden into the next street, pausing before Grace turned right into the street and headed towards the church at the bottom of the road.

As Grace walked down the dark street, she tried to keep her breathing calm, but every noise made her jump and by the time she made it to the church Grace was a bag of nerves. She slowly opened the church gate and moved around the side of the church to the graveyard. Opening the graveyard gate, Grace moved between the gravestones as if she had done it a thousand times, which of course she had. Coming to a gravestone Grace stopped and knelt down, and by the light of the moon, she read the inscription:

> ***Ruth Gloria Backer***
> ***Loving daughter of Grace and Tom Backer***
> ***Taken before her time, now with the angels***
> ***Tom Backer Loving Husband and father***

Grace had added 'Tom Backer loving husband and father'; although Tom was not actually there, it gave her a place of pilgrimage and a place of solace since the war had ended. Grace would come every Sunday and some Sundays Tom would accompany her to lay flowers on the grave, and while Tom wandered off she would talk to both of them.

Grace sat on the suitcase and waited. After about an hour, Grace heard her name being called in a whisper. "Mater, mater." Grace stood up out of the darkness and held her arms open. Tom immediately ran to her embrace, and sobbed into her shoulder. Tom clung to her in such desperation he made her heart weep.

After a time Grace held him at arm's length, and asked him, "Did you do it?"

Tom looked straight into her eyes and said, "No, mother, I promise," which was all the confirmation she needed.

They both sat on the ground huddled together, whispering; Tom explained that he and Sally had argued after school. Some of the kids were going to the park to drink and smoke and fool around. Tom was trying to get Sally not to go, as she was getting a reputation at school for being a slut. Tom had punched a few boys over certain comments they had made about Sally, but he realised he could not fight the whole school over her. Tom tried to appeal to her better nature to stop, but Sally had laughed in his face, and Tom angrily grabbed her arm which Sally shrugged off. Sally then ran, saying, "I hate you, Tom Backer." Shocked, finally Tom ran after her up to the end of Brick Lane where she disappeared from view; once Tom had lost sight of her, Tom then went back to school to see Mr Douglas.

Grace explained all that had happened since he had run. Tom said, "I just panicked, as everyone was pointing and calling me a murder, so I ran. You know me, mother, I would never have hurt Sally." Grace told Tom about the police coming to the house and she thought they were watching it, waiting for him to return. So London was no longer safe for him.

Grace took out the brown envelope and gave it to him, and said, "This is all I have; use it well." Passing him the suitcase, Grace said, "Go to the docks, pier eleven. There is a merchant ship hauling coal called the Red Star, bound for Odessa in Russia. Ask for the captain, Ivor Sharapova. He is expecting you."

Tom wondered how his mother had managed all of this in such a short time, but knowing she would not tell, he knew he would be eternally grateful to her. They hugged for what seemed like an eternity, finally breaking and looking deep into each other's eyes; both wondering if this was their last meeting ever. Grace kissed him on the cheek and pushed Tom towards the way he came, and said, "Go, go now and don't look back, remember I will always love you."

Tom turned and said, "Thank you, mother," before disappearing into the darkness.

Once alone, Grace's knees gave out and she sank onto the grave, sobbing uncontrollably. Not for one minute did she consider her actions incorrect, there was no way her Tom was going to be hanged for a murder he never committed.

Grace eventually returned to her empty home, knowing it would never be full of happiness again. Once inside she made a pot of tea, sat down, and slowly drifted off into another world.

Over the coming days, the police returned many times, and questioned Grace over the whereabouts of Tom, and she truthfully answered she did not know. After all, she did not know where the Red Star was, so to Grace it was not a lie. People on the street would gossip, but after time the incident faded into people's memories and although the case was never solved, it was eventually closed. Life carried on as normal, Grace returned to work at the hospital but every day she wondered how her Tom was doing.

Years later, one morning she heard a knock at the door. She looked at her watch and thought it must be the postman, but she could not remember ordering anything large enough for him to knock. Opening the door, there stood Captain Ivor with a big grin on his face, and a large bunch of flowers. Grace stood and stared at him in total shock. "Ivor, my dear god," said Grace.

"Well, am I invited in?" replied Ivor.

"Of course, where are my manners, please come in," said Grace.

When they were in the kitchen, Ivor presented the flowers to Grace, and said, "Something to brighten your day."

Smiling, Grace said, "How on earth did you find me?"

"You are not the only one who can play at being Miss Marble," said Ivor. Grace looked at Ivor in total puzzlement. "Have I not said it right? The lady detective Miss Marble."

"Oh, Miss Marple, you mean Miss Marple," said Grace, laughing.

"Arr, yes, Miss Marple," replied Ivor, also laughing. He went on, "The other day when we docked, I went to the hospital you cared for me so well at, to see if I could track you down, and to my surprise after all these years you still work there, and they knew who you were immediately. Matron Grace, now head of Nursing. You have done well for yourself, Nurse Grace," said a smiling Ivor.

Grace blushed. "Get away with you, you silver tongued devil," said a laughing Grace; this made Ivor throw his head back and roar with laughter as well. Grace asked, "Can I get you a cup of tea, Ivor?"

"That would be most pleasant, thank you Nurse Grace," replied Ivor.

While Grace was busying herself making the tea and sorting the flowers, she asked over her shoulder, "So, Ivor, why the need to track me down after all these years?"

"I think you know the answer to that question yourself, Nurse Grace," said Ivor softly.

Grace put the tea pot hard down on the kitchen table. "My Tom."

"Yes, your Tom," said Ivor, smiling at Grace. Grace closed

her eyes for a second, and when she opened them, they were filled with tears. "Please my dear Nurse Grace, I did not come here to cause you distress," said Ivor on seeing Grace's face.

"No it's not you, Ivor, it's me, after all these years of wondering if he was safe. Please go on, tell me your news."

Ivor went on and explained to Grace about Tom's escape and how well it went, his friendship with his nephew Sebastian, there company they created together and his forthcoming marriage to his niece Natasha. After Ivor had finished talking, Grace sat with a smile on her face.

Grace said softly, "Thank you Ivor, you are so kind to track me down and let me know my boy is doing well."

"Nurse Grace, it was my pleasure," replied Ivor, smiling. "Before I go and forget," said Ivor, passing Grace an envelope, "this is from Tom."

As Grace reached for it, Ivor placed his hand over hers, and said, "Please only read it after I have gone."

Grace smiled and said, "Of course, Ivor."

After Ivor left, Grace sat at the table staring at the envelope. Grace did not care about the contents of the letter, as she now knew her Tom was safe and thriving and living his life to the full, which is all a mother could possibly hope for. Grace slowly opened the envelope and removed the letter and read:

My dear Mother

I am so sorry it has taken me so long to write to you, and let you know I am now safe. I hope you have not been too disappointed by my lack of contact, or think my love for you has diminished because we are not together, because nothing is further from the truth.

I hope you know now from Uncle Ivor that I am well and run my own business here in Odessa, Russia. Life is good for me, I am in a month's time getting married, Natasha is her name, who to me is the most beautiful woman in the world, she makes me so happy, and mother, she reminds me a lot of you, in her manner and outlook, I think when you meet you will become firm friends. I know our parting was not ideal and I did not have a chance to tell you things perhaps I should have before I left so suddenly, this was a big regret on my part. But I want to now tell you, the reason I am the man I am today is solely down to you, and the way you brought me up, and the guidance and encouragement you gave to me during the years we were together.

I can never repay you for what you have done for me, the sacrifices you endured to give me a happy home life and a loving environment, I only hope that if I am blessed with children, I can teach them the lessons I learnt from you on how to be a loving parent. One day I will return and hold you once again, this I promise to you. But until then, know you are always in my heart and thoughts.

Your ever loving son
Tom

After Grace had read the letter five or six times, she replaced it back into the envelope and closed her eyes. Tom was safe and well, that all she ever wanted to hear. Grace said a silent prayer, before standing up and realising if she did not get a hurry on she would be late for work for the first time in years. Grace went upstairs singing.

Odessa

Tom kept to the shadows all the way down to the docks, instead of making for the front gates. Tom knew these would be guarded and no doubt the police would have a man stationed there looking for him; also they would have passed out his description to all the dock workers, no doubt some would know him by sight. He slipped into the docks via the coal heaps, through a hole in the fence he used to use when he played there as a child. After entering the docks, he waited behind an abandoned coal shed, to see if the alarm had been raised or if he had been spotted. While crouching in the half-light he realised his next problem was to find pier eleven, as in the moonlight all the ships looked the same. Checking that no one was about, Tom walked down to the main intersection of the docks and read the signs to pier eleven; following the arrow towards pier eleven he stayed in the shadows where possible, stopping every few feet to make sure he had not been spotted.

Finally Tom found pier eleven, and looked up at the Red Star for the first time. She look like a dark, foreboding colossus, which made Tom shiver. He moved cautiously to the gang plank heading up to the ship; he had kept in the shadows most of the way without being spotted, once or twice it was close as dockers passed by, but they were not looking for him so they did not look too hard in the shadows.

Slowly he crouched down and ran up the gang plank onto

the ship. Just as he took his first step on the ship, a large hand shot out of the darkness and grabbed him. Tom nearly fainted with the shock of being grabbed. The hand encompassed his whole neck. Tom felt the pressure from the hand and realised one squeeze could snap his neck like a twig. Tom did not move; the hand went loose and he turning around and looked into the face of the biggest man he had ever seen, with a scars running down his face from temple to chin. The man did not speak but dragged Tom towards an open door. Once inside the door the man released Tom, and look down at him and said in a heavy weighted Russian accent, "You must be young Tom Backer, Nurse Grace's son," to which Tom nodded; the man smiled, showing a perfect set of white teeth.

"I am Ivor Sharapova, Captain of the Red Star, I have been expecting you. We saw you skulking along the pier towards us. Come follow me." The captain led Tom into the interior of the ship and showed him into a small cabin. The captain said, "Get some sleep in here; I will be back for you once we have cleared harbour and are at open sea."

Tom thanked the captain and entered the small cabin. Once the door was closed behind him, Tom sat heavily on the bunk and for the first time in hours breathed normally. Tom placed his suitcase on the top bunk, placed his head in his hands, closed his eyes and sobbed. After a time Tom looked around the cabin noting the sparseness of it, a bunk bed with mattresses, both with a pillow and a blanket folded up on them, a table extending from the wall which allowed you to sit on the bottom bunk and use it as a work top, and a small lavatory in the corner with a neatly placed, folded concertina door. The whole room looked practical without showing any warmth. Tom felt exhausted so he lay down on the bottom bunk and closed his eye and slowly drifted off into a troubled sleep.

Tom came awake by a loud knocking on the door. The door was then opened by a young blond-haired boy, not much older than Tom was. The boy smiled at Tom and said something which Tom presumed was Russian, and at the same time beckoned Tom to follow him.

Tom followed the boy through the maze of the ship, coming eventually to what Tom could smell as the galley. Tom realised he was starving; he could not remember the last time he had eaten a proper meal. The boy beckoned Tom inside and handed him a plate and spoke again while gesturing towards the food steaming on the side.

Tom took a plate full of eggs, bacon, sausage, toast and a large cup of tea, which was thick and dark. The blond-haired boy led Tom to an unoccupied table and together they eat in silence.

After breakfast, Tom leaned back and patted his stomach and smiled. The blond-haired boy did the same and they both burst out laughing. For the first time since being on the ship, Tom felt comfortable and at ease. The blond boy picked up his plate and returned it to a large trolley at the end of the table; Tom followed suit, then the blond-haired boy once again beckoned Tom to follow. Eventually they arrived at the bridge. The bridge was a hive of activity, with at least four seamen and the captain, who was sitting on a chair in the middle of the bridge. The seaman were either sitting at work stations, or scanning the horizon; they were all busily working away to keep the ship afloat and straight towards their destination.

Finally the captain turned in his chair towards Tom and beckoned him over to his chair. Tom went and stood next to the captain. Tom looked out of the windows and all he could see was dark grey sea, with waves crashing against the bow and side of the ship as she ploughed her way eastwards. "Next stop, Russia," said the captain, smiling at Tom, which brought a smile to Tom's face, but for the life of him he could not fathom out why. The captain stood up and spoke to someone on his left, who acknowledged his orders and went and sat in the captain's chair. The captain said to Tom, "Follow me," and he strolled from the bridge with Tom and the blond-haired boy in his wake.

The captain led them down the corridor back to the galley; they all took a seat around the table and the captain shouted something, and eventually appeared a man dressed in a white coat carrying a tray of three steaming hot cups of tea. After passing out the cups they all sat in silence, slowing sipping from the steaming cups. The captain placed his cup down and Tom followed suit. The captain looked at Tom and said, "Well, master Tom, what a fine mess you have gotten yourself into," to which all Tom could do was blush, which made the blond boy giggle.

Tom said, "Captain Ivor, I appreciate your help and will never forget your kindness and," but before Tom could finish, the captain had put up his hand and said, "Master Tom, this is no cruise ship, I do not carry passengers. You will work for your passage to the motherland, and let me assure you," said the captain, leaning in close, "you will pull your weight on my ship, or over the side you will go." The captain laughed at his own joke, but Tom knew by his manner he was deadly serious, which made him shudder. The captain told Tom he would be working in the galley with Sebastian, waving at the blond boy, "He will show you your duties. Plus I also have a favour to ask of you, I want you to teach my nephew English," pointing to the blond-haired boy, "and no doubt he can teach you some Russian, so by the time we reach the motherland, you might become useful to me." Still laughing at his own jokes, the captain stood and left the room.

Tom and Sebastian sat staring at each other when the captain had gone. Eventually Tom tapped his chest and said, "I am Tom," and pointing at Sebastian, "you are Sebastian." Sebastian pointed at Tom and said, "You are Tom." They both smiled and nodded.

Over the next few weeks, Tom had got the hang of his duties and the navigation of the ship down to a fine art. His duties were quite simple: he had to make sure before every meal the galley was stocked up with enough cups, plates and cutlery to last the meal. After each meal, clear all the dirty dishes from the galley. He had to keep the galley floor and tables clean at all times. Wash and dry all the dirty dishes and cutlery and return them to the galley ready for use. As the crew worked different watches, Tom and Sebastian became quite good at knowing how many were coming to the galley at each watch beginning and each watch end. After two weeks, Tom and Sebastian had become inseparable.

After a month they were both able to speak to each other, switching from English and Russian and back again. Sometimes Sebastian would get stuck on a sentence, but Tom was quick to translate for him, which became an annoyance to the some of the other crew members who did not understand the whole conversation. Even Captain Ivor was impressed at the speed with which Tom had picked up Russian. He spoke it like a native without an accent; this Tom had learnt from listening to the crew. The Red Star stopped twice on the way to Odessa, but both times no crew members were allowed to leave the ship.

Most nights Tom and Sebastian would sit up late in the galley and talk about the worlds they came from, both learn-ing about each other's lives. One night Tom asked Sebastian about his uncle the captain, which made Sebastian smile. "Uncle Ivor. But I am not allowed to call him that on ship, it's always captain," said Sebastian giving a mock salute, which made them both laugh. He told Tom that the captain was his mother's older brother and had been at sea all his life, since he was fourteen. "He had been away at sea when my mother and father died, Uncle Ivor with my Uncle Vlad became my and my older sister Natasha's guardians." He had taken him on this trip to see if a life on the ocean was in his blood, but Sebastian said, "I think my uncle knows I am not cut out to be his protégé and a life at sea is not really in my blood. I think I am destined to be a land lover," which made them both laugh again.

Tom then asked how the captain knew his mother, and Sebastian explained that during the war his uncle was working on the Russian convoys bringing goods into the UK. Out in a pub one night, he got into a fight with another Russian over a woman and he got stabbed in the chest twice and his faced slashed. "He was in hospital for nearly two months while he recovered; as fate had it, the ship he was sailing on was torpedoed on the way back to Russia, with all hands lost, so you can say he was the lucky one. Your mother was one of his nurses who cared for him, she was the one that stitched his face up and saved his eye. She was very gentle and she would visit and sit with him and she taught him basic English. I think he was a bit in love with her, but he was always in her debt, so when she sought him out and asked about you, he did not even hesitate to help."

One night whilst Tom and Sebastian were chatting, Sebastian asked, "Have you decided what you are going to do once we reach Odessa, Tom?"

"To tell you the truth, I have not really given it any thought," replied Tom.

"How would you like to go into partnership with me when we reach Odessa?" Sebastian asked.

"What kind of partnership?" Tom replied.

"I want to start a delivery business. We will take any goods anywhere it's required within our range, with no questions asked."

For the next two hours Sebastian laid out his basic plan to Tom, and after he had finished Tom said, "Bloody hell, you certainly thought things through." Tom agreed with Sebastian; although he has enjoyed his time on the Red Star, Tom did not think he was a natural seaman either and held out his hand to Sebastian and said, "Partners."

Sebastian shook Tom's hand and said, "Partners," and they both then started to laugh again.

Over the next few days Sebastian and Tom discussed their plan. Sebastian had managed to find an old unused notebook, so between them they wrote down a few ideas and plans for the future. One night Sebastian looked at Tom seriously and said, "What we are short of is capital."

Tom smiled and for the first time really felt part of the process. Taking the brown envelope that his mother had given him, he placed it on the table and said, "Will this help?"

Slowly picking up the envelope, Sebastian opened the envelope and whistled, "Must be a fortune in here, more money than I have ever seen. How much is here?" asked Sebastian.

Tom said, "There is over 300 UK pounds there."

Sebastian said, "We will have to exchange it to Russian roubles. Natasha will know how." Sebastian just sat looking at the money and finally tipped his head back and howled, and start laughing. Seeing Sebastian's joy it was infectious, and it made Tom howl and start laughing as well.

Finally land was spotted and the ship made its slow process in to Odessa. The ship was a hive of activity over the next few days and Sebastian and Tom did not have a lot of time together.

Sebastian and Tom were on the upper deck looking out at the vast city while they were docking. Sebastian turned to Tom and holding out his arms, said, "Welcome to my home." Tom smiled but felt apprehensive about the next stage of his life. As Tom scanned the sprawling port of Odessa, he thought how different it was from the port he had left in England; everywhere Tom looked there was every kind of military ship, and before Tom could ask Sebastian he said, "Russian Black Sea Baltic fleet, best navy in the world." Tom stared; never had he seen so many ships congregated in one place.

A crew member found them on the upper deck, and told them the captain had called Sebastian and Tom to his cabin. It was the first time Tom had actually been to the 'Captain's Cabin'. As he stood outside with Sebastian, the door finally opened and a crew member walked out with a smile, so Tom deduced it was good news. Sebastian and Tom stood before the captain, who handed both boys an envelope. "Take this, you have earned it. I have been impressed by you both. I hope someday we can ship out again."

Tom shook the offered hand which engulfed his, as did Sebastian. Both turned to go when the captain said, "Don't let some hussy relieve you of that in the first hour of being on shore," to which the captain started to laugh. Tom and Sebastian looked puzzled, and both looked at each other and shrugged.

Tom said he would meet Sebastian at the top of the gang plank once he had collected all his belongings. Whilst he packed his suitcase, Tom pulled out the envelope given to him by the captain, and on opening it was surprised there was a stack of Russian roubles. Although Tom had no idea how much it related to in English pounds, Tom thought perhaps he needed to stop thinking in English pounds and go with the local currency, which seemed like a plan to him; but for his own curiosity, he would ask Sebastian how much they had made from this trip. With his suitcase in hand, Tom stood at the top of the gang plank and waited for Sebastian. Five minutes later Sebastian joined him with his own suitcase, and together they went down the gang plank to their new future.

Tom had been raised in London, so seeing a city like Odessa should not have come as such a shock, but it did; the place was a hive of activity everywhere you looked, stalls selling anything and everything, and Tom wondered that in such a place you can buy or sell anything. Tom then realised that Sebastian's plan might not be so daft as he first thought. These traders will need stock and they could be in a position to help. One thing Tom did notice straight away was that unlike in London, people did not call out their wares, plus people were not smiling or laughing, but kept their heads down going about their business; but it was still a bustling city like any other in the world.

Sebastian led Tom to a tram stop. As they waited for the next tram Sebastian gave Tom a running commentary of Odessa, pointing out places and explaining sights to Tom, but Tom was still amazed that unlike London, which was crammed into a small area, Odessa was sprawling and vast.

Eventually the tram arrived and Tom and Sebastian took a seat at the back; the ticket collector came and Sebastian paid for the two tickets, not before the ticket collector gave them both a hard stare, as if they were up to no good.

Tom asked Sebastian, "What's his problem?" to which Sebastian answered, "In Russia everyone spies on everyone else. You will get used to it my friend, the trick is knowing who to trust and who not to trust."

"Him I do not trust," which made them both laugh, which made the ticket collector turn and stare again.

Finally Sebastian nudged Tom and said, "This is us." Sebastian pressed the bell and the tram slowed and halted. Both Sebastian and Tom departed just before the tram moved off again; they both stood and waved at the ticket collector and laughed again, but he just stared after them. Tom looked about and they were surrounded by tall apartment blocks, each one identical to the next. Tom said, "How the hell you supposed to know what one you live in? They all look the same," which made Sebastian laugh. Slapping Tom on the back, he said, "This way, comrade."

Sebastian walked diagonally from the tram stop toward the apartment block in the corner. Once there, Tom saw an old lady sitting in front of the entrance who appeared asleep, but as Sebastian approached he called her name; she raised her head and smiled at Sebastian. Sebastian told Tom, "We only live on the fourth floor so we can walk up the stairs."

Tom asked Sebastian why he was reluctant to use the lift; Sebastian said, "My friend, if you want to try Russian lift, we will try Russian lift, but it will be your one and only time."

Tom thought, daft, it's only a lift. Sebastian pulled the double gates open and stood back to allow Tom to enter, and after Tom got in Sebastian closed the double gates. Sebastian said, "You can do the honours," pointing at the lift buttons.

Tom said, "Here goes," and pressed the number four button.

Tom looked at Sebastian, who had a worried look on his face and was hanging on to the side for what to Tom looked like dear life. Tom was just about to say something, when the lift took on a mind of its own; it started to violently shake from side to side and make the most death-defying screaming noise, which Tom thought no doubt the whole building could hear. The lift then shot up at a rapid rate of knots. Tom was sure his feet actually left the ground, as the lift ascended upwards. At the fourth floor, the lift stopped with a shudder and finally with a bang settled on the fourth floor. Shakily, Sebastian and Tom left the lift. Tom stood and closed his eyes and took deep breaths; he turned to Sebastian and said, "I have never been so scared in my life, I am never going to repeat that experience," and laughing, Sebastian slapped Tom's back and said, "I told you so."

Sebastian walked to a brightly coloured painted blue door and knocked; Sebastian turned to Tom and winked. The door was opened by a young woman not much older than Sebastian, but it was obvious she was Sebastian's sister; she had the same blonde hair and the same bright blue eyes. She hugged him, then kissed him on each cheek, held him at arm's length and then she peppered him with a thousand questions. Tom was unable to keep up with the verbal onslaught. Finally Sebastian gestured towards Tom and for the first time, the young woman looked at Tom.

Tom thought his heart would jump from his chest, as the young woman stared at him and smiled and said, "So it was you who made the racket with the lift." Tom tried to smile back, but only managed to go red.

Sebastian said, "Stop it Natasha, you are making my friend embarrassed." Tom tried to protest, but the young woman had already turned laughing from the door and entered the flat.

Tom followed Sebastian into the flat and closed the door behind him, both dropping their suitcases in the hall. Sebastian went and stood next to Tom and said, "Natasha may I introduce Mr Tom Backer who is my best friend and new business partner. He is from London, England."

"I know where London is, Sebastian," said Natasha. Natasha

held out her hand and smiled at Tom. "Welcome to our home Mr Tom Backer, please treat our home as yours."

Tom took Natasha's hand and said, "Thank you, Natasha, for your warm welcome."

"You speak Russian well for someone from England," said Natasha.

"I am a quick learner," said Tom, smiling.

Natasha, still smiling, said, "You two hungry?"

"Yes," they both said in unison.

"Good," said Natasha, turning, and retreating to the kitchen.

Natasha emerged from the kitchen with a tray of steaming food, which she placed on the table; both Tom and Sebastian devoured the food. Natasha returned to the kitchen, leaving them to eat in peace.

After having their fill, both Tom and Sebastian agreed there was nothing like a good home made meal. Sebastian picked up the dishes and returned them to the kitchen, Tom sat and closed his eyes, and for the first time thought about his mother and home. He could hear Sebastian and Natasha chatting in the kitchen, and before long he had drifted into a deep sleep.

Tom slowly came round, and although his eyes were still closed, his other senses were fully alert. It was silent apart from a hum of an electric lamp. He opened his eyes and blinked; the first thing he saw was Natasha sitting opposite him, reading a book. She slowly put the book down and smiled. She said, "Sebastian went for a lie down. You looked so peaceful so we left you."

Tom stretched and asked her how long had he been sleeping; Natasha replied six hours.

Natasha asked Tom if he wanted anything. "Please can I use the bathroom," to which Natasha pointed, "First door on the right," and raised her book again, Tom got up and walked to the bathroom. Afterwards Tom came and sat back opposite Natasha, but the silence was deafening.

Both Tom and Natasha started to speak at once, which made them both laugh, and seemed to break the ice, and after a few minutes they were chatting like old friends.

Natasha asked, "How did you end up in Odessa?"

Tom replied "My life was going fine, I was brought up by my mother, she was a loving, and kind person, who I love very much. School was brilliant, I had just passed my exams to go to grammar school."

Natasha could see Tom was getting upset as he was going on, so she said, "Do not say any more if it will bring you sadness."

"No," replied Tom, "I think I need to tell someone."

"OK, if you are sure," said Natasha.

Tom went on, "I had a best friend Sally, we used to be so close, do everything together, but over the last few months she changed, mother explained the difference between men and women to me," which made Tom blush as he thought about his mother's lecture.

Natasha tried not to laugh but she could not help herself, but she quickly said, "I am sorry I did not mean to laugh, when my Aunty Victoria explained it all to me, I felt embarrassed, so please do not worry, it happened to us all." Natasha smiled at Tom, which made Tom feel better.

Tom carried on his story. "Sally and me had a row after school one day, I tried to grab her and she told me she hated me. That was so hurtful, I felt so confused that I tried to run after her and talk to her. But she had vanished, so I went to see Mr Douglas my school master, on the way home. People were pointing and calling me a murder, I did not know what they were talking about. Then someone said Sally had been found murdered. I was physically sick. How could people think I could have done that to Sally? She was my best friend.

"Just then, two policemen spotted me and called my name and started to run after me. I just panicked and ran." Tom stopped speaking and had tears in his eyes; Natasha leaned over and took his hand in hers and smiled. Tom finished off his tale by explaining how his mother knew her uncle Ivor and she got him to take Tom from England.

Natasha asked, "What would have happened if you had stayed and handed yourself in?"

Tom thought for a few minutes and softly said, "I think they would have hanged me for Sally's murder."

Natasha nodded and said, "Then I am glad you did not stay. I think we are going to become good friends as well." This made Tom smile.

Tom said, "OK, your turn."

Natasha told Tom she did not really remember her mother or father, she and Sebastian had been brought up by Uncle Vlad and Aunty Victoria, with Uncle Ivor when he was back from sea. She went to state school, and graduated with a diploma, so she could choose any career or further education if she wanted to, but decided on helping Aunty Victoria in her bakery, a job which she loved. "The smell of baking bread is the best smell in the world," she said. This made Tom laugh. Tom knew most of the story from Sebastian, Natasha just filled in the parts Sebastian forgot or did not want to mention.

Eventually Natasha yawned and said, "I must go to bed, I am up bright and early." Tom looked at his watch and was amazed that they had been chatting for over five hours; he realised himself he felt tired and a good night's sleep was needed. Natasha showed Tom where he was sleeping and bid him good night before entering another room and closing the door quietly behind her.

Tom noticed Sebastian had already placed his suitcase on the bed. He could hear Sebastian quietly snoring in the other bed, Tom quickly undressed and for the first time in months slept in a bed that did not move.

Next morning Tom woke before Sebastian. He quickly dressed, made his bed and went into the kitchen where he found Natasha already busy. Once Natasha saw Tom she greeted him with a smile and asked if he had slept well. Tom nodded and smiled; she then poured him a cup of coffee, which Tom took and sat at the kitchen table, chatting to Natasha. Eventually Sebastian appeared, still looking half asleep; Natasha smiled at him and said, "My little brother was never a morning person, were you," as she ruffled his hair, which brought a 'get off' from Sebastian.

After Natasha had left for work, Sebastian told Tom they would go down and see what was on offer to use as a delivery van. Tom thought it strange way of putting it, 'what was on offer', but he was about to find out.

Sebastian led Tom down the road back towards the city centre. Sebastian explained they were going to the local garage; once there, Tom realised what Sebastian had meant by 'what was on offer'. There were five assorted types of vehicles in the car lot, and not many of them.

As Tom and Sebastian were moving towards the first car, a man appeared from a porta cabin, and with arms wide and a big smile said, "Welcome comrades, how can I help you?" While Sebastian was talking to the man, Tom wandered, looking at the vehicles on offer. Tom thought to himself that he had seen better burnt out wrecks on Brick Lane's waste ground then were here, and wondered if any actually ran.

One was so rusty that Tom could not determine its original colour; this brought a smile to Tom's face. Eventually Tom wandered back to Sebastian who was in a heated negotiation with the man over a small-sized greenish van; Tom thought this man must have seen every Hollywood film that portrays a car lot owner, as his actions were so American, even down to the hand gestures. The man said a price, Sebastian shook his head, Sebastian said a price, the man shook his head, and waved his arms; so it went on, until Sebastian pulled out a wad of roubles, and then the man's attitude changed, as here was real cash and a real chance of a sale. Eventually the man and Sebastian agreed on a price, both shook hands, the man slapped Sebastian on the back, and said, "Let's step into my office and complete the paperwork." Tom shook his head and was still grinning.

Sebastian eventually appeared waving the keys to Tom. Tom said, "All paperwork sorted?" Sebastian waved the keys again and said, "Paperwork."

Tom said, "Where is the log book and paperwork?" which by the confused look on Sebastian's face was the keys, which he now had. Tom looked toward the heavens and said, "Saints preserve us from dodgy deals," which made Sebastian laugh. Sebastian unlocked the van door and stood back for Tom to enter.

Tom tugged at the door handle and was surprised it opened without any effort.

"O ye of little faith," said Sebastian. Tom climbed in as Sebastian was opening the driver's door and getting in. Sebastian placed the key in the ignition and Tom held his breath, and to both their surprise it purred into life. Both were elated as they drove back home, both singing at the top of their voices, and when Sebastian saw someone he honked the horn and they both waved; of course no one waved back, but only stared after the two laughing young men in a dirty green van.

Sebastian parked outside the block of flats, and they both got out and checked out the back. It was clean and spacious. Tom tested the suspension, and it seemed OK. Sebastian said, "Tomorrow we will go and see my Uncle Vlad, he will point us in the right direction for some work." Tom thought this was a good plan, and both made sure the van was locked and secure and went upstairs to the flat.

While they were sitting at the kitchen table discussing the next steps and future, Natasha came in from work carrying some groceries. Tom went to help, but she shooed him away and said, "I can manage." Tom apologised but did not feel foolish as Natasha had a glint in her eye and a smile on her face, so he knew she was teasing him.

Natasha joined them both at the table and asked what they were talking about. Sebastian explained they were discussing their business plan. Natasha said, "First you need a name."

Both Sebastian and Tom felt a bit stupid as neither had even considered having a company name, and Natasha laughed. "How do people find and use you if you don't have a company name?"

Tom said to Sebastian, "Perhaps we should ask Natasha to join us, she seems to know more about business and have more sense that both of us," which made Sebastian nod his head and Natasha laugh.

Tom and Sebastian both put forward some ideas of a company name, which brought about a heated argument between them both. Eventually they were both on their feet shouting at each other; Natasha sat still until Sebastian reached for Tom, then she stood, and slapped the table and said, "STOP, will you two sit down, you are acting like a couple of school children." Both apologised and sat down.

Natasha said, "Let's compromise and call your new fledgling company S&T Imports." Both Tom and Sebastian mulled it over for a few minutes, and then both agreed it was a fine name for a company, which made them all laugh.

Sebastian told Natasha his plan to go and see their Uncle Vlad to see if he could help with a few contracts, which Natasha agreed was a good place to start. Sebastian proudly placed the keys to the van on the table and beamed with pride. "Our first acquisition."

Natasha looked at them both and said, "You don't mean that rust bucket sitting outside is yours?"

"Why, what's wrong with it?" said Tom.

Natasha smiled and said, "Nothing, I was teasing you again," which made them all laugh.

Natasha asked how much money they had to start off with, both Tom and Sebastian stood and returned a few minutes later holding their respective envelopes. Both placed them on the table; Natasha opened them and counted the money out, three hundred and twenty five UK pounds from Tom's mother, three hundred roubles from Tom's trip on the Red Star, and one hundred roubles from Sebastian, but Sebastian did protest when he saw the look on Natasha's face.

"I did buy our only asset," he said, looking wounded.

Natasha said, "Men of wealth," which made them all laugh again.

Tom asked Natasha what they were going to do about the UK money, obviously it was no good as it was. Natasha said, "Tomorrow I will take it into the city, and go to the money exchange and see the best price I can get for it." Tom did not doubt for one minute that Natasha would be cheated out of anything, she was too shrewd.

Natasha also said, "You need to have a company structure," which brought a puzzled look to both Sebastian's and Tom's faces. Natasha went on to explain that all businesses have directors with allocated jobs titles, proper recorded minutes, regular board meetings, an asset register, correct accounting for profit and loss, and of course salaries paid to employees. Tom and Sebastian both looked at each other and in unison said, "Mrs Business, impressive."

Natasha replied "I read books, perhaps you should sometimes," which made all three of them laugh.

Natasha stood and went into her bedroom, eventually returning with a large pad. Returning, she placed it on the table, and smiling she said, "OK, let's get down to business." Over the next few hours, they decided on the company name: S&T Imports. They all agreed Tom would be the Managing Director, and Sebastian the Commercial Director, and of course Natasha the Company Secretary.

On a sheet of paper Natasha wrote at the top 'minutes of the first board meeting of S&T Imports', wrote the date and listed the items they had discussed so far. Tom finally said, "Can we have a break, my head hurts." When Sebastian agreed, they all decided on a short break. Natasha went into the kitchen to make some food and drinks, while Tom and Sebastian sat on the settee, staring out of the window at the weather. Eventually Tom turned to Sebastian and said, "I did not realise being a manager director could be so exhausting," which made Sebastian laugh.

Natasha called them both back to the table where she had placed a large plate of sandwiches and a large pitcher of orange juice. Tom poured each a glass of juice before taking a sandwich and munching away. They all ate in silence, and once the plate was empty, they cleared away ready for more discussion. The only point that caused bitter argument from them all was the salary they should be paid.

They had previously agreed that Natasha should also be the accountant and hold all the company's money. Natasha tried to object, but Tom pointed out Sebastian and he would only spend the money foolishly; after a pause Natasha smiled and agreed with Tom, which made them all laugh again. They agreed that if they required to purchase anything for the company then it had to be by a majority vote. As for the salary Natasha said she did not really feel right about asking for one, as she had not really contributed, which brought a storm of protest from Tom and Sebastian, both pointing out that without her then S&T Imports would not have come into existence and therefore it was only right she took a salary as well.

Eventually Natasha agreed, Sebastian and Tom would have fifty roubles a month and she would take twenty five roubles a month. Natasha raised the first vote asking if she could purchase some stationery on behalf of the company, asking all those in favour and three hands shot up. Smiling she said, "Those against?" theatrically looking between them all; laughing, she said, "Carried."

On a sheet of paper Natasha wrote a list of questions that Sebastian needed to ask Uncle Vlad. When she passed it to Sebastian, Tom leaned over his shoulder and read it as well; Tom whistled and said, "Amazing," and realised how much of an asset Natasha was turning out to be.

The next day Natasha was up first, followed by Tom then later by Sebastian. After a light breakfast, Natasha, together with Tom's UK money and her list of supplies, left before them both. They both eventually left as well. Driving towards the city, Sebastian turned off before the city signs, and eventually came to a block of shops; two boarded up and two that looked like they were closed for business. Sebastian told Tom the end shop was his Uncle Vlad's shop. "He sells anything to do with electrical items."

To Tom the shop looked deserted, but Sebastian strolled up to the door and pushed. Once the door was open, a bell sounded somewhere in the shop and a man appeared who looked like an older version of Captain Ivor but without the scar. Once he spotted Sebastian he smiled and came and embraced his nephew. Sebastian introduced Tom to his uncle, who smiled, and they shook hands. Vlad said, "Ivor has given me good reports about you, young Tom," smiling at Tom. Vlad beckoned them both further into the shop's interior. Tom looked around the shop and was in amazement: everywhere he looked were electrical parts. Some he recognised, like radios and vacuum cleaners, but nowhere did he spot an actual appliance completely made.

Vlad led them into the back of the shop, which was laid out like a comfy room; Tom thought Vlad obviously spent a lot of time in this back room. Once they were all seated Sebastian explained to his uncle Vlad their newly formed business venture, and all the time Vlad was nodding without interrupting his nephew. Eventually Vlad took out an old battered pipe and placed it in his mouth. After Sebastian had finished talking, Vlad took the pipe out of his mouth and, pointing at the two boys, said, "Maybe I can help you get some work," to which both Tom and Sebastian smiled. Vlad went onto explain he had an acquaintance in the city who he had worked with before, and did similar work to what they wanted to do, and sometimes was oversubscribed with work; he was sure for a small percentage he could place some work their way.

Tom thought, even in Russia, a communalist country, capitalism lives where money talks.

Sebastian stood to leave when Tom poked him in the side and said, "List."

Sebastian said, "Oh yes," and pulled out the list Natasha

had given him, passing the list to his uncle, who studied it and after a time, took a pencil and wrote next to each question. He passed the list back to Sebastian, who carefully placed it in his pocket. Back at the front door, Vlad once again hugged Sebastian, and said, "Don't be a stranger," and shook Tom's hand once again and said, "Nice to meet you Tom." As they both left he said, "Be safe you two," and closed the shop door behind them.

Vlad watched them both go; his brother had been right, Ivor was a good judge of character as he was. Tom seemed to be very resilient and intelligent, and as he smiled he knew he saw something in Tom that he had not seen in many apart from himself when he was his age. Vlad picked up the phone and dialled a number; after a brief call, Vlad went back to his paper, still smiling.

Back on the road heading into the city to speak to Vlad's contact, Tom said, "He was nice, your uncle."

"Don't let the old man act fool you, Tom," said Sebastian. Tom looked out of the window and wondered what Sebastian was on about.

Sebastian drove carefully and quickly to the designated address given to them by Vlad, and found it was a warehouse off one of the major road junctions not far from the port they had arrived at on the Red Star. Sebastian parked and they both walked to a side door of the warehouse; Sebastian banged on the door, which rattled in its frame but did not give. After a time the door slowly opened and a large man filled the entrance and asked "What?" in a not too pleasant voice. Sebastian told the man he was here to see, and looking at the paper Vlad had given him, repeated the name. The man said, "Come."

Both Sebastian and Tom followed the man into the dark interior of the warehouse towards a well-lit office area. In the office were sitting six men, all whispering together. All stopped once Sebastian and Tom entered.

Sebastian again repeated the name, and a man at the desk nodded; Sebastian said he was from Vladimir Sharapova. On hearing the name the man sat up a bit straighter. Sebastian explained who he was and why he was there; the man listened to Sebastian's proposal, all the time nodding, and then eventually smiling. The man stood and extended his hand towards Sebastian, who shook it.

The man explained that if they came every day before nine am then he would more than likely have a delivery job for them, but any time after he could not guarantee a job. Sebastian and Tom both nodded in agreement. "As for payment," the man said, "How does twenty per cent sound?"

Sebastian said, "Five per cent," then the man laughed and said, "Fifteen."

Sebastian said, "Ten," and the man, still laughing, said, "OK OK. Just like the old bear Vladimir, a chip off the old block," said the man, which made Sebastian smile and Tom feel more relaxed than he had been since arriving at the warehouse.

On the way back Tom said to Sebastian, "Was it me or did that man seem a bit more relaxed after he knew who you were and from who we came from?"

Sebastian thought about it for a bit and said, "Not to me."

"Plus," said Tom, "he seemed to cave a bit quickly over the price."

Sebastian said, "No, it was me. I am a natural in business."

Tom thought to himself but did not say that in his opinion it was more Vladimir Sharapova's name, and by Tom's thinking his reputation that won them such as easy prize.

Back at the flat Natasha was already home, and she called from the kitchen, "Hungry?" and in unison they said, "Yes," realising that they both had not eaten since breakfast. After dinner was finished and cleared away, they all sat around the table again. Natasha said "I will go first," and both Tom and Sebastian were smiling, as she looked so eager to share her news that to prevent her would have been cruel.

Natasha first cleared her throat and said, "I went to the City Exchange and for Tom's money I got two thousand two hundred and sixty roubles at the local exchange rate." Both

Tom and Sebastian looked shocked. "I know," said Natasha, "I was shocked by the amount, as well. I did not realise the UK pound was so strong against the rouble."

Natasha went on, "Before I left the shop I did not know what to do with the money, I have never seen so much money in my life. I did not trust my purse, which could be stolen at any time, so I panicked and placed the money down my knickers." This made Tom and Sebastian burst into laughter. Natasha looked at them both and looked indignant and sat with folded arms, huffing. But after a time even Natasha was laughing with them; once she realised what she had said, her hands flew to her mouth and she went red, which made Tom and Sebastian laugh more and Natasha look even more embarrassed.

After they all had calmed down, Natasha showed them her purchases for the company. She placed on the table an 'accountancy book', where she showed she had started entering in the columns already, plus a 'minutes book', and once again she had completed the first pages with the last meeting's record. She passed the book to Sebastian and said, "Read and sign," and said the same to Tom.

Tom noticed that Natasha's written hand was beautiful, but he looked embarrassed at her and said, "I can speak Russian, but I am afraid I cannot read or write it yet." Natasha took the book from Tom, read the pages to him, and then passing it back, pointed to the place for him to sign. Natasha said next time she would read the minutes of the previous meeting at the new meeting, and both Tom and Sebastian nodded in agreement. Sebastian passed to Natasha the piece of paper she had handed him with her question to Uncle Vlad; reading, Natasha smiled and said, "Perfect."

After the meeting Natasha said to Tom, "Perhaps we can help each other out."

"How?" said Tom, looking confused.

"Well, I will teach you to read and write Russian, if you teach me to read and write English."

Tom looked at Natasha. "I did not realise you wanted to learn English."

Natasha said, "All the best books are in English, and although some are translated into Russian, I think the translation misses the point of some books."

Tom nodded and agreed. "OK," said Tom, "you got yourself a deal," holding out his hand which Natasha shook, making them both laugh.

After a few months Tom realised he had the worst of the deal; Natasha was relentless in her pursuit of knowledge, and he thought it was going to be an easy ride. Natasha's grasp of English far outstripped his learning of Russian, and sometimes she would scold him to achieve more. Eventually Natasha dispensed of Tom's teaching and went on her own; Tom was secretly pleased.

Years later Natasha, Sebastian and Tom were sitting around the table with a glass of champagne each, celebrating another outstanding year of trading. "To the three of us," said Tom, smiling.

"To us," the other two said in unison, and they all laughed. Natasha said, "Keep this up, in a few years' time you will be very rich men, perhaps one day you will find partners and get your own houses, and settle down."

"What about you, Natasha," asked Sebastian, "You got your eye on anyone in particular?"

Laughing, Natasha went bright red and said, "Sebastian, sometimes you are a small minded person," which made Sebastian laugh even harder. Tom sat looking confused over the siblings' exchange.

A few days later Sebastian said, "When are you going to ask her out?"

"I don't know what you mean," said Tom, looking sheepish.

"Oh come on, it is so obvious the way you two look at each other."

"I don't know what you mean," said Tom.

"Do you want me to ask her for you?"

"No way," said Tom. "I can do my own asking."

"Well, you better hurry up, I saw that bloke from flat six taking an interest, plus a few at the bakery, and if she thinks you are not interested, well."

"Oh shut up, Sebastian."

"You really think she would go with some else," Sebastian was laughing so much. "Tom you are a fool, just ask her."

Next evening after dinner had been cleared away, Sebastian made an excuse to leave, leaving Natasha and Tom alone. Tom was so far out of his depth, he wished his mother was here; she would advise him on what to say. While Tom was thinking about his mother, Natasha said, "You OK Tom? You look worried."

"No, not at all," said Tom too quickly.

Natasha smiled and took Tom's hand. "Tom, it looks like I will be an old maid before you ask me out, so I better ask you. Tom, will you take me to the park tomorrow? If it's a lovely day we can feed the ducks."

All Tom could do was squeeze Natasha's hand and nod and grin like the Cheshire Cat. Next day, Tom could not concentrate in the morning, so that in the end Sebastian said, "OK, let's call it a day, you are about as much use as a baby."

"I have a lot on my mind," said Tom, laughing.

Sebastian said, "Don't be silly, it's only Natasha. As long as you don't try to get fresh, you will be fine."

"Get fresh? Don't understand," said Tom.

Sebastian said, "You know, try to kiss her and try for a hand full of breasts."

Tom went bright red, and said, "I am a man of honour."

"Should think so too, that's my sister we are talking about," said Sebastian.

Natasha and Tom walked close down to the duck pond. Natasha handed some stale bread to Tom, and they both stood throwing it to the ducks; eventually when they had finished

Natasha went and sat on a park bench, and Tom followed. "Do you not like me Tom?" said Natasha quietly.

Tom looked at Natasha and went red. "I am sorry, Natasha, I am still a bit unsure around women, after my experience with Sally."

"My poor Tom, I did not even think, please forgive me," said Natasha.

"No, it's my fault, Natasha," said Tom, taking Natasha's hand, and taking a deep breath. Tom said, "Natasha Sharapova, I have loved you since the first moment we met, you captured my heart with your first smile, I want us to be boyfriend and girlfriend."

Natasha looked deeply into Tom's eyes and said, "Tom Backer, I have wanted to tell you that for months." Leaning over they, embraced and kissed until the sun was just visible over the horizon.

A few months later while out for a walk, strolling arm in arm, Tom thought he would never be as happy, as he was now.

"Penny for them."

"Sorry?" said Tom.

"Penny for your thoughts, that's how the English saying goes."

"Yes, sorry, I was miles away."

"I know that," said a laughing Natasha.

"I was thinking of my mother."

"You do not speak much about her, do you?"

"No, to tell you the truth it was all a bit messy, my leaving. But hey, every cloud has a silver lining. If I had not left, I would not now be the happiest man alive walking in the sun with the most beautiful girl in the world."

"Stop it, you old romantic," said Natasha as she pushed him away, laughing.

A year later, Sebastian was sitting at the kitchen table reading the paper, when Tom wandered in and asked where Natasha was. Sebastian did not look up from his paper but just shrugged.

"Good," said Tom. "Sebastian, I want to ask you a question. I am going to ask Natasha to marry me, what do you think?"

Slowly, Sebastian made a big theatrical show of folding up the paper and placing it on the table. Arms folded, he turned to Tom and said, "Well, as the man of the house, it is custom in Russia, for the bride's family to be asked, and we then decide if your fortune is good, and you can keep my sister in the style she has become accustomed to."

"That's daft," said Tom.

"Tradition my friend, tradition," said a smiling Sebastian.

"Let me get this right, before I ask Natasha," said Tom.

"First you got to ask the family," said Sebastian, interrupting, who was sitting with the biggest fake grin he could muster.

"So let's get this right, we've got to get the whole family together then I ask them, you lot decide yes or no, before she can answer yes or no?"

"Yup that's about it."

"What happens if the family say no and she says yes?"

"Then, my dear Tom, you have a problem," said Sebastian smiling.

The next day Tom asked Natasha casually if it was not about time her family had a party. Natasha flung her arms around Tom's neck and said, "Oh yes, please." The Gathering, as Tom called it, was scheduled for three weeks, due to the fact some members of the family would need notice to get there.

"How many are in your family?" asked Tom one day.

"We are only a small family, about two hundred will be there."

Tom whistled. "Two hundred, that's more people than I have known in my entire life."

Natasha said, "Tom, just be yourself, you will be fine."

"I would not be yourself," said Sebastian.

Natasha threw a tea towel at Sebastian and said, "Sebastian, stop winding him up, he is too nervous as it is."

"Well all I can say is uncle Boris, after a few bottles."

"Oh yes, forgot about him," said Natasha, looking at Tom.

"Who is uncle Boris?" and then Tom looked at both Sebastian and Natasha and realised they were making fun of him. "Funny, ha ha," said Tom, as they both laughed.

The Gathering was held in the community hall, not far from the flats. Tom was surprised to see so many people, and realised that Natasha and Sebastian were not joking about the size of their family. Tom met so many people who wanted to give him advice, that by the end of the evening his head was buzzing. The buffet was lavish and plentiful, and of course an endless supply of alcohol. Tom thought the Sharapova family sure knew how to throw a party. Just before the band started, Vlad came to the stage, and tapped the microphone, and everyone stopped talking and turned towards the stage.

"Welcome the Sharapova family," which brought a large cheer from around the room. "As you know, we are here to decide the fate of our little Natasha," which brought another cheer as people near her took her to the stage. "So our little Natasha, you have found a man who can put up with your bossy attitude," which brought another loud cheer, and a blush from Natasha.

"Where is he, Tom," Vlad said, scanning the room; someone shouted, "Done a runner already," which brought a laugh from the crowd. Tom held up his hand and walked towards the stage. As he went, people were smiling and patting him on the back. "So you wish to ask our little Natasha a question, Tom," Vlad said. The whole room went silent; you could hear a pin drop. Everyone was holding their breaths. Tom smiled at Natasha, and went down on one knee and said, "Natasha Sharapova, will you marry me?"

Natasha quietly said, "Yes, with all my heart," and took Tom's hands and helped him stand.

Vlad said, "And what does the Sharapova family say?" and as one, the room exploded with whistles, cheers and clapping.

Tom hugged Natasha and whispered, "Nightmare," and

Natasha whispered back, "Not over yet, my love." Tom was dragged away from Natasha towards the bar, where all the men had gathered, and Tom noticed Natasha was taken away to where all the women had congregated.

Vlad thrusted a large glass into Tom's hand and, holding his own glass up, said, "To a happy union." All the men repeated the toast, and drank their drinks down. Tom drank the clear liquid and wished he had not; Vlad smacked him on the back, and laughed.

After that, the night was just a blur. Tom lost all sense of time, reason and composure; his last memory was trying to arm wrestle Ivor. With singing in his ears, he slowly slid down the bar before passing out cold.

Tom woke the next morning. He knew he was awake, but his eyes would not open; he felt a dull thud in his head, and all his body ached. Eventually he opened his eyes, and scanned the room; he was in his bed still fully clothed, minus his boots. Slowly placing his feet on the ground he tried to stand up. The world spun, and he sat back down again with a bump. After a few deep breaths, he tried to stand again, felt better; he slowly walked to the kitchen. After drinking what seemed like five pints of water, and feeling a little better, he looked and noticed Sebastian sitting there with a large grin on his face.

"Morning comrade," said Sebastian.

"Morning," whispered Tom, and sat down opposite Sebastian.

"What a night," said Tom.

"Will go down in family lore," said Sebastian, "but you, my friend, were the star of the show."

"Really?"

"Trying to outdrink uncle Ivor and uncle Vlad was not your greatest idea, but fun for the family."

"I cannot even remember leaving."

"That was down to Natasha, she came and rescued you from your fate, and with some help, brought you home."

Tom asked, "Talking about Natasha, where is she?"

"Gone shopping my old mate, she is now a bride to be, so a lot to organise."

The wedding was set for three months' time; they would be married in the local church with the reception held in the same place as the family gathering. Tom was not really included in the wedding preparations; every time he asked Natasha, "Can I help?" he always got a smiles, and an 'all in hand' comment.

One night Uncle Ivor was sitting with Tom and Sebastian on a quick visit; he said he had to make a quick trip to England. If the trip was not so lucrative, he would have turned it down, "But as you are all businessmen you cannot overlook a good opportunity." Both Tom and Sebastian nodded in agreement. Going on, Ivor said, "I will be back in plenty of time for the wedding celebration, don't fret, even if I have to walk back I will not miss it for the world," which made them all laugh.

Tom asked Ivor, "Do you mind doing me a huge favour when you are in the UK? I would not normally ask but, with the wedding."

"Please ask, Tom."

"If I write a quick letter to my mother, can you deliver it for me?"

Putting a large hand on Tom's shoulder, Ivor said, "Tom, I will personally place it into Nurse Grace's hand."

"Thank you," said Tom, who left to write the letter for Ivor.

A week later, as Tom was sitting reading the paper, Natasha came and handed him a piece of paper. "What's this?"

"Your list of things to do for the wedding." Tom scanned the list and smiled. Later that day, when Tom and Sebastian were finally having a break, Tom made a big show of producing the list.

"What you got there?" said Sebastian, trying not to look interested.

"It's my wedding list from Natasha, thing I need, and have to do."

"Oh good, about time she gave you something to do."

Ignoring Sebastian, Tom went on. "First thing on the list, 'find a best man'."

Sebastian sat up a bit straighter.

"Now where can I find a best man? Do you reckon Dimitri from the docks would do it? He seems a decent guy."

"Are you joking? Dimitri? Why would you pick such a loser, plus he…?" Sebastian stopped talking and looked at Tom, who had a big smile on his face; he realised Tom was taking the mickey out of him. "Very funny," said Sebastian. "OK, you got me. But you need to ask me properly, or I won't do it," said Sebastian, now looked annoyed.

"Sebastian, will you be my best man?"

"I will check my calendar and get back to you."

Tom punched Sebastian in the arm and they both started laughing.

Tom was surprised how Sebastian had taken his best man duties so seriously, even taking the list from Tom that Natasha had given him and completed everything. Even Natasha was impressed by her brother's efficiency. Tom and Sebastian were having a cup of coffee when Natasha appeared carrying a suitcase.

"Oh my god, she has finally seen sense and is running away," said Sebastian.

"Idiot," said Natasha. "I am going to Aunty Victoria's, as I cannot stay here."

Tom asked, "Why?" looking concerned.

"Because, my love, tomorrow is our wedding day, and the bride should not see the groom before the day."

"Tomorrow," said Tom, pulling a face at Sebastian.

Natasha turned and said, "Men." Both Sebastian and Tom burst out laughing. Natasha turned and said, "Sebastian, make sure Tom is on time tomorrow." Sebastian stood and saluted his sister, still laughing.

Once Natasha had gone, Sebastian rubbed his hands. "Got a little surprise for you." Tom looked apprehensive. "Don't worry," said Sebastian, "you will love it." Just then the doorbell rang. "On time," said Sebastian, and after going to open the door, returned with a smiling Ivor and Vlad, with arms full of bottles.

Ivor said, "We waited until we saw Natasha leave," then Vlad said, "Tom, we need to give you a good send-off."

"But you've been giving me send-offs all week."

"Arrr, but this is the real one, the rest were practice. Tonight is your last night of freedom. After tomorrow, you will need permission to fart." This made everyone laugh.

The next morning, Tom woke feeling alive and excited. Today, he was getting married today. He shook his head, he could hardly believe it. Since leaving England, his life had changed so much; thinking of England sometimes made him feel a little sad, he wished his mother could have been there, but sending the letter made him feel better. He knew she would be proud of the man he had become, but strangely he did not miss home so much nowadays or his old life; this was now his home. And he could not wait to start his new life with his new bride.

Tom looked over at a snoring Sebastian and smiled. He had slipped the party quite early, only leaving when he was sure the others would not miss him. He went to the kitchen to put the kettle on and smiled at Ivor and Vlad sprawled out on the floor softly snoring. He knew he was a lucky man to have such a loving and strong family who had accepted him into their world.

Driving to the church, Sebastian was keeping up a string of chatter, which Tom was not really listening to. It was only when Sebastian prodded him, and said, "You listening to me?"

"Sorry," said Tom, "I was miles away."

"Well, get your head back in the game, we are here now," he said as he pulled up in front of the church.

As Tom walked down the aisle toward the front of the church, he was getting more and more nervous, and the people who wanted to shake his hand or slap him on the back were not helping. Tom turned to scan the church; there was not a spare seat, the place was packed, and it seemed every face was smiling at him.

Sebastian said, "You OK Tom? You don't look well."

"To tell you the truth, Sebastian, I am shitting myself."

Sebastian slapped him on the back and said, "Breathe and it will be fine."

"You got the ring," asked Tom.

"What ring?" replied Sebastian, pulling his list from his pocket. "I see no ring on my list," showing Tom the list. Tom turned white. Sebastian looked at Tom and laughed, "Don't worry, Natasha gave it to me yesterday."

"Please don't joke," said Tom.

"Breathe my friend, and enjoy your day," said Sebastian, looking over at Tom who was deep breathing with his eyes closed. Sebastian just smiled.

Once the music started, Tom and Sebastian turned in unison to look back down the church. There coming towards them was Natasha, on the arm of her uncle Vlad. Tom gasped; Natasha was dressed in a beautiful flowing white dress, covered with mother of pearl, with her face covered in a veil that nearly touched the floor. Tom caught his breath and fought back tears; he had never seen anything more beautiful in his life than Natasha looked today. Even Sebastian said a whispered, "Oh, sister."

Tom and Sebastian turned back towards the priest, and waited for Natasha to join them. Once Natasha was level with them, she stopped. The priest asked, "Who gives this woman to this man?"

Vlad lifted Natasha's veil and said, "I do," passing her hand and placing it in Tom's. Tom turned and looked at Natasha, and once again caught his breath as she smiled at him. Tom knew he would always remember this minute for the rest of his life, the way Natasha looked at this very moment.

To Tom the rest of the ceremony was a blur; he spoke when he was asked to, but all he could think of was how beautiful

Natasha was, and how he was definitely the luckiest man alive, and he knew that she was now and would always be the only women he could ever love.

The priest said, "I now pronounce you man and wife," which brought a cheer from the congregation, which made Tom and Natasha laugh.

"Kiss her," whispered the priest, nodding towards Natasha. Tom looked confused, then realised what he was saying; taking Natasha in his arms he kissed her passionately, she kissed him back just as passionately. Turning, Natasha linked arms with Tom and they walked back down the church as man and wife towards the cheering crowd.

Back at the reception, the food and drink was flowing. After some time, Vlad stood and tapped his glass for hush, and the place immediately went silent. Vlad said, "Family and friends, welcome," which brought a cheer. "We are here to celebrate the marriage of a wonderful couple," which brought another cheer from the audience. "Tom, Natasha I wish you all the lucky in the world in your future life," which once again brought a cheer. "Ivor, Victoria and I thought long and hard what to get you for a wedding present and we decided on this." He passed an envelope to Tom; Tom opened it and showed Natasha, and they both looked at Vlad in confusion. Vlad laughed, the crowd were shouting, "What is it?"

Vlad held up his hand to silence the room. "It is a deed to some land just outside the city near the lake, where you can build you own house." Tom and Natasha sat shocked.

Next was Sebastian's turn, Sebastian stood and theatrically cleared his throat, which brought laughter from the audience. Holding up his hand for silence, "Family and friends," he started and then went on to deliver an amusing speech which at times had both Tom and Natasha squirm and the crowd in uproar.

"Finally," he said, "I also was struggling what to get my favourite sister and my best friend for a wedding present, so I decided on this," also passing an envelope to Tom, who once again opened it and passed it to Natasha. Again they both looked puzzled, but before anyone could speak, Sebastian said, "I have just passed over the building permits for a two storey house to be built on the land purchased by Uncle Vlad Aunty Victoria and Uncle Ivor, and by the time you come back from honeymoon it will hopefully be built, if all my lazy cousins can do an honest day's work," said Sebastian, holding his arms out wide to the audience, which brought another round of laughter.

Sebastian sat down beaming, then Tom stood up.

Tom started as the others did. "Family and friends, what can we say we are both speechless on the generosity of you all." He embraced the room with his arms. "But on behalf of my wife and I," which brought a cheer, and made Tom blush as he had just realised what he had just said, which made everyone laugh. Turning to Natasha he made her stand. Taking her hands, he said, "I know we discussed a honeymoon and decided on a few days in the country, but I did not say which country." Passing an envelope to Natasha, Tom said, "Three weeks in Egypt on an all-inclusive resort." Natasha opened the envelope and there were two passports and two airline tickets, and all the relevant paperwork for their honeymoon; Natasha flung her arms around Tom's neck, which brought a standing ovation from the crowd.

Later the next day, Tom, Sebastian and Natasha took a drive over to where their new house was going to be built. They all wandered around the plot of land discussing various positions of things; Natasha said she wanted a south facing living room, so it could have the dying sun in the evening. Tom also put his ideas forwards, and all the time, Sebastian was taking notes. Sebastian said, "Don't worry, it will be beautiful for when you get back."

Natasha said, "You sure you can build the house in three weeks?"

Sebastian said, "Don't worry sister, I have an army ready to work," which made them all laugh.

Sebastian drove them to the airport, and after a tearful fare-well, left them. Natasha squeezed Tom's hand, and said, "I am so nervous my love. I have never been on an airplane before."

Tom looked at Natasha and smiled. "Me neither, darling," which made them both laugh; together they walked into the airport to start their honeymoon.

Next morning, Sebastian was at the site early, sitting having a flask of coffee waiting for his small army to arrive. He did not really expect most to turn up, as most promises of help had been given in a drunken stupor at the wedding reception; although loads of promises and handshakes were given, some he knew would cry off or forget their drunken conservations. All of a sudden he heard horns honking and, looking up, saw a fleet of trucks driving down the track towards him. He smiled, and punched the air. Sebastian and all the family worked tirelessly to complete the house on time; at times, Sebastian realised how big a project they had taken on, and at night worried if the house would ever be completed on time, but the disappointed look from his sister and his best friend drove him on, and he worked and badgered people to excel. Occasionally Vlad would come to oversee the project, and if any part had fallen behind, miraculously, the next day workers would be on site to get the project back on course.

Eventually after three weeks of chaos, a house now stood where once there was a vacant plot of land. Vlad placed his arm around Sebastian and said, "Well done boy, well done," as they stared at the finished house. This made Sebastian smile and feel elated, even though at times he wondered if it would ever be finished, but now he was confident the house was the best it could be.

Sebastian was waiting for them as they came out of the airport. When Natasha saw him she ran and hugged her brother; Sebastian held her at arm's length, and said, "Blimey, what a lovely colour you are," and, "you look pos-itively glowing." Finally Tom caught them up, and they embraced. "Wow you look a lovely colour as well. I take it you had a good time?"

"Wonderful," said Natasha.

"Perfect," said Tom.

On the drive home, Sebastian asked, "Are you tired?"

"Worn out," they both agreed.

"OK, the house can wait until tomorrow."

"No," they both said in unison. "We must see it now," insisted Natasha.

"OK, OK, but promise me you will not be too disappointed on the house so far."

"Promise," Natasha said, not sounding too convinced. Sebastian winked at Tom who just smiled.

Sebastian was driving down the road, when through the trees Natasha spotted a house. "What a lovely house," she said, tapping Tom on the shoulder.

Tom looked over and said, "That's a posh house, never noticed that last time we were here." Sebastian was just smiling. Both Tom and Natasha were dumbfounded when Sebastian turned into the drive and drove up to the house they had spotted from the trees and stopped.

Slowly climbing from the car, Sebastian said, holding out his arms, "Welcome to your new home."

Natasha said, "This is our house. I never imagined it would be so beautiful." Turning to Sebastian, she hugged her brother and whispered in his ear, "Thank you, little brother."

Tom went and stood next to her, and just stared in wonder. Sebastian joined them and shook the keys at them. "Go explore, everything is ready for you. I will be back tomorrow morning for you."

As he turned to go, Tom said, "Not too early tomorrow, mate," winking at Sebastian, who gave him a mock salute in return. They both stared as Sebastian drove up the drive and out of sight.

Tom and Natasha stood staring at the house for ages, taking in all the beauty of it; finally Natasha said, "Never in my wildest dreams did I ever imagine I would live in such a beautiful house." Tom just stood nodding in agreement.

Tom opened the front door and turned to Natasha and said, "Tradition. Need to carry you over the threshold." Natasha giggled and lifted her arms to allow Tom to pick her up, and carry her inside. Inside, both wandered from room to room, both excitedly pointing out things, and acting like children on Christmas morning. Finally returning to the hall, Natasha, turning to Tom with tears in her eyes, taking his hand said, "I love you so much Tom. I just know we are going to be so happy in this house."

Tom smiled back and said, "Always and forever, my love."

Over the next few months, while Natasha busied herself with making the house a home, Tom went back to work with Sebastian. Every evening when Sebastian dropped Tom off, he would enter the house and call Natasha's name, and she would call back, "In here," and he would find her, beavering away with a new project.

One night after dinner, while Tom was reading the paper, Natasha turned to him, and said, "The second spare bedroom, can we decorate it?"

"Suppose so," said Tom, not really listening.

"Well, I think pink is a lovely colour for a girl."

"Guess so," said Tom. He slowly lowered the paper at a smiling Natasha, and said, "Say again."

"I said I think pink is a lovely colour for a girl."

"That's what I thought you said." Then the penny dropped. Tom's hands flew to his mouth and all he could say was, "Bloody hell." Tom took Natasha in his arms and with tears in his eyes kissed her, and said, "I love you so much my darling."

Natasha said, "Always and forever, my love."

For the next few months Tom was getting on Natasha's nerves; in the end, she exploded and said to him, "Look Tom, I love you more than life itself, but I am not ill, I am pregnant. I can do things for myself. Do not fuss over me. Us Sharapova

women have been having strong healthy babies for genera-
tions, so stop fussing."

Tom, looking shocked by her outburst, whispered, "Sorry."
Natasha saw his little school boy sad look, took him in her
arms and kissed him deeply.

The family was elated that Natasha was pregnant; another
generation to carry on the family name, plus it was a reason
to have a family celebration. Sebastian especially was elated he
was going to be an uncle.

Tom had taken Natasha to the hospital for her six monthly
check up, now she had a pronounced shape of a pregnant
woman. Her cravings were amazing even Tom's imagination,
changing daily and keeping him on his toes, looking for her
new combinations of food.

On the way home, Tom asked Natasha if they could stop
off at uncle Vlad's shop; Tom needed a few parts for his pet
project, and Natasha said, "Why not? Not seen uncle Vlad in
ages."

Parking across the street from the shop, Tom noticed
Sebastian's van parked outside. Tom smiled; even after all these
years, Sebastian still clung onto that rusty first van they ever
bought. Tom started to walk across the road when Natasha
called him back and said, "Wait for me please." Tom stopped,
and waited. Just then, Sebastian emerged from the shop and
spotted Tom and Natasha, waved and shouted a welcome.

The next thing Tom knew was a flash of blinding light followed by a rush of hot air that blew him off his feet and back
towards Natasha. Luckily, she had been standing behind the
car, and was out of range of the blast area. Tom slowly got up;
his first concern was for Natasha. She was leaning on the car,
and as Tom reached for her, she said, "We are OK, go help
Sebastian." Tom's ears were still ringing as he ran over the road
towards the shop. The dust was still billowing about and it was
hard to see; eventually Tom came to Sebastian's van, which
had been mangled and turned over on its roof, as though it
was a toy car left abandoned by a child.

Tom shouted Sebastian's name several times, but Sebastian did not reply, Tom was shouting his name, getting more frantic with each shout, then Tom tripped over something, and nearly went down; as he put his hand out to stop himself falling, he touched what seemed like a leg. Just then, a small opening in the dust showed Sebastian laying in the dirt.

Tom went down on one knee and took Sebastian's head in his arms; Sebastian looked like he was fast asleep. The only indication something was not right was the steady trickle of blood from each nostril. Tom knew Sebastian was dead, and he laid him on the ground again, and went to find uncle Vlad. The shop had been blown into two parts, so it was easy to search the wreckage. As Tom was beginning to search, he heard sirens in the distance getting closer; as he looked over he could see Natasha had reached Sebastian and was holding her brother's head and wailing.

Tom found Vlad under his desk; Tom checked Vlad was still breathing, before he beckoned over the arriving fire crew to dig Vlad out.

Tom went to Natasha and slowly lifted her up. "Let the paramedics do their job," he told her; she nodded and stood back to allow them access. The paramedics asked Tom and Natasha some questions which they answered as best they could. Just then a policeman came up and asked for a word.

Tom answered all the police questions as best he could; Natasha filled in parts that Tom was not sure on. The policeman thanked them, and said he would be in touch. They brought Vlad out on a stretcher and took him to the waiting ambulance; Tom spoke to the paramedic, and told Natasha that Vlad had been stabilised, but was still critical. Tom said, "I am going to the hospital."

Natasha said, "I am coming too," and Tom knew by her look it was not a time to argue with her.

At the hospital they both sat in the reception area, and after giving Vlad's details to the receptionist, waited for news. Eventually a doctor came and sat with them.

"Your uncle is stable, but he has a punctured lung, and two broken legs; the head scans were clear, so no long term damage."

"Can we see him?" asked Natasha.

"Of course you can," said the doctor, "but he might drift in and out of consciousness, but that will be the drugs he is on."

"We understand," said Tom.

"Before you go," said the doctor, "I need to ask an awkward question."

Both Tom and Natasha looked at the doctor and he went on, "We need someone to formally identify the body brought in with your uncle Vlad."

"That was my brother Sebastian," said Natasha softly.

The doctor apologised and said, "Sorry, I did not know."

"You go see Uncle Vlad, and I will go see Sebastian," said Natasha.

"You sure?" said Tom.

"Of course, I will be fine." The doctor pointed the way to Vlad's room for Tom, then took Natasha by the arm and led her towards the mortuary.

At the mortuary, the doctor pushed the buzzer on the wall next to the large steel door, which was immediately opened by a man in a white coat, the doctor said, "We have come to formally identify the body brought in from the explosion." The man in the white coat stood back to let them enter.

The mortuary was a stark, well lit room, with two single tables in the middle. The thing that Natasha noticed first was the smell – strong disinfection – which nearly made her gag. Seeing she was looking in distress, the doctor asked the man in the white coat, "Can we hurry this up?"

The man nodded and went to a large drawer and pulled. The body was laid out covered with a pristine white cloth; Natasha thought she had never seen anything so white. The doctor turned to her and asked if she was ready, to which she nodded. The doctor nodded to the man, and he pulled the white sheet down uncovering the head.

Natasha walked towards the outstretched body, and looked into the sleeping face of her dead brother; Natasha lifted her hand and stroked her brother's cheek, and softly said, "Yes, that is Sebastian Sharapova." Natasha leaned forward and kissed Sebastian on the lips and whispered, "Goodbye my little brother." Turning, Natasha with tears in her eyes asked the doctor to take her to see her uncle Vlad.

Tom found the room quite easily from the doctor's directions. Opening the door, a nurse turned and smiled at Tom. "Be patient with him," she said.

"Does he know his nephew is dead?" asked Tom.

"No, not yet," said the nurse.

Vlad turned when Tom approached, and by Tom's face knew something bad had happened. "It's Sebastian," said Tom. Vlad closed his eyes and breathed deeply; when he opened his eyes they were full of tears.

Vlad reached for Tom's hand but the tubing prevented him from raising it too high. Tom took Vlad's hand and sat down next to the bed. Vlad started to speak, and Tom listened. "I wanted to spare my sister's children, my business interests, so I purposely left Sebastian and Natasha out of it."

Tom said, "I don't understand, Vlad."

Vlad went on, "I run the Odessa Bratva."

Tom looked shocked. Of course he had heard of the Bratva or Russian mafia; who hadn't? The most feared organisation in Russia. If you wanted to do business in Odessa, you paid the Bratva first; even Sebastian and Tom had to pay their contributions or work would have stopped.

Vlad went on, "I tried to protect Sebastian and Natasha from it all, but sometimes the only way to get to me and my organisation is through family. The people who did this were after me, not Sebastian, but now they have made it personal." Vlad closed his eyes and drifted off.

Tom's thoughts were racing; it all made sense now. The shop that looked abandoned was just a front, plus how easy it was for Sebastian and him to get work. Contracts denied to others were suddenly presented to them. Sebastian put it down to luck, but Tom now knew it was down to uncle Vlad, and the fear his organisation held over Odessa.

Tom stood and stared out of the window, his thoughts miles away. Tom heard his name being called softly; he turned and saw Vlad was awake again. Tom returned to the chair and took Vlad's hand again. "My family have always been Bratva, we decided to keep Sebastian and Natasha out of it because of their mother, my sister; she married a man who was not in love with her, but saw the marriage as a way to advance himself in the organisation. But he became over confident, arrogant even, to a point he thought he could beat her and we would not say anything. One night when Sebastian and Natasha were but three and one, in a drunken stupor he beat my sister to death. This I could not let go, so I killed him, and took the children and became their guardians, vowing to keep them away from the ugly side of the family business.

"When Sebastian returned from the UK, with you in tow, we decided to let you run with your business venture, and helped when we could. And after time, you and Natasha became close and married, and I could see how happy you made her. I saw in you, Tom, something I did not see in Sebastian; he was never serious about anything and he led his life like that. But you are different, I know family is important to you, and you would do anything for them; you also have that ruthless streak in you, I noticed it in your eyes the first time I met you, I had the same look at your age, and over the years I have watched you grow into a confident man." Tom sat and nodded while Vlad was speaking.

Pointing to the closet, Vlad said, "My jacket. Inside pocket, a wallet." Tom went to the closet and took the wallet from the inside pocket of Vlad's jacket and handed to Vlad. Vlad placed the wallet in Tom's hand and said, "Open it." Tom opened the wallet, and it contained a large metal Red Star, with a gold border, with the Russian symbols for BO engraved on the Red

Star. Tom looked from the wallet to Vlad, and said, "I don't understand, uncle Vlad."

Vlad said, "This is the symbol of the family. All my top people carry one, but with this one you are head of Bratva in Odessa, and can on behalf of me find who killed Sebastian and make them pay." Vlad gripped Tom's hand hard, and looked him in the eyes. "Promise me you will do this for me and the family."

Tom said, "I promise, uncle Vlad."

"This injustice cannot be allowed to go unpunished or the family will be seen as weak, and we cannot allow that." Tom nodded and understood. Vlad was finding it hard to breathe after the effort of speaking. Vlad gripped Tom's hand again and said, "Go see Alexei at the warehouse, he is one of my lieutenants, he will steer you in the right direction."

Just then Natasha walked in. Tom quickly placed the wallet in his jacket pocket. Tom noticed Natasha had been crying; he looked at her with concern in his eyes, but she said, "I am OK," so he let it drop. Standing and letting Natasha sit, she took Vlad's hand and started to cry again.

After an hour a nurse came in and said, "Visiting time is over, he needs his rest, come back tomorrow."

Natasha stood and lean over and kissed Vlad on the forehead, and said, "See you soon, uncle Vlad."

Tom gripped Vlad's arms, and said, "Don't worry, uncle Vlad, I will sort it." Vlad just smiled and closed his eyes.

Back in the car, Natasha asked Tom, "What was all that about?"

"Sorry, not with you," said Tom.

"You and Uncle Vlad acting all suspicious," said Natasha.

"Family business," said Tom.

Natasha said, "I understand," and remained silent until they were home.

Next morning Tom drove to the warehouse, and knocked on the same side door he and Sebastian had done all those years ago. It was opened again by the same large unfriendly man, but this time Tom was not afraid. He asked to see Alexei, and the man stepped to the side and Tom walked towards the same well-lit office. Tom entered the office and took an empty seat; this made the six men in the office stop talking. Alexei said, "What do you want?" in a non-friendly voice. Tom slowly took the wallet from his pocket and opened it and placed it on the desk.

Alexei and the other six men just stared at the Red Star on the table. Tom said in a soft voice, "So where are we in finding the scum that dishonoured our family?"

Alexei immediately sat up straight, and said, "We have only just started to find out, we been worried about Vlad." The other men in the room nodded.

Tom said, "Uncle Vlad is going to live, but is not happy that the investigation has not yielded any bodies yet." Tom stared hard into Alexei's eyes and said, "So he sent me to sort you all out, and get results."

Alexei gulped and said, "OK, where do you want to start?"

For the next few days Alexei brought Tom up to speed on the family business, Tom then gave orders to each of the six men in the room, who were pleased to be once again active. Tom tasked then to spread the word that the family had a new enforcer and he was on a mission of vengeance.

A few months later Alexei told Tom they had located the man who had made the bomb, and they were bringing him in, for a chat. The man who sat on the chair looked terrified, and was sweating heavily.

Tom sat opposite the man and smiled. The man was physically shaking. Tom said in a soft voice, "We don't blame you, you only made the bomb. You don't blame the man who made the car in a car crash, now, do you?" The man shook his head. "All we want to know is who you made it for."   The man licked his lips and said in a hesitant voice, "I don't know his name, he just came to my work shop with a design and ask if I could build it."

"And these plans are still in your workshop?"

"Yes," said the man.

Tom nodded towards one of the men, who immediately left. Tom asked, "What did this man look like?"

"Russian, tall, built like a gorilla with a bald head, well dressed," said the man.

Tom asked, "What was special about the design of the bomb?"

The man said, "It was a remote detonation, directional bomb, designed to only target and devastate a small area. I have never seen this type before. It is an American design, I think."

"What was the range of the trigger?" asked Tom.

"No more than five hundred yards," said the man.

"Thank you," said Tom, still smiling, then shot the man between the eyes. Tom asked, "Does anyone recognise the man from this scum's description?" waving at the dead man on the floor.

"I do," said one of the men.

Tom turned to him and said, "Well?"

"Sounds like Anton Bullski. He works as an enforcer for the Yashin family who runs Kiev," replied the man.

The man who Tom had sent to retrieve the bomb plans returned an hour later, shaking his head. He said, "We were too late, the place had been ransacked and everything had been taken."

Tom turned to Alexei and said, "Obviously they were watching his place, and saw you take him; these people are clever so we need to up our game."

Alexei made the appointment with the head of the Yashin family for Tom. As they drove to the abandoned warehouse with just Tom, Alexei and a driver, Alexei said, "I don't trust these Yashin scum Tom, this smells like a trap."

"Well, let's hope they stick to the term of the agreement," replied Tom. As they drove up, the Yashin family car was already parked up. Tom ordered the driver to park ten feet away from the other car facing it; the driver obeyed Tom's order. Tom and Alexei both got out of the car and stood in front of it. The Yashin family finally left the car and stood in front. Both parties started to walk towards each other.

When both parties were two feet away they stopped. Tom looked at both men; one was small and Tom guessed in his late seventies, the other was tall and hard looking, and never took his eyes off Tom.

"I am sorry to hear about Vladimir's accident," said the old man.

"No accident," said Tom.

"Please pass on my best to him when you see him next," said the man, ignoring Tom's comment. "So why have you called this meeting?" asked the old man.

"I am Tom Sharapova, chief enforcer of the Sharapova family," said Tom.

"I know who you are, young man. Made quite a name for yourself in such a short time. Vlad picked well. Plus you are family, which helps," said the old man, smiling. "You have still not answered my question, why have you called this meeting?" he asked.

Tom replied, "The bomb that tried to kill Vlad but managed to kill his nephew was ordered by one of your men. This has angered Vlad and he has instructed me to ask you if you could do the decent thing and hand over this man who tried to kill him."

"Can you be sure of your information?" asked the other man, speaking for the first time.

"Yes, we had the bomb maker and he described the man in detail, and one of my team recognised him by his description. Anton Bullski," replied Alexei. The older man turned and whispered something to the younger man, who turned and walked back towards the car.

"If your information is correct, then I will hand him over," said the old man, "and hope this will be the end of the trouble between our two families."

Tom smiled at the old man and said, "I will pass on your

regards to Vlad and I know he will be pleased this problem has been settled quietly and quickly, and I am sure he would like me to leave your mind at rest that this is the end of the trouble we have between our families."

The old man smiled, bowed at Tom, turned, and walked back towards his car.

Three days later a carpet was dumped outside the warehouse with the remains of Anton Bullski wrapped up in them. Pinned to his chest was a '*with compliments*' slip, and a note: *not sanctioned by us, try the Americans.*

A few weeks later, one morning, Natasha said to Tom, "I think the baby is coming." Tom looked shocked that the day was finally here; they had been ready for months, with a few false starts. This was it, the waiting over. Helping a very heavily pregnant Natasha slowly to the car, Tom drove as recklessly as he possibly could to the hospital. Once there a nurse sat her down in a wheelchair and said to Tom, "Follow me."

While they wheeled Natasha into the delivery room, the nurse told Tom to wait in the waiting area. Tom was pacing up and down; every time he heard Natasha scream out, he wanted to go in and comfort her. He was becoming seriously worried and had started to sweat. He could not settle, his mind was racing; all he could think of was Natasha on her own with strangers, he should be in there. He had just about convinced himself to barge in and suffer the consequences, when a nurse appeared and said, "You can come in now."

Natasha smiled as Tom entered, and said, "Come, meet your new daughter."

Tom slowly walked to the bed and looked down at his daughter for the first time, and with tears in his eyes, said, "She is the most beautiful thing I have ever seen in my life, apart from her mother." Tom leaned over and kissed the baby on the forehead and then Natasha on the lips.

Natasha passed the baby to Tom, who held her for the first

time. "What shall we call her?" said Natasha, and without any hesitation Tom said, "Grace."

Natasha smiled. "Grace. I like that."

While Natasha and the baby were getting some sleep, Tom went to see Vlad, who after all this time was sitting up and generally being a pain to all the nurses. When Vlad saw Tom he smiled and waved him over. "Tom, tell this nurse I don't need my temperature taken every hour I am fit as a horse again."

Tom said, "I would do what they say, uncle Vlad, they know best," which brought a smile from the nurse and she retreated from the room.

"So my boy, I hear good things about you, you have made a reputation and have brought honour back to the family."

"Still a long way to go, Vlad, but every lead throws up more leads, so we are confident we will eventually get the bastard who ordered the hit."

Vlad looked seriously at Tom and said, "Sit down, Tom." Tom sat as ordered, and Vlad went on, "As you know, Ukraine is trying to get popular support to eventually break away from the Russian Union, but Odessa Russians are still very loyal to mother Russia, so the powers behind the Ukrainian movement are trying to push their agenda here in Odessa, where they feel the most resistance will come from."

Tom asked, "Who is behind the breakaway movement for Ukraine?"

"I suspect the Americans and the British, as they seem to have most to gain from a Russian union broken up in pieces."

"This can complicate things," said Tom.

"I know," said Vlad, "but we will leave these things for another day. Now take me and show me my new great niece, and for her sake I hope she takes after her mother," which made Vlad laugh as he slapped Tom on the back.

Tom sat staring out of the window when he heard the car pull up, and a high pitch voice ring out around the house, "Papa,

papa." Tom smiled; had it really been four years since the birth of little Grace? The time had flown by.

Grace raced into the room and flung herself into Tom's arms, and Grace said, "Miss me, papa?"

"Always," replied Tom, smiling. Tom looked over his daughter head as Natasha walked into the room.

Natasha smiled at Tom. "Your daughter was her usual self today, at dance." Tom knew Grace had been her usual bolshie self, as Natasha always called her 'your daughter' when she had been naughty and when she was good 'our daughter'.

Tom held Grace at arm's length and said, "What is mama going on about, young lady?" in a stern voice.

Grace, with tears in her eyes, explained to Tom that horrible Miss Blaskaski had been mean to her because she had not practiced her 'Rand de Jambre', so Grace sat and refused to take part anymore. Tom had not got a clue what a 'Rand De Jambre' was but suggested to Grace that perhaps, "Miss Blaskaski, being the teacher of many years, might know more than a four year old student."

Grace looked at Tom and said, "Perhaps you are right Papa. Next time I will apologise to Miss Blaskaski. Thank you papa," said Grace as she leaned in and gave Tom a kiss and a hug; he put her down and Grace skipped off to her room.

Laughing, Natasha said, "Nicely done, papa."

Tom hardly noticed Vlad's limp anymore but he still insisted on walking with a cane; this, Tom suspected, was more for show than necessity. Vlad said, "Let me walk you outside. I would like to see Grace and Natasha, not seen them for over a week now."

Tom looked and could see the car slowly coming down the road. He smiled, and as Tom and Vlad sat on the wall waiting for them to enter the car park, they discussed a new up and coming business venture.

Vlad was the first to spot the fast approaching black Mercedes. "Shifting a bit," said Vlad. Tom looked and noticed the erratic way he was driving, coming on too fast. When the car was level it did a neat handbrake turn and stopped; the window were already down, so a quick sting of gun fire rang out towards them. With lightning speed Tom pulled Vlad backwards over the wall with himself, as the gun fire peppered the wall where an instance ago there were sitting.

Tom quickly took out his pistol and returned fire. He accurately fired two shots into the open windows, which made the car speed away back the way it came. As the Mercedes sped away, it was crossing lanes and slamming into oncoming cars, of which one was Natasha's. One car was flipped over, one was shunted into two parked cars, and Natasha's car was pushed into a low wall that made the car somersault and land on its roof.

Tom shouted to Vlad to call an ambulance as he ran as fast as his legs would carry him towards the car. Tom's heart was in his mouth and he crouched down to see Natasha slumped in her seat; he shouted Grace's name but heard no response. By this time a large crowd had gathered and Tom was shouting at people to help him get Natasha and Grace from the car before it blew.

They managed to get Natasha and Grace from the wreckage just as the gas tank blew; everyone turned away from the searing heat from the explosion. Finally the emergency services arrived. The paramedics lifted both Natasha and Grace on to stretchers and placed them in the ambulance. Tom said, "My family – I am going too."

The paramedic nodded, and just as Tom was going to climb into the ambulance, a strong hand grabbed him, and he turned to look in the face of Vlad, and with tears in his eyes, said, "We will not let these bastards get away with this insult."

Tom sat alone in the waiting room all night. Every time a nurse or doctor went past he stood in hope they wanted him. Early next morning while Tom was sitting dozing, he felt a presence next to him; coming wide awake, he looked into the eyes of a young doctor.

"Sorry did I startle you?"

"No, not at all," said Tom.

The doctor said, "Fancy a cup of coffee?"

Tom said. "Look, doctor, I know you are a busy man, just give it to me straight."

"OK," said the doctor. "First your wife, she has major internal injuries and I don't think she will last the day. We tried to stem the blood but the internal organs were too damaged. We have made her as comfortable as we can, so you can see her when you are ready."

"My daughter," said Tom.

"She is just as badly injured. We have sedated her for the time being to let her settle before we try and operate again, but she is a fighter."

The doctor took Tom to where Natasha room was. Slowly Tom entered and stood at the side of the bed, staring down at a sleeping Natasha, hooked up to various monitors, one keeping a steady beep, beep. Tom moved around and sat on the chair next to the bed. Tom took Natasha's hand in his, and kissing her hand held it close to his chest, and sobbed.

Tom must have dozed off. As he came awake, for a second he wondered where he was; opening his eyes, he saw a smiling Natasha looking at him.

"Hi," she said.

"Hi," said Tom. "My darling, how do you feel?"

"Terrible," joked Natasha.

"Are you in pain?" Tom asked.

"No, not at all," said Natasha. Tom realised the drugs they have given her must be making her feel lethargic. Tom remembered the doctor's warning – 'she can slip away at any time'. This made Tom's eyes water.

As he looked at Natasha, he kissed her on the lips and said, "I never loved anyone but you. From the first meeting I knew I would love you always, you stole my heart."

"Took you long enough to ask me out. In fact, did I not ask you?" This made them both laugh, and in doing so brought a sharp intake of breath from Natasha.

"Shhh my love, take it easy."

Natasha turned to Tom and said, "Promise me something, my love."

"Anything, my darling."

"Look after our baby when I am gone. Make sure she always remembers me with love."

Tom could not hold back the tears, and promised his dying wife something that was out of his control.

A few moments later Natasha took her last breath and died while holding Tom's hand. The only sound that could be heard was a single continuous beep from the monitors.

The nurse came in and said, "Your daughter is asking for you." Trying to wipe his eyes, Tom left his wife and went to see his dying daughter. Tom entered Grace's room and the first thing he thought was how tiny she looked in the bed with all the monitors around her.

Grace turned and smiled and said, "Papa, where is mama, is she OK?"

Tom sat and took his daughter's hand and tried hard not to cry, but the tears just streamed down his face. "Mama is in the next room, she will be here soon to see you."

Grace smiled and said, "I am so cold, papa."

Tom took another blanket and placed it over Grace, leaning over he kissed her on the forehead, and said, "My brave darling, papa loves you so much."

"I love you too, papa," said Grace, who just smiled. Tom sat and softly spoke to Grace, while holding her hand, until she finally drifted away.

Tom sat and stroked Grace's hair and face, not accepting that in a space of thirty minutes he had lost the two people who made up his world.

Tom looked up to see Vlad and Ivor standing there, both with tears in their eyes. Ivor slowly walked over to Tom and lifted him to his feet and said, "Come, let's leave this place." Tom allowed Ivor to steer him away and out of the hospital, not registering anything around him. Tom was in a dark place where no one could follow.

Three days later Tom, Ivor and Vlad stood around the freshly dug graves of Natasha and Grace, in the Sharapova family plot. They buried them next to Sebastian. The same church that Tom and Natasha had married in, and the church Grace had been christened in. Tom stared at the single simple headstone which read:

Natasha Sharapova
Loving wife and mother
Grace Sharapova
Loving Daughter
"We shall one day be reunited"

Vlad said, "We traced the car and the driver. The car was abandoned at the docks, with the driver still in it. Single gunshot wound to the back of the driver's head, classic execution, but some better news is it looks like you got a lucky shot away. Blood was over the back seat. Looks like you managed to clip one of them. We followed the blood trail into the port."

"Spoke to the Harbour Master," said Ivor. "Only one ship sailed in the last week, and that was an American container heading to Belize."

"Belize is good a place to start looking as anywhere," said Tom.

"We leave on the dawn tide," said Ivor.

Tom told Ivor he would meet him at the ship. Tom and Vlad went to Tom's house so Tom could pick up some personal stuff. Tom asked Vlad to come; he did not trust himself to stay in control, as this was the first time he had been back since the accident, and Tom knew it would be full of Natasha and Grace's memories.

Tom and Vlad quickly went from room to room and collected the relevant items Tom required. As he went, Tom placed small green objects. As they were driving down the drive, an explosion ripped through the house leaving nothing behind. Tom stared out of the windows as Vlad drove him to the ship and Belize.

Vlad and Tom embraced on the pier. "I have sent a message to our family contact in Belize," said Vlad, "here is his address." He passed Tom a folded piece of paper.

Tom nodded at Vlad. Holding Tom by the arms, Vlad said, "If you ever need anything let me know, the family and I are ready to help you."

"Thank you, uncle Vlad," said Tom, "but this time it is personal."

Vlad embraced Tom one more time and as the Red Star blew its horn, Tom turned and walked up the gang plank.

Ivor found Tom standing on the upper deck of the Red Star, staring out at the docks of Belize City. "Warm night," said Ivor.

"Warmer than home," said Tom. Although it was midnight, the temperature was still in the mid-thirties.

"I have sent a man to see if the American ship came in, and where it is moored."

Tom nodded.

"I do not like this place," said Ivor. "Too warm, I prefer the cold wind of Siberia." This made Tom smile.

"When you off?" asked Tom.

"Four, five days depending on loading and paperwork," replied Ivor.

"I will be out of your hair by then, Uncle Vlad gave me a contact in the City, Max. Another distant cousin of the extended Sharapova family," said Tom laughing.

"Do not knock it," said Ivor. "We Sharapovas are well travelled," he laughed with Tom. Ivor took Tom's arm, and said, "You sure you want to do this? Once started it's hard to stop."

Tom looked at Ivor and smiled. "I know, uncle Ivor, but they were my world and I cannot let it go unpunished, the family cannot let it go unpunished."

"Forget the family," said Ivor, "I never understood the

obsession my brother Vlad had with family honour and all that stuff. This is not about family honour, this is about you and your soul turning into something you may never be able to return from."

"It's something I have to do, uncle Ivor," said Tom softly.

"OK my boy, I understand. I will be popping by occasionally so if you need me, let Max know," said Ivor. "Now come give your old Uncle Ivor a hug, before you leave."

Tom opened his arms and, smiling, said, "Always knew you were a big girl at heart." Ivor hugged Tom, laughing his head off.

Belize

Next morning, Tom made his way through a bustling busy Belize City, getting lost once or twice but eventually making his way to the address supplied by Uncle Vlad. The apartment block looked tired and run down, and Tom noticed he was being watched from various doorways; Tom smiled and entered the apartment block with no front door. The apartment he wanted was on the second floor.

Knocking on the apartment door, Tom waited for a few minutes before the door opened with the safety chain still attached. "Yes," asked a voice.

"I am Tom Sharapova, uncle Vlad's nephew." Immediately the door was opened by a large rounded man, with a big Mexican moustache, and a big smiling face.

"Please come in Mr Tom, I am Max, I think we are lots of cousins removed but still family," said a laughing Max. Tom entered the well decorated and nice apartment; unlike the exterior, the place was homely and cool.

Offering Tom a chair, Max shouted something Tom knew was Spanish. a pretty woman came and placed a tray of cold drinks on the table and smiled at Tom. "This is my wife Silva," said Max. Silva smiled at Tom and offered her hand. Tom shook Silva's hand and smiled.

"If you need anything else, just holler," said a laughing Silva, returning to the kitchen.

Max looked toward the heavens and said, "Women." Tom smiled. "Down to business," said Max. "I have heard from Captain Ivor's man, the American ship docked two days before you did. Captain Ivor's man had a few drinks with the American ship's crew, and they confirmed they did pick up two passenger whilst they were docked in Odessa; one was attended to by the ship's doctor as soon as he came on board. Both men stayed in their cabins the whole crossing to Belize and both left as soon as the ship docked. The crew member who took the men their meals said one did not speak, but the injured one spoke with an English accent."

"Thanks Max, you've done well," said Tom.

"Anything to help the family," said a smiling Max.

"Few things I need you do for me," said Tom.

"Anything, just ask," replied Max.

Tom asked Max if he could find a suitable place for him to work from, out of the way, plus some transport, not too conspicuous. Tom also told Max that money was no object, placing a large envelope full of money on the table. This made Max smile.

Max made some notes and said, "Give me twenty four hours and I will see what I can do."

Standing, Tom shook Max by the hand. Tom said, "To a long a fruitful partnership."

Max puffed out his chest, and said, "For family."

Next day Tom met Max outside his apartment block. Tom said, "How we doing, Max?"

"Think I have found what you are after, Mr Tom," replied Max.

Tom smiled and said, "Excellent, Max."

"Follow me," said Max.

Tom followed Max to the back of the apartment block and opened a garage; there stood an old battered run down Jeep. Tom smiled and said, "Perfect."

With Tom driving, Max directed Tom on the road out of

the city. About ten miles down the road Max told Tom to slow down, and stop. Max pointed out a few geographic features and land markers, to enable Tom to orientate himself to where they were. Tom nodded and told Max he understood. Max then told Tom to turn off right into a small opening.

Tom drove for about a mile down a dirt track that was overgrown; sometimes they both had to duck because of low lying branches. Eventually Tom pulled into an opening and stopped. Tom looked at a large run down single storey warehouse totally hidden from view. Tom and Max took a tour of the warehouse and surrounding area; they also walked down to the jetty, where a boat was half submerged.

Tom turned to Max, and said, "Max, you have outdone yourself, I am so impressed, and this is just perfect," with his arms out wide. Max had a beaming smile on his face. Max told Tom that he had purchased the land cheaply and that Tom owned twenty square kilometres of land around the warehouse. Tom looked at Max and said, "Max, I can see you are going to be a credit to the family," knowing this was what Max wanted to hear and would make him feel special. Slapping Max on the back, Tom once again said, "Well done, I am impressed."

On the drive back to the city, Tom gave Max a list of things he needed. They worked out a system so Tom did not have to go into the city every day. Max said he would get his men right onto it, and let Tom know when he had his list ready.

Dropping Max off, Tom drove back via the British Embassy; stopping over the road from the embassy, Tom wondered how he was going to proceed tracking down the man from the American ship.

Before Tom returned to the warehouse, he went to the main post office and purchased a PO Box, and paid for six months' rental. Tom then drove to the Belize Central Bank and parked up; entering the bank Tom strolled to the reception, and asked to see someone so he could open a local account.

As Tom was sitting flicking through a magazine, a young

smiling man approached. "Tom Sharapova, I am Mr Stevens, the assistant manager," he said. Tom smiled and stood up, they shook hands and the man said, "Follow me please, Mr Sharapova." Tom sat in the offered chair and the young man sat behind his computer opposite.

"So, Mr Sharapova, how may we help?"

Tom said, "I want to open a local account and transfer some money from a Russian account into it."

Mr Stevens nodded and said, "No problem, we can complete your request now, if you have time."

Tom smiled and said, "All the time in the world."

After completing the forms for the new account, Mr Stevens said, "That's all complete, we will have a new bank book ready in a day or two, just pop back in for it; in the meantime you can use any of the counter staff, using your bank details." Mr Stevens passed over a small card to Tom with his new bank details on them. "Now, you said you wanted to transfer some money from a Russian Account to your new local one?" asked Mr Stevens.

Tom passed over the account details on a piece of paper; Mr Stevens took the piece of paper, smiled and started to type on the computer. While he was typing, Mr Stevens' face changed from indifferent to amazement; looking up at a smiling Tom, he said in a quiet voice, "Your Russian account seems to be rather healthy, Mr Sharapova. How much do you wish to transfer?"

"About three million Russian roubles into the local currency," replied Tom. Mr Stevens' face dropped. "Three million," replied a stunned Mr Stevens. Standing, Mr Stevens said, "Please wait here sir, I need the manager's authorisation to transfer such a large amount, won't be a minute," as he rushed from the room.

Tom sat and smiled to himself and thought, from a plain Mr to a Sir in the matter of a few keys strokes on a computer screen; money certainly talks the world over.

In a matter of seconds Mr Stevens returned with a puffing

small man. "This is Mr Rodrigues, the bank manager." Tom stood and shook his hand.

"I apologise, I was busy with another client when you came in Mr Sharapova, hope my assistant was satisfactory," said a worried looking Mr Rodrigues.

Tom said, "Mr Stevens has been impeccable and a true asset to your bank and your stout leadership."

"We always try to be here at the Belize Central Bank," said a smiling Mr Rodrigues. "Now, sir, you wish to transfer some money between accounts?" asked Mr Rodrigues. Tom told him the same amount as he had told Mr Stevens, but also added that periodically he would be transferring more money between accounts. Mr Rodrigues completed the money transfer, and personally walked Tom out of the bank with Mr Stevens in his wake. Outside in the sun, Tom smiled. He had no doubt next time he visited the bank his reception would be different.

Next day Tom woke early, as soon as the sun filtered through the windows of the warehouse. First job, Tom thought, was to hack back the overgrown jungle around the warehouse and down to the jetty.

After days of hard work, Tom sat on a broken chair outside the warehouse and surveyed his handy work; he had cleared back the jungle and rubbish to a good five metres out, so he was now able to walk around the warehouse and all the way to the jetty without being stopped by any obstacles. The next task was to see if he could salvage the submerged boat.

Tom jumped down into the boat, and realised it was not as bad as he first suspected. The boat was in a pretty good condition; metal construction with a large gaping hole in one side the size of three hand spans. Tom knew he could patch the boat and pump it out to get it to float again, get the engine working. Tom stopped himself and started to laugh out loud. Tom sat on the jetty and thought to himself, one step at a time my old mate, one step at a time.

Just then Tom heard a loud honk of a horn getting closer.

All of a sudden a large truck emerged from the opening that led to the road; a waving, smiling Max was sitting in the front of the truck. Three trucks in all parked next to the warehouse. Tom thought, that's one job I don't need to do now, the path up to the road; the trucks would have done a far better job than I could have, thought a smiling Tom.

Max and his men quickly unloaded the trucks in an efficient manner; even Tom was impressed by their work. After they had finished Tom thanked them all, and handed a large wad of money to Max, saying loudly, "Max, buy all these fine fellows a few drinks on me." Everyone climbed back onto the trucks, laughing and joking and with large smiles.

After they had left, Tom went and checked on the merchandise that Max and his men had dropped off. Tom stood and smiled; they had placed all the crates in the correct part of the warehouse. Tom first decided to set up his home area, as he called it. The men had laid down a large plush carpet that covered a third of the warehouse floor, near the kitchen area, so Tom began there. After a time Tom sat on a sofa and looked about. Not bad. The kitchen area consisted of a fridge and a freezer, a Calor Gas oven and stove; neatly partitioned off by screens were a small screened room with a cot bed, and the large area with two sofas opposite each other with a low table in between, and a large table with six chairs around it. Nice little home from home, thought Tom.

Over the next few days Tom unpacked all the crates and placed the items in their own places. Tom left one large crate until last. Before Max had left, Tom had asked if one of his men were good with electrics. Max smiled and said, "Already ahead of you, Mr Tom. Sparky," Max called, and a smiling man carrying a large tool bag came over. "Sparky, Mr Tom will show you what he requires."

Sparky smiled at Tom and said, "Lead the way, Mr Tom."

Tom admitted Sparky had done a really good job with the electrics; the whole warehouse had been wired inside and out, all the way down to the jetty, and the small room in the back was particularly well wired. Over the next few days, Tom wandered the warehouse and surrounding area setting up cameras and sensors. After Tom had set the last one, he said, "Right, let's go see it any of it works."

Sitting in front of eight large monitors Tom turned them all on. In turn they all came on and different views of the warehouse and area became visible. Tom switched between different camera angles and realised he needed to adjust a few, but overall no one would get close without him knowing about it, which made Tom feel, for the first time since his arrival, more relaxed.

Next day, Tom decided to tackle the boat again, now he had the right equipment. First, using the underwater acetylene tank he welded the patch on the side of the boat with a large metal plate. Once this was done, he cleared all the debris from around the bottom of the boat and inside. Lastly, pulling the boat from the side that was still above the water line he managed to right the boat, although it still sat low in the water. Hours later after painstakingly hand-baling water from the boat, Tom sat on the jetty watching the boat finally bob on the water. Tom was surprised that boat was in such good condition for its age.

Finally, after days of hard toil, Tom took the boat for its maiden voyage. Passing out of the small lagoon, Tom took the boat up to the busy Belize City Port, and located where the civilian boat harbour was so he could purchase fuel for the boat and any other items he might require. Also, Tom found out where the harbour master office was situated.

After Tom had returned to the warehouse, he sat at the table and wrote a list of things he still had missing for Max. He had decided to pay Max a visit tomorrow to continue with his mission, now his base of operation was up and running. Next morning Tom took the Jeep into Belize City, and he had been correct about the path leading up to the main road; the truck had cleared a really nice path for the Jeep to pass along.

Arriving at Max's, Tom knocked on the door to the

apartment, which once again was opened a few inches, then fully, by Max. Tom passed his list over to Max, who studied the list and nodded, and said, "Give me a few days, Mr Tom, and I will send a truck to you with it all." Tom smiled and thanked Max.

"Now, Max," Tom began, "I know you have not been fully brought up to date by uncle Ivor on why I am here." Max nodded, looking sombre. "Well, I need your expertise and contacts in the area to trace that man for me."

"Go on," said Max.

"I also need to keep busy, while I am hanging about waiting for events to unfold, so I was wondering if you could find me some occasional work to keep me busy."

After a few minutes, Max said, "As for the work, I have no doubt we can pass some interesting work your way, for a man of your talents, if the rumours are true that have come out of Odessa about Tom Sharapova. Even here your reputation has preceded you," said Max. Tom smiled at Max, and held out his hand which Max shook, smiling.

Days later, as promised, Max sent another truck to the warehouse stocked with all the items Tom asked for, plus a few extra items Max thought Tom might need. Tom smiled as he unpacked each crate. Max certainly knew his business and Tom realised Max was a good asset to have in his quest.

A few months later Max got a message to Tom to urgently contact him. Next day, Tom drove to speak to Max. After taking a seat in Max's apartment and refusing the offer of anything, Max finally sat opposite Tom and passed him a folded piece of paper. Tom read the single piece of paper, smiled, closed the piece of paper and passed it back to Max. "Well done Max, you came through for me once again."

"Glad to be of service," said Max.

Tom slid over a large envelope stuffed full of money towards Max, who quickly scooped it up from the table, smiling.

Later that week, working on the information Max had given him, Tom sat outside a small bar. When the waiter approached, Tom ordered a coffee. Tom casually watched a smart apartment block in the posh end of Belize City, mainly occupied by foreigners. Tom watched as a man with his arm in a blue sling came out of the building, turned right and walked down towards the city centre. Tom drank his coffee, left some money on the table and casually followed the man. Eventually the man walked up to and entered the British Embassy. Tom smiled; he knew he had found his prey.

Over the next few months, Tom watched the man's routine; the man never deviated much from his daily routine, only stepping from the embassy at lunch time or to go home. At lunch time he was normally accompanied by other embassy workers, so Tom decided the best time was when the man was at home.

Next day after Tom had watched the man depart for work, Tom took a small box and wandered up to the man's apartment block, pretending to study the list of apartment numbers. A voice behind him said, "Please can I help you?"

Turning, Tom smiled at the little old lady in front of him. "Yes I hope so, I am in a bit of bother," said Tom, trying to sound scared.

"Let's see if we can sort it out for you," said the old lady, smiling at Tom.

Still smiling, Tom said, "You would be an angel if you could."

"The problem I have is this box need to be delivered urgently, and I have left the paperwork back in the office, if I go back the boss will surely sack me for being lazy again."

"Who is it for?"

"That's the problem," said Tom. "I only saw the man briefly in the shop but I remembered part of the address of this building, from the paperwork."

Still smiling, the little old lady said, "Try and describe this man to me and I can see if I can place him for you."

"Well," Tom started, "he is about six foot tall," said Tom using his hand to show the old lady his height. "Also," went on

Tom, "he is as slim as me, plus he had his arm in a blue sling thingy on his arm," explained Tom, holding his arm up.

The little old lady started to laugh. "Oh, you are describing Mr Adam, from the British Embassy."

Tom smiled at the old lady and said, "You sound confident from my very bad description."

Still laughing, the old lady continued. "Mr Adam Banks, flat ten, second floor," said the old lady, looking pleased with herself.

Tom said, "You, old mother, are a marvel of the mind." Leaning over, and kissing her on the cheek, Tom also started to laugh with her.

"You can leave it with me if you like, young man."

"That's so nice of you, old mother," said Tom, bowing deeply to her. Tom placed the parcel on the counter and quickly left, smiling as he went.

Adam Banks was bored. He had been in this arsehole of a place for over a year, and it was like he was being punished for the cock-up in Odessa; it was not his fault the stupid driver had decided, instead of doing a U-turn for the shoot, to do a handbrake turn. He obviously had watched too many bloody Hollywood movies. This had thrown the whole operation into chaos, it had warned the two men sitting on the wall of their presence, and although they got a few bursts of fire off, they did not hit the intended target. Then, as they returned fire, he got a round in the shoulder for his troubles. Speeding away, the driver started to panic and hit a few parked cars, and several oncoming cars. As they arrived at the docks, the American decided to despatch the driver. Adam smiled; the American was just as pissed off as he was, and no doubt did it out of frustration. At least he helped him to the ship and medical attention.

The ship's doctor had done a botch job of removing the bullet and had damaged a few tendons in his shoulder, and if left as it was would have eventually left him without the use of his arm, so after a further five operations by the embassy doctors to repair the damage, he was on the road to recovery. So here he was, stuck in Belize City awaiting further orders. He had been told to rest and recuperate and take it easy. He had been placed on light duties in the embassy, which was boring; at least they had found him a decent place to live.

Returning home, Adam was just about to enter the apartment complex door when the old trout at reception stopped him. "Mr Adam, I have a package for you." Adam wondered who could have sent him a package here; immediately he became wary. His mind working overtime, he knew a parcel would have been delivered to the embassy not his home residence.

Thanking the old lady, Adam went and sat at a bench just inside the door. The post mark was local, which did not give any clues. Slowly opening the small package, all he found inside was a brochure: 'Welcome to Odessa'. Adam immediately panicked. Forbidden to carry a pistol, even for protection, he knew he had one in his apartment; should he go for the pistol, or return to the Embassy and report this? Deciding to arm himself first, which would make him feel better, he took the stairs to his apartment. On opening the door, he did not stop but went straight to the bedroom side cabinet and took out the 9mm Browning Automatic.

Just then Adam heard a noise behind him. Turning, Adam saw a man was standing in front of him, smiling. "Hello Adam," said Tom.

"Who the fuck are you?" asked Adam.

"I am the man you tried to kill in Odessa."

Adam went white as a sheet; not being left handed, the pistol felt strange in his left hand, but still he knew he could not miss a target as close as this man was. Adam smiled and said, "And now I get to kill you correctly." Adam slowly raised the pistol and pulling the trigger five times.

It took Adam a few seconds to realise the pistol was not working; no rounds were coming out. Adam looked confused until the man waved the firing pin at him and said, "Not today," pulling a 9mm silenced Glock of his own out and pointing it at Adam's heart.

"Sit," said Tom. Adam immediately sat on the bed.

"What do you want?" asked Adam.

"Information," said Tom.

"Fuck off, I am saying nothing," said Adam.

Tom smiled. "Typical British stiff upper lip. But you will tell me what I want to know," said Tom, smiling as he shot Adam in the foot.

Adam felt the pain rip through his foot and leg, and rolled back onto the bed. Tom went on, "Let me tell you what I know already, then you can fill in the blanks." Adam just stared at Tom with hatred in his watering eyes. Tom continued. "You and an American agent were dispatched to Odessa to kill Vladimir Sharapova, but you missed, took a bullet in the shoulder, took a ship here to Belize to recover. All correct so far?" asked Tom, waving the 9mm at Adam. Adam just sat and stared at Tom. "Now, tell me why your government intelligence agencies along with the Americans were so keen to kill Vladimir Sharapova. Don't feel like talking?" asked Tom, shooting Adam in the shoulder again, which made Adam pass out with pain.

Adam finally came round; he was unsure how long he had been out but his shoulder was on fire. Adam was sweating heavily and he was feeling nauseous. He stared at the man, and said in a weak voice, "What has that got to do with you?"

Tom smiled and said, pointing at Adams shoulder, "Twice now I have shot you in the shoulder."

Adam immediately knew who he was. "Tom Sharapova," Adam said.

"At your service," replied Tom, smiling. Adam realised there was no point in stalling him anymore; he was the ruthless enforcer for the Sharapova family, and Adam knew he was a dead man already, so why not give the man what he wanted to know? Over the next hour, Adam told Tom everything he knew about that fateful day, or what he knew of the events.

"Who was the American agent?" asked Tom.

"Never gave his name, only met him that morning before the attempt, and afterward, he dispatched the driver, helped me onto the ship, once here, I never saw him again."

"Who was your handler, next in the chain?" asked Tom.

"Stuart Pendall."

"Adam, you have been so co-operative," smiled Tom.

Adam for a second smiled and thought Tom was going to let him live, but a split second later two rounds took his head off.

The Duke

The day couldn't have started better for Tom; he had had a really good sleep, only because he possessed a rare condition, one that left his body clock un-affected by jet lag. After a shower, he lay on the bed and slept for three hours. After he woke he felt revitalised, and after another quick shower, he quickly dressed, checked his room and went down to the hotel lobby.

Tom spotted him as soon as he came out of the lift, and smiled. Even he was impressed; the UK agencies must be getting better. Found him already, and he had been in the country for less than twelve hours, most impressive. Ignoring the man, he strolled to the reception desk and handed in his key, then turned towards the exit doors, and passed through onto the pavement where he turned left and started to stroll down the road.

As he slowly walked down the street he spotted a coffee shop on the opposite side of the road. He crossed the road and pretended to study the menu in the shop window, but really he was counting the number of government agents; he spotted five scattered about doing various tasks trying to blend into urban life. Some were doing a really good job, others were like fish out of water. He was just about to enter the shop when he paused. Six agents: he nearly missed the old lady at the bus stop opposite. He then entered the coffee shop, and ordered a black flat coffee to go from the spotty teenager behind the counter. Tom paid, then went and added milk and sugar, left the coffee shop, and sat on an unoccupied table outside.

His mind went back to the note passed to him by the receptionist. The note he knew was from Lord Grenville St Louis, twelfth Duke of Hampshire. There had only been a phone number on the piece of paper, which Tom had chewed into a ball and flushed down the toilet after his morning ablutions. Tom would give the duke a call later, but knew the phone was a burner and would only be active for one call; after that it would be useless. He had to sort out a few things first. It would come as a complete surprise to the security services if they knew his best friend and contact was none other than a peer of the realm who sat in the upper house of the establishment, and ran one of the most successful businesses in the country.

How this strange turn of events came about was after a weird sequence of events, which happened in Belize many years ago. The Duke, as Tom always called him, was the second son of the eleventh Duke of Hampshire, so not likely to inherit; so he duly played the part of the second son, reckless and carefree. Whilst on a gap year from university, he was backpacking with a friend in Belize, when they happened to be in a bar at the southern end of Belize at a place called Punta Gora. The two friends were playing darts with two local lads. Tom just happened to be in the bar at the same time, waiting for a contact, not really paying attention to the darts game taking place, when all of a sudden it turned nasty in the blink of an eye; a knife had been drawn and one of the party was on the floor with blood oozing from a cut to the shoulder. All of a sudden Tom heard a plea for help, from a voice of impeccable English. It had been years since Tom had heard such well-spoken English, and for some reason, even to this day unknown to himself, decided to interact, and break a golden rule: 'never get involved unless you are involved'.

Tom moved with lightning speed, smashing the bottle in his hand over the aggressor with the knife's head, who went down like a dropped sack. Tom moved with the fluency of years of training and had rendered the other assailant harmless even before he knew what had hit him. Tom quickly looked at the two friends, who looked stunned with what had just gone on in a split second.

Tom said, "Grab your stuff and follow me if you want to live." He walked towards the door and down the road; the two recently sobered friends grabbed their belongings and staggered in his wake.

After reaching the harbour Tom jumped onto his boat, and told the friends to jump aboard. Running to the cabin he quickly switched on the engine and it roared into life. He shouted for one of them to cast off the jetty. Just as they were pulling away from the jetty, a stream of screaming locals were running towards them, stopping short on the jetty as by now they were far into the fast flowing river, quickly disappearing from view.

After about an hour Tom made sure they were not being followed, throttled back the engines until they were on idle and let the river's current take them along. He then moved to the back of the boat to greet his guests. The two friends were huddled in the bow of the boat, both looking shell-shocked by recent events; an hour ago they were having a fun game of darts in a local bar whilst having a few beers with the locals, now they were on a tug boat heading up a river to god knows where, with a complete stranger.

Tom introduced himself to them both and asked if he could look at the cut, and explained in these parts an untreated wound could fester and can go gangrenous in hours if not treated. Tom held out his hand in friendship, which the other man took, and said, "Grenville St Louis, eleventh Duke of Hampshire, second son."

"Blimey," Tom said, "that's a mouthful, I will call you Duke," to which they both laughed.

Sensing the tension broken, the other friend after shaking Tom's hand introduced himself as Jonathan Spencer, "Or Spence, if you like."

Spence asked where Tom was from and Tom replied, "Originally the East End of London," but never ventured any other information.

Tom explained to Duke and Spence what had occurred in the bar. He told them, "The local Creoles are very passionate about their darts, so being beaten by a couple of Angles who were playing to win was, to them, unfair."

Duke asked Tom where they were, and Tom explained they were following the river to the coast then up towards Belize City, the capital of Belize, where he would drop them off, and from there they could catch transport anywhere they like; the trip would take about three/four days depending on the authorities, current and other river traffic.

From this, Duke got the impression that Tom was some sort of pirate, and not strictly working within the law. Tom patched up Duke's shoulder, which luckily enough turned out to be only a minor cut; the knife had not penetrate too deep. This would only leave a light scar, plus also it did not require stitches. Tom told Duke that his shoulder would feel stiff for a few days but nothing permanent; he had been lucky, Tom told Duke, he had seen knife fights become brutal and often leave one or two dead.

Duke thanked Tom for his timely intervention. Duke and Spence both realised how lucky they had been, and if Tom had not been there, then they could have landed up in an unmarked grave in some part of a forgotten jungle. This thought seemed to have an impression on both men, and both now looked on Tom as some sort of saviour.

After a day following the river, they came to the open sea and Tom followed the coast up towards Belize City. Tom was sitting in the cabin slowly steering the boat when Duke came and sat next to him, passing Tom a steaming cup of coffee. Tom asked how Spence was getting on, as from the offset it become apparent Spence was not a born sailor and had spent most of the trip so far hung over the side. Duke, looking toward Spence, said, "Poor lamb, not having a good time of it, think this is going to put him off boating forever," which made them both laugh.

Duke had also found his place on the boat; he had become the designated chef, and Tom was impressed with the standard of food he produced in the tiny cabin below deck. Tom had not had decent food in a long time. After three days the water was becoming busier, as bigger boats and even ships were appearing all heading in the direction of Belize City Harbour. Tom managed to manoeuvre the small boat between the larger crafts, using most to mask his approach towards the docks. After a few hours, Tom steered the boat away from the main channel towards a disused part of the docks. Once they had tied up, all three finally stepped onto dry land for the first time in four days.

They followed Tom down an overgrown path that looked well maintained but like it had never been used to an abandoned warehouse, which also looked like it had been condemned years ago. Moving to the side, Tom pushed open a door which opened without any force. Tom moved into the darkness and after a few seconds the interior and exterior was lit and the other two stepped inside. Duke and Spence were amazed by the difference between the exterior and interior of the building; the inside was clean and the floor covered with carpets, and on one side it was set out like a small apartment, with a bed, sofa and chairs, kitchen area and a bathroom, everything neat and clean and ready to use. The other side of the building was stacked with boxes of every size and shape.

"Make yourself at home," Tom shouted over his shoulder as he disappeared into another part of the building. Duke and Spence both inspected the inside of the building and were impressed at the standard Tom had achieved in making it like a home. Spence flopped down on the sofa as Duke went into the kitchen area to make a coffee. Tom eventually arrived back ten minutes later. By this time Duke had found everything he needed to make a decent coffee; as he handed Tom his cup, he saluted him with his own and said, "All the comforts of home."

Tom saluted back with his own cup and said, "It does for now." Tom suggested they all get some sleep and tomorrow he would run them into Belize City and drop them off, wherever they wished.

The next morning Duke was first up and made everyone breakfast of fresh fruit and toast with coffee, the smell bringing the other two into the kitchen area.

So Tom said, "Where you do want to go?"

Spence said, "The British Embassy will do for a start," which brought a nod from Duke.

Tom agreed and said, "It will take me about twenty minutes, just need to rebuild the Jeep," which brought a puzzled look from the other two. They both followed Tom outside and at the back of the building sat an old rusty Jeep shell on bricks. Tom explained that although this place was remote and no one ever came around here, it was always best to have the appearance of neglect, that way it avoided further investigation. After all, if you found a derelict building with a brand new Jeep sat outside, would you not become curious? And, as Tom explained, curious people are never friendly. They both helped Tom replace the wheels and seats, which surprisingly was not any effort. Lastly Tom replaced the steering wheel and once again it looked like a roadworthy vehicle.

Lastly he filled the jeep with petrol, so at last they were ready to leave. Tom drove down a track, which to Duke and Spence did not look like any track they had ever seen. Tom drove with care and precision like he had done this journey many times before; eventually Tom stopped, and then slowly he moved forward and finally they were on a tarmac road. Turning left, Tom sped up to a steady speed and finally they all saw a sign that said 'Belize City ten miles'. Tom drove with skill through the hustle and bustle of the city, eventually arriving at the British Embassy gates.

Tom parked opposite the Embassy and turned off the engine. Spence immediately jumped out of the Jeep, but Duke stayed put, which brought a puzzled look to Spence's face.

Spence looked at his friend and said, "Come on, home awaits," to which Duke answered, "I am not coming, I am going to stay here with Tom, if Tom doesn't mind," which brought a nod and a smile to Tom's face. He had missed company, and he and Duke had become fast friends in the short time they had known each other.

Duke said, "Look, Spence, what have I got to look forward to going home? It's not like I will be welcomed with open arms, and so I will stay and have an adventure."

"OK, if you are sure," replied Spence.

"All I ask is you let my mother and father know I am safe and well, and if you see my brother tell him he is still a prig," which brought a smile to his friend's face. They briefly hugged and after he shook hands with Tom, he turned and headed toward the Embassy gates. Before he crossed the road Tom ran up to him and gave him a piece of paper, and after a quick few words and another handshake, Spence turned and did not look back until he was through the Embassy gates, by which time the Jeep had gone.

After they had pulled away, Duke looked at Tom and asked, "What was the note?" to which Tom replied, "If you ever need to be contacted, that's the PO Box I use for mail," to which Duke nodded, and somehow felt better about staying.

Tom parked in a rundown part of the city, and told Duke to stay in the Jeep, and went on to say, "Trust me, it will be easier until we have given you some training. Remember the bar," which made Tom laugh but Duke frown. Duke felt like a school boy again being told to stay in the Jeep, and felt seriously pissed off until he noticed he was being watched and people were staring at him. He realised perhaps Tom had been right after all.

After five minutes Tom came out of a building without any doors, got in the Jeep, started the engine and pulled away into the traffic. It was about a mile heading out of the city before Tom eventually spoke. "My contact was not happy I was unable to fulfil my contract, but I explained the circumstances so he gave me another chance."

Duke then asked a question that had been burning him up for days. "What do you actually do?" to which Tom answered, "Import/export, you know, normal stuff."

Duke just nodded, not knowing what 'normal stuff' covered. They both remained silent until they were back outside the warehouse. After stripping the Jeep down and making the place look abandoned once again, they both went into the building and Duke sat heavily on the sofa with Tom sitting opposite.

Over the next few days Tom explained to Duke his life story so far and how he had ended up a smuggler in Belize, to which all Duke could say was, "Wow," and was shaking his head in amazement.

Duke asked Tom if he could ask some questions just to get the picture clear in his mind, which made Tom smile and say, "OK, but only if I can ask some of mine," which Duke agreed. After what seemed like an age, Tom and Duke finally stopped asking questions, and they both realised the sun was setting and it was turning dark, so Tom moved over and turned on a side light which although did not illuminate the whole area, gave enough light to be practical. Eventually Tom said, "God, Duke, I feel like I spent hours in a police integration room," which made them both laugh. Tom said, "Let's get some sleep and start afresh in the morning," which Duke agreed.

The next morning after a light breakfast, Tom said to Duke, "Come sit down and let's start," which was making Duke more pensive as time went on. Tom sat staring at Duke for over ten minutes before finally saying, "First, we go to do something about your appearance. You look like a typical English boy. Little Lord Fauntleroy, with all those lovely long curly locks." Duke looked offended but did not say anything. "Plus," Tom went on, "We need to change your whole appearance. The whole Carnaby Street fashion look you have going on is not really going to blend in, especially the places we are going to frequent," which made Tom laugh, and Duke feel gutted.

Tom went on to explain that if you looked and appeared

rich, then most poor people will perceive you as rich; after all, the aristocracy had been getting away with it for years, plus no one noticed poorly dressed people as they all look the same. "You, my friend, in your present state, look like you are a typical English high born ponce on a road trip," to which they both laughed.

Tom smiled at Duke and said, "This is going to hurt you more than me," after which he started to cut Duke's hair. All Duke could do was close his eyes and think merry thoughts. After some time, Tom stood back and admired his work and said, "Go look at the new you." Duke went over to the mirror and hesitantly peered at the new person staring back at himself.

Tom had cut Duke's hair down to the scalp and coloured it, so it was no longer blond but more a dirty brown. Even Duke was impressed; he looked a different person. Tom said, "Put some dirt on your face and you will blend in perfectly." Next Tom told Duke to strip. He then threw Duke some trousers and a T shirt which Duke immediately tried to protest at, but Tom stood firm and told him once again he needed to blend in. Duke sighed and realised his fate and dressed quickly. Tom passed him a pair of trainers that had seen better days, and after Duke had put these on he did a twirl and said, "How do I look?" to which Tom replied, "Not like a stuck up toffee nose school boy, that's for sure," which made them both laugh.

Tom looked at Duke and said, "Just one more thing." Tom moved to a large box, and opening the lid, rummaged for a few minutes before emerging with something rolled up. Passing it to Duke, Duke realised it was a webbing belt with a large sheathed knife.

Duke pulled out the knife, and said, "You have got to be joking," and Tom said, "For protection," but Duke was not convinced. Putting the belt on and feeling the heavy knife on his hip, he did admit it made him feel a lot bolder and more confident about the place, better in fact since he had arrived in the country all those weeks ago.

After a light lunch, Tom gave Duke a tour of the warehouse.

Apart from the living area, Tom showed him the 'control room'. Duke was amazed; set up were twelve monitors, all with different views of the outside and inside of the building, from the landing pier where the boat was tied up to the road they use to go to the city. Tom explained that in his world it was never a good thing to be caught unawares and a golden rule was 'always have a plan'. He also showed Duke the security precautions of the building. The whole building was rigged with explosives ready to blow if compromised, also there were pressure and laser sensors all around the perimeter all fitted with silent alarms connected to a portable device Tom had in his pocket. So even before they arrived, Tom would know if any intruders had been about or were lying in wait for them. Duke was impressed at the layout; what first appeared to be a rundown derelict site was in fact a highly technical advanced hideout.

Lastly Tom showed Duke the many products he had stored in all the boxes. Duke was impressed and said, "Harrods would be so jealous," which made them both laugh out loud.

Over the next few months, Tom took Duke through a basic self-defence course, showing him both defence and attack techniques, without weapons and with weapons. Duke was unsure he could actually strangle someone with his bare hands, but did not mention this to Tom. Tom took his teaching very seriously so Duke had to reply in kind. It was during one lesson that Duke was not taking it seriously when Tom grabbed his arm, threw him over his back, and knocked the wind out of Duke. It was then Duke realised they were not playing games, and this was real life and death, and Duke was left under no illusion that Tom would expect him to uphold his end. After they had finished for the day, and sitting under the front porch watching the sun go down, Tom said, "We need to go back to Punta Gora and pick up the merchandise I left last time, before I got distracted and saved your arse," which made Duke blush, but he knew Tom was joking.

Duke looked at Tom and in his most serious face, held out his hand and said, "Tom, thank you."

"What for?" said Tom.

"For allowing me the privilege of entering your word and sharing it with you, you have also given me a purpose in life."

Tom looked at Duke's face, and said, "Oh my god, don't go all mushy on me now," which broke the tension in the air and Tom took the offered hand then slapped Duke on the back and said, "Coffee, my lord?"

Tom walked Duke through the security systems and fall back sites – all stacked with enough equipment for a clean getaway if required – until he knew them off by heart, even in the dark. Tom gave Duke a final test during the day and at night, before declaring Duke was ready, Tom was impressed by how quickly Duke had become accustomed to the procedure, but as Tom explained so many times over the last few weeks, 'always have a plan' and 'sloppy people end up dead people'.

Tom and Duke made sure the warehouse was set ready for their return, and headed down towards the boat. Once on board Tom started it up and Duke cast off, and before long Tom was navigating towards the busy river estuary and heading out to sea towards Punta Gora. On the way down Tom taught Duke how to navigate the boat, and after a few days even Tom was impressed at how quickly Duke had become proficient with the boat.

After three uneventful days at sea, they finally made their way up the tidal river towards Punta Gora. Finally Tom stopped at the jetty, and Duke jumped off and tied up. Tom looked over at Duke, who was looking apprehensive. "Don't worry," said Tom, "not even your own mother would recognise you, let alone some bar scumbag," which brought a smile to Duke's mouth, but not to his eyes.

They both made their way up to the local bar, which over several months before Duke and his friend John had been entertaining the locals in. Just before they entered, Tom turned to Duke and whispered, "Better leave the talking to me," which brought just a nod from Duke. Tom scanned the bar and noticed only two tables occupied; no one raised their heads when they walked in.

Tom went to the bar and ordered two beers, and placed a ten dollar note on the counter which was swiftly removed by the bar keeper in case Tom changed his mind. Duke turned and headed to the corner table, and Tom smiled and thought, Duke is learning.

Over the cold beer, Tom and Duke re-scanned the bar and Tom explained to Duke, "Always look at the person behind the bar, if they seem relaxed then probably all is well, if they look agitated then it's time to leave."

Duke noticed the man behind the bar looked bored, or was one hell of an actor. Eventually the bar door opened and two men walked in; one walked straight up to Tom and Duke's table and sat down and smiled, the other stool by the bar watching. The man said, "You have the merchandise?" Tom nodded and the man stood and turned. Tom and Duke stood and followed the man, who was joined by the man from the bar, out of the door.

They followed the two men down a dirt track between several shacks. Duke noticed women and children peering out of the windows as they passed by. Eventually the two men stopped outside a gated yard; just then, a man carrying a gun slung over his shoulder walked across and opened the gate. The two men beckoned them both in. Tom and Duke followed the men to a side door which was opened for them and they all went inside. A big man in greasy overalls approached and smiled at them, and said, "Shall we do business?" to which Tom lifted his shirt up and removed his belt.

He then opened and placed the merchandise on an old upturned oil drum. The big man looked at the merchandise and smiled. With a quick nod of his head, someone from the shadows stepped forward and placed four large plastic bags wrapped in black tape next to the merchandise. Tom quickly took two of the packages and handed them to Duke and he took the other two, and smiled at the man and said, "Nice doing business with you."

Tom was about to turn and walked back toward the open door when the large man said, "You not going to check it, you trust me?" and laughed; this brought on a laugh from the rest of the room. After the laughter had died down but before the large man had stopped, Tom leaned over and looked at the man and softly said, "If it's not right, I will be back." The man stopped laughing as something in Tom's eyes and manner made him realise this was a very dangerous individual who you didn't cross.

Tom turned and glanced at Duke to follow. Just then, one of the man grabbed Duke's arm and bringing his face close to Duke's, he said, "You sure we not met before?" to which Duke said, "Don't think so, and I suggest you try mints," which the man looked puzzled at, but before he had time for a reply Duke shrugged him off and he followed Tom from the building.

Both Tom and Duke walked quickly, but not appearing to rush back to the boat, closely followed by the two men from the bar. At the boat, Tom jumped aboard and quickly started the engine and Duke cast off. Duke did not breathe until he was sure the gap between the boat and the jetty was far enough apart for anyone to jump into the boat. Once back in the river, Tom asked Duke, "What was that about?" and Duke answered, "One of the men from the darts match."

"Oh I see," said Tom, and was still laughing an hour later.

After a hassle-free trip back to the warehouse, both Tom and Duke felt exhausted, and both decided once they had dropped off the packages they would have a few weeks' rest. A few days later, while Tom and Duke were lazing under a big tree not far from the warehouse, Duke asked, "How do you know you have a job on?" to which Tom replied, "Follow me."

Tom followed the trail up to the road. Tom stopped short of the opening to the road, and pointed across the road at a tree, and explained, "When there is a coloured ribbon around that tree, we have a message, so you only need to wander up until you can see the tree, so as not to arouse any suspicion from passing traffic."

"Neat," said Duke and they both turned back towards the warehouse. Duke and Tom took it in turns twice a day to check the tree, and after a month a blue ribbon was fluttering on the cool breeze late one afternoon.

Driving into town the next day, Duke asked Tom, "Don't you ever get curious at what you are transporting?" to which Tom replied, "No, I told you curious people are dead people. As long as I get paid I don't care, it's just business." At the same run-down building, Tom parked the Jeep and they both entered and went up one flight of stairs to a door at the far end of a corridor, knocking once on the door, and after a minute or so the door was opened slightly with the chain still across, and a face appeared and studied them both for a few seconds. The door closed and then re-opened fully to allow them to enter.

Sitting at a table with a cigar stub hanging from the corner of his mouth sat a man who Duke thought looked like every picture he ever imagined of a Mexican bandit. He smiled and stood and held out his hand and said, "Mr Tom, welcome."

Tom shook his hand and said, "Max, this is Duke, my friend," to which Max smiled at Duke and held out his hand and said, "Welcome Mr Duke, a friend of Mr Tom's is always welcome in my home." Duke shook Max by the hand, before both being offered the chairs opposite Max.

Max asked if they both wanted some refreshments, both declined. Max smiled and said, "Mr Tom, always business with you." Max said something to Tom in a language that Duke did not recognise, but Tom spoke it back to Max like a natural. After some ten minutes of dialogue, Max stood and went into a side room and returned with a large brown envelope and placed it on the table. Max and Tom spoke some more, and Duke could tell by Max's voice as he sounded more stressed as he went on that he was not happy about this.

Eventually Tom and Max stood and shook hands. Duke stood also and shook the offered hand from Max. As they both turned to leave, Max said to Duke, "Please make sure Mr Tom is careful, I can tell you are a good friend of his, tell him not to take risks." Duke nodded and followed Tom from the building and back to the Jeep.

After a silent drive back, Duke noticed Tom was deep in thought and did not want to bother him; he knew he would explain once he was ready.

Next day when Duke woke, he was surprised to find Tom missing. After checking the control room monitors, he was nowhere to be seen; everything else looked all in place, the boat, the Jeep, the perimeter. Just then he spotted on one of the monitors a few boxes being moved at the very end of the warehouse, so Duke went to investigate. Tom was moving boxes looking for something.

Duke asked, "Can I help?" to which Tom replied, "I got it covered," so Duke shrugged and went to make some coffee. After a time while Duke was sitting drinking his coffee, Tom returned carrying a crate which, by the way he moved, looked heavy. Tom placed the heavy crate on the table and sat down. Duke had made him a coffee; Tom took a big swig and said, "OK, I know you are dying to know what's going on," to which Duke replied, "I was wondering."

Tom explained he had known Max since he had arrived from Russia, and was his contact. They were speaking Russian the other day. Tom explained that Max did not always get import/export contracts for him, he also tracks people down and the new name was making Max nervous, as the man with his contacts was extremely dangerous. So he tried to persuade Tom to forget it. Tom said, "How hard can it be? Only dropping in for a chat." Duke did not look convinced.

Next day, Tom and Duke took the boat towards the busy City Marina to fill the boat with fuel. Also Tom filled several jerry cans, paying in cash. Tom and Duke were once again heading for the open sea.

During the trip down coast, the large crate that Tom & Duke had manhandled on board was sitting in the middle. Every time Duke went past he either caught his toe or knee, which always brought a laugh from Tom after Duke's profanities, and Tom would always say the same thing: "Language, my lord," which made him laugh more and Duke swear more.

After several days of keeping to the coastline, Tom finally turned the boat towards the coast. Duke noticed he was heading towards a small tributary. Cutting the engine, Tom allowed the boat to drift into the small river mouth and once out of site of the sea, Tom let the boat ground on the shore. Tom smiled at Duke and said, "We will camp here," to which Duke nodded and went to put the kettle on.

Later that night, Tom explained to Duke that they were meeting a container ship and the man he wanted to talk to was on it. Still smiling, Tom said, "Nice and easy," which still gave Duke a bad feeling in the pit of his stomach.

While Tom was getting some sleep, Duke decided to look in the large chest they had manhandled on board. Slipping the locks Duke opened the crate, and using the light of the moon, looked inside. Duke was astonished to see it full of weapons and assorted battle-ready equipment. Duke quickly closed the lid and went to lie down.

Tom watched Duke and smiled; he's getting good, I must admit, thought Tom as he closed his eyes again. Next morning over a cup of coffee, Tom was scanning the horizon with a pair of binoculars when he said, "Find what you were looking for last night?"

"Sorry?" said Duke.

"Last night," said Tom, "in the crate."

"Arrr," said Duke, "sorry old man, could not resist. Apologies and all that," looking rather sheepish.

"You only had to ask," said Tom, smiling.

Just as Tom was about to speak again the radio squawked, and Tom heard the boat's call sign. Tom quickly answered, and smiled at Duke. "On for tonight."

"Deep joy," said Duke, still feeling uncomfortable.

"So," said Duke, looking serious, "what do you want me to do?"

Tom said, "Just pilot the boat out to the cargo ship. Wait for me to return."

"And if you don't?" said Duke with his most serious face, which Tom replied, "Well, Duke, my old flower, you got a bitch of a trip back home without me," and laughed. Duke laughed as well, but did not see anything funny in it.

Once it had got dark, Tom dressed all in black with his face also covered with black camouflage, opened the crate and put on a combat style vest; also a double pistol holster, which he placed after checking two hand guns; two thigh holsters with also two checked hand guns in; two short snub machine guns which Tom slung over each shoulder; and finally, he picked up a single short barrel pump action shot gun.

"How do I look?" said Tom, smiling.

"Deadly," said Duke, only seeing Tom's flashing teeth in the moonlight.

"OK," said Tom, "this is what I want you to do. When the cargo ship anchors off the coast, motor out to it, but before you get there, cut the engine, and drift into the ship; you will be watched from the ship, they should lower a ladder down to you, so drift towards it, but take your time. As by then I will have slipped over the side and up the anchor chain onto the ship."

After midnight, Tom and Duke were watching the ocean for the ship. Eventually a large black object came slowly into view, not more than a mile from their position; they both heard the screw of the ship, and eventually they heard the anchor being slipped and falling into the sea.

Tom slapped Duke on the back and said, "Ready?"

"Not really," said Duke.

"Don't worry," said Tom, "do your part and all will be fine."

"OK," said Duke, before switching on the engine and pushing the throttle to forward and slowly manoeuvring the boat towards the large black object stationary at sea.

As Duke steered the boat towards the cargo ship, Tom was crouched down in the stern of the boat. Duke headed toward the bow of the ship, passing under its great arched front. Once level with the ship's stern, Duke cut the engine and steered the boat down the side of the ship. Duke heard the splash but was concentrating too much on not hitting the ship with the boat to worry about Tom.

The boat finally came to a halt halfway down the starboard side of the ship, gently kissing the side of the ship with the boat. Duke felt pleased with himself; he was more than apprehensive about his ability to do what Tom had asked of him, but now he was in position, he felt so relieved.

Tom slipped over the side, and started to climb the anchor chain, once he reached the chain locker where the anchor enters the ship, Tom stood on the anchor chain and removed from behind his back a small crossbow, aiming up over the ship Tom fired, an audible hiss propelled the hook and line up over the bow of the ship, Tom felt the hook catch he gave it a few hard tugs, it held fast, holding his arms above himself he pressed the button on the side of the crossbow and he slowly ascended up to the gunwale where Tom climbed onto the ship.

Tom made his way down the side of the ship, keeping to the shadows, passing the open hatch to the bridge Tom paused briefly as a voice said "Cabin four", Tom move on to the next hatch opening the hatch Tom paused for sounds, only hearing the low hum of the electric generator Tom moved down two flights of stairs to the level of the cabins. Tom opened the door and moved down the corridor. Stopping outside cabin four made Tom nearly giggle; how prophetic, thought Tom, this was the first cabin he stayed in when he first came aboard the Red Star all those years ago.

Tom knew that Ivor would have explained to his passengers that he was stopping to pick up extra cargo, and not to worry when they stop for an hour. Tom stood until his breathing had gone back to normal. He placed two small charges on each of the side bolts of the door. Holding the remote in his hand, Tom knocked on the door with the barrel of the shot gun placed over the eye piece, waited five seconds, he then pulled the trigger and remote at the same time.

The door blew inwards at such a speed, the shot gun had done its job and killed the first man looking through the eye piece, sending his dead body and the door towards the three sitting men, sending them into confusion. Tom quickly entered the room and, changing to a silenced sub machine gun, shot both men sitting to the left and right quickly, before they had time to react or draw their firearms. The man in the middle looked confused, looking about at his three dead body guards, and the man standing in front of him dressed all in black pointing a sub machine gun at him; the man started to sweat even more than he had been doing.

Tom slowly walked over, still with the sub machine gun pointing at the man.

"Please don't kill me," said the man, "I will tell you any-thing you want to know."

Tom removed his black mask and smiled and said, "I have no doubt you will." Taking a chair and sitting opposite the man, Tom still smiling, said, "So where do we begin, Mr Pendall? Let's talk about Odessa and Operation Blackstone."

"I don't know what you mean" said the man a little too quickly.

"Come now, Stuart, don't make out we are both stupid."

"What has Operation Blackstone to do with you anyway?" asked Stuart.

Tom smiled and said, "My name is Tom Sharapova, and I have everything to do with Operation Blackstone." This made Stuart Pendall look more scared. "So I see you know my name," said Tom.

"I know who you are, of course," replied Stuart.

"I had a nice long chat with Adam Banks and he gave you up."

"Adam Banks, should I know him?" asked Stuart Pendall.

Tom stared at the man with cold eyes. "I can see you need

me to jog your memory," he said as Tom shot the man in the left knee cap.

The man, after some time, said in a whisper, "OK, I know Adam Banks, I was his handler, it was me that put his name forward for Operation Blackstone."

"Go on," said Tom.

"It was run out of Kiev Office, we were both stationed there at the time."

Tom stared at Stuart Pendall, and said, "The names of the American agents, if you don't mind, Stuart."

"I don't know the name of the agent tasked to go with Adam, but his handler was Simon Muscrat," said Stuart.

"Thank you," said Tom, he then shot the man twice in the heart.

Picking up the man's large duffle bag, Tom left out of the cabin, moving down the corridor to a door, opening the door and going back up two flight of stairs and opening another door, Tom was back on the deck, Tom moved down the side of the ship towards the ships ladder, just as Tom was moving down the ladder to the landing platform, a voice said, "You owe me for a door and a cabin re-fit."

"Send me the bill," said Tom, laughing as he slipped over the side and down the ladder.

As Tom had said, the ship lowered its side ladder. Duke slowly drifted the boat towards the landing platform. As Duke waited, he tried to see the name of the ship but from where he was it was too dark to make out; as the minutes ticked past, the tension mounted and became anxious.

After thirty minutes while waiting in the dark, under the looming ship Duke's mind started to ask questions he should not be asking at a time like this. Finally Duke said out loud, "Stop it now, you are being stupid, get a grip," to which a voice behind him said, "Talking to yourself is the first sign of madness."

Duke must have jumped about three feet in the air, as

standing there was Tom with a smiling face. "Bloody hell old man, talk about give a poor chap a heart attack,"

"Sorry," said Tom.

"Everything alright?" said Duke.

"Perfect," said Tom, "let's go home," to which Duke acknowledged with an 'aye captain' and a mock salute, before turning on the engine and pushing the throttle to full and heading back towards Belize City and home. As they were moving away, the Red Star had already started to pull up its anchor and start its engines again.

On the way back, Duke asked Tom what happened on the ship. "Well," said Tom, "first I had a chat with the Captain, then a chat with the man in cabin four, who told me everything I needed to know before I killed him."

"OK, but did you have to kill the captain?" was all Duke could say.

Tom smiled, "It's OK Duke, me and Captain Ivor Sharapova are family. It was him who put Max onto the man I wanted to speak to. Ivor will dump the bodies once he is out at sea."

"Bodies?" said Duke.

"Well, he had, three bodyguards, who would have objected to me chatting to their employee."

"So you found the next link in your chain," said Duke.

"Yes," was all Tom said? Duke nodded and stared out of the boat's windows, pretending to steer the boat.

Once they had docked and everything had been stored away and they were back in the warehouse, Duke was making a coffee and Tom shouted over, "We will go and see Max tomorrow and check the mail box," to which Duke replied, "Sounds like a plan."

"Oh yes, got us a present," said Tom, throwing Duke the large over-stuffed back pack.

"Splendid, love presents," said Duke. Duke caught the large duffle bag, and was surprised at how heavy it was. Slowly Duke opened it and looked in. His eyes nearly popped out of his head as he looked up from the back pack towards Tom, who was laughing.

"See, not a total loss trip, was it?"

Duke could not believe his eyes as he tipped the entire contents of the backpack on the table. Both stared at the pile of money on the table.

"How much you think is there?" asked Duke.

"Not sure," said Tom, "it's all in difference currencies, so hard to judge."

Duke just sorted out the English and American. As he recognised the dollars, after a time he whistled and said, "500,000 English pounds, and 300,000 US dollars, and if the rest are the same amounts, depending where you exchange them, this is a small fortune," said Duke, smiling.

Duke then spotted a large brown pouch that was hidden in the pile of money; taking the pouch, he opened it and for the second time that day was speechless. Tipping the contents of the pouch on the table as well, it formed a heap of pure cut diamonds which sparkled in the sunlight. Duke just stared at the diamonds, and finally said, "I don't think I have ever seen so many diamonds in one place, not even the queen of England owns this many." Tom laughed, and finally Duke raised his head and howled, which made Tom laugh even louder.

Tom extracted Max's commission from the money and diamonds, and placed them in a small backpack. The rest Tom placed in an old battered safe in the Communications Room.

On the drive into Belize City, Duke turned to Tom and said, "This killing lark is quite lucrative," which made Tom smile.

"I am not in it for the money," said Tom, which made Duke's brain turn somersaults with possibilities.

The meeting with Max went well, as Max was so relieved to see Tom again. Max said, "He was a tricky bastard, that one," to which Tom agreed. Max asked, "Did he tell you everything you wanted to know?"

"Yes he did, and here is the next name to trace for me." He passed Max a piece of paper. Max took the paper and said, "I will see what I can do."

After leaving Max, Tom and Duke drove to the post office to collect the mail from the PO Box; also, Tom paid the rent for the next six months on the box while they were there.

Once back at the warehouse, Tom was flicking through the pile of mail, when he stopped and said, "Oh this is for you, Duke."

Duke looked puzzled. "Me? How strange." Duke did not recognise the writing on the envelope, which made the mystery even greater. Duke opened the letter and then stood and went outside.

After it had gone dark, Tom wondered where Duke could be. Going looking for him, he found him sitting on the front porch. "Everything OK, Duke?" said Tom.

"Not really," said Duke, "here, read this, it will explain it." Tom took the letter and read:

My Dear Grenville

It is with a heavy heart I write to you, and I apologise for being the bearer of bad news.

You older brother Stephan was killed in a car accident on the way back from London to your country estate, also in the car was his future bride who fortunately survived the car accident.

Your Mother and Father have asked me if I knew how to contact you, and persuaded me to write to you, and let you know the terrible news that has befallen your family; as you are now the rightful heir and next in line, both your parents are eager for you to return so you can rightfully take your place as the future Duke and run the family estate.

Your Father asked me to point out the family motto to you "Officium antequam glorificetur", "Duty before honour". He knows you will do the right thing.

Your friend

Jonathan Spencer

Tom folder the letter back up and passed it back to Duke, who placed it in his top pocket. "Sorry," was all Tom could say. He patted Duke on the shoulder, stood and went back inside. Duke sat and thought about his family motto, 'Duty before honour'. Duke instantly thought of his late Grandfather, and smiled. He remembered the time when he was a little boy, and his Grandfather had first shown him the family motto at Hampton Hall; Duke frowned as he imagined his father dictating the letter to Jonathan, old bastard thought Duke, just like him to tug the heart strings to get his own way. He had never really seen eye to eye with his father, always a disappointment; he never fitted into the role he was meant to be. Second sons of dukes are meant to go and slip quietly into the shadows; all Duke wanted to do was to be free from all restraints. He was pleased in some way to be the second son, no pressure to achieve, unlike his brother Stephan who was constantly reminded he was the heir, and depended upon to do the right thing always.

He had never been close to his brother; they were separated by three years, so they did not really mix. Even when they were together at holidays, the both went their separate ways. He tried to remember the last time he had spoken to his brother; it was nearly three years now, at the last family dinner before he left for Belize. The last thing his brother said to him was, "Grenville, my dear chap, you are a waste of space." Duke smiled when he remembered that; he probably was, but now he was a rich waste of space.

Duke tried to feel sad at his brother passing but could not conjure any emotion, he just felt normal, not even a tear, but he did feel sad when he thought of his mother and father. They would be feeling the loss, and no doubt his mother was anxious for him to return home. Also in the letter Spence said that in the car with his brother was his future bride; he never knew his brother had any feelings apart from the one he had for his own self-importance, to have feelings for someone enough who wanted to marry him. Then Duke smiled. The Farthings girl, what was her name? Something beginning with S, he was sure… oh yes, Sara. So she finally tied Stephan down, good for her, thought Duke.

Next day Tom asked Duke what he was going to do. Duke said, "To tell you the truth I am not sure." Tom did not push the matter, as he knew what Duke was going to do, even if he did not; Tom knew people, and Duke would decide to go home and become what his family required of him. Tom felt a bit sad; he would miss Duke, they had become close.

As they both drove into Belize City to visit Max, Tom asked Duke, "You know you will have to at least write home, or contact your family, to prove you are still alive before your father sends the cavalry to find you?"

"I know, I know," said Duke, sounding annoyed, which made Tom smile but he did not speak again until they reached Max's place.

When they arrived at Max's place, they were both surprised to see a police car parked outside. They both entered the building and went up to Max's apartment. The door was ajar. Tom gently knocked and it was opened by a policemen, who asked, "Yes, can I help you?"

"Friend of the family," said Tom, smiling and peering over his shoulder. Tom noticed Max's wife Silva and waved; a voice from behind the policeman said something and the policeman stood aside to let them both enter.

Tom went directly to Silva, who looked like she had been crying, as her eyes were red and puffy. Tom sat next to her and took her hand in his and asked gently, "What's going on, Silva?" to which she replied, "Max is dead."

Tom stared at Silva, not believing what she had just told him. The policeman standing next to her said, "We found Max's body in a dumpster outside the Flamingo club, do you know it?"

"No," Tom lied.

"To us it looked like a robbery, nothing was on the body apart from this piece of paper with a name on it." The policeman passed the paper to Tom and he recognised his own handwriting on the bloody piece of paper immediately. "Do you recognise the name?" asked the policeman.

Once again, Tom lied.

The policeman said, "If there is anything thing else you can remember," passing a card to Silva, "please contact us." Silva showed the two policemen out and came and sat back down next to Tom.

Tom said to Silva, "OK, tell me everything."

Silva went on to explain that after he left last time, Max made a few phone calls and last night told her he was on to the name that Mr Tom had given him, he said he had to meet a man at the Flamingo club at seven pm. Tom asked, "Did Max mention who he was meeting?"

Silva nodded. "Yes, Juno Broutini."

"Never heard of him," said Tom.

"He was one of Max's contacts," said Silva. Tom looked at Duke, who shrugged. Tom took out a large wad of money and passed it over to Silva. "What is this for, Mr Tom?" said Silva.

"It is what I owed Max," replied Tom.

"Thank you," said Silva, "he loved working for you, Mr Tom," said Silva, "as Max always said, family is important."

"Too true," said Tom. "If you ever need anything, you will let me know."

"No, it's OK Mr Tom, Max left me and the children well provided for. And just be safe, Mr Tom." Tom left Silva with a smile.

Back at the Jeep, Duke turned to Tom and said, "Poor Max, he seemed a nice man."

"He was," said Tom, "plus he was family, so this makes this even more personal."

"So I take it we are off to the Flamingo club for a few drinks and a snoop?" asked Duke.

"Got it in one, partner," said Tom with a smile after starting the engine.

Arriving at the Flamingo club, Duke said, "Not the Carton

Club, is it?"

"Carton Club?" Tom asked.

"In London, very exclusive. One day, old man, I will treat you to lunch there."

"Sounds like a plan," said Tom. "Bet it looks better inside," said Tom, smiling.

"That I doubt," said Duke, laughing.

Walking up to the main door, Tom pushed and found it was locked. "Perhaps it's too early for opening hours?" asked Duke.

"Doubt it," said Tom, "more like it's members only." Tom knocked on the door and a hatch opened. "Two please," said Tom, passing some notes through the hatch. The hatch closed and the door opened and they entered.

"Money talks," said Duke.

"Always," said Tom.

Tom was wrong; the inside was no better than the outside. Along one wall was a bar, the other side a stage, and several tables with chairs scattered about. The place was fairly empty at this time of day. Also dimly lit, it was hard to see the entire room. They both walked up to the bar, as Tom smiled at the oncoming barman. "Two large rum and Cokes," said Tom.

"Large?" said Duke in a whisper. "Pushing the boat out a bit, aren't we?"

The barman retuned with the drinks, and said, "Twelve dollars," which Tom handed over. Tom passed one of the drinks to Duke, who took a sip.

Tom asked the barman, "Where you from? Your accent is not local."

The barman looked at Tom and said, "Germany."

"One of my favourite places," said Tom. "Whereabouts?"

"You would not know it," said the barman.

"Try me," said Tom. "Tell you what, if I do, next round's on you."

"Deal," said the barman.

The barman said, "I come from a place called Paderborn."

The barman looked pleased with himself, a free drink coming his way.

"Paderborn," said Tom, "Near Sennelager where the British Army have their firing ranges, great place."

The barmen looked shocked. "You've been to my home town?"

"Yes," said Tom, "here, have a drink with me." He passed a 100 dollar bill across the counter.

"Thanks," said the barman, "nice one." The barman returned with three glasses, and took a special bottle from under the counter after pouring, held up one and said, "Prost."

"Cheers," said Tom and Duke in unison.

"Wonder if you could help me," said Tom.

"Of course, my friend," said the barman.

"I am looking for someone who comes in here."

"Who is that?" said the barman, looking a bit apprehensive. "Juno Broutini," said Tom.

Looking around, the barman said, "He is not in yet today."

"OK," said Tom, "can you point him out when he does? We will be sitting over there."

"Sure," said the barman. Tom placed another hundred dollar bill on his change and followed Duke to a wall table.

"Impressive," said Duke.

"Easy really, the accent was a dead giveaway, plus the place name Paderborn; hoped there was only one Paderborn in Germany, so mentioned the British Army Firing Ranges in Sennelager."

"Amazing," said Duke.

"Knowledge," said Tom.

To pass the time, Tom once again asked Duke what he was going to do.

"Well old man, I think it's best if I return home to face the music."

"Thought as much," said Tom, smiling.

"Really," said Duke, "am I that predictable?"

"Yup," said Tom. "I am going to miss you."

"And me you, old fruit. But I have been wondering about that."

"Oh really?" said Tom.

"Yes, I can carry on your quest with you."

"What do you mean?"

"Now Max is dead, you need help in the future so what if I become your contact, tracker down of people for you?"

"Hang on a minute my lord, I cannot ask you to do that."

"Of course not, that's why I am asking you. After all, who would suspect the heir to a dukedom helping you?"

Tom thought about it, and said, "I will sleep on it."

Just then the barman nodded to the door; a small, scruffily-dressed man had just entered the bar with another man. They sat at a table near to Tom and Duke and one of the men went to the bar and brought back two beer bottles to the table.

Tom told Duke to stay put, and look out for any surprises; not sure what kind of surprise Tom was referring to, Duke said, "OK," and watched as Tom casually walked over to the table where the two men were sitting.

Grabbing a chair as he walked past and taking it to the table with him, Tom sat down and said, "Evening."

One of the men said, "Who the fuck are you?" which made the other one laugh.

"Only want a chat," Tom said, "nothing heavy."

"What if we don't want to chat?" said the man.

"Well, perhaps I can persuade you." This brought a laugh from the man again, but before he could finish his laugh, Tom moved as a blur and straight handed him across the throat; the man's eyes went wide, his face turned purple and he slumped onto the table.

Tom looked at Juno Broutini. "Now, about that little chat," said Tom, smiling.

Juno was looking from Tom to his dead friend. "What do you want?" he said in a trembling voice.

"Information," said Tom.

"OK," said Juno.

"Last night," said Tom, "You asked Max to meet you here." Juno went white when he heard the name. "And after meeting you, he ended up dead. Now, how did that happen?"

Juno told Tom, "I did meet Max. Max was my friend, I fed him useful information from time to time. He had rang me a day or two ago with a name he wanted some information on, I said I would find out and get back to him.

"While I was asking about the man Max was looking for, I got a phone call from a man; he did not give his name, only it was definitely an American accent, he asked me who was looking for the name, I told him, so he told me that I had to meet Max last night in here at seven pm, and tell him the man he was asking about had left the country."

"Go on," said Tom.

"That's all I know, I promise, I met Max, we had a beer and I left. If I had known what was going to happen I would never have met Max, he was my friend."

"But you being you, you waited outside to see what was going down."

"No, no," said Juno too quickly.

"Juno, why are you lying to me? Your friend annoyed me and look what happened to him."

Juno stared at his dead friend and then at Tom, gulped and said, "OK, OK. I waited outside to see Max come out."

"OK, what happened?" said Tom.

Juno told Tom, "As Max left the bar, a black car came and parked next to the club. A large white man with a bald head, smartly dressed, got out and called Max by name. Max looked scared and tried to run into the alley, but the man was too quick for him and slammed him against the dumpster. He had Max pinned against the dumpster and had a big knife against his throat, asking him questions; I could not hear the conservation, I was too far away. The man was getting angry, but Max kept shaking his head, then Max spat in the man's face, and laughed which seemed to freak the man out. He was yelling at Max, and I heard him shout that Max was just a dumb commie bastard; he then just slit his throat and let him fall to the ground. The other man in the car came running over and they both had an argument, while pointing at Max.

"The big man shrugged the other man off and went back to the car, the second man, rifled Max's pockets and took everything, including his watch, and then threw Max in the dumpster. The car then left, and about five minutes later when I felt it was safe, I ran."

"Did you get the registration of the car?" Tom asked.

"No, but it was one of those big black ones the embassies use for their people."

Tom patted Juno on the face, and said, "Listen, Juno, we never had this conservation. You don't want me to come back for another chat, do you, if I hear you've been talking?"

Juno shook his head and was trying not to imagine what another chat with his man could be like. "No, I promise."

"Good lad," said Tom, patting his face again, and for the first time since Tom had sat down, Juno smiled, just before Tom killed him.

Tom nodded to Duke and they both left the bar. "Well," said Duke. "Max was set up by that scum bag in there."

"But the plot thickens, Max seemed to have opened a hornets nest asking about, the name on the paper, and the wrong people got to hear about it, and did not like it."

"So what happens next?" asked Duke.

"Well, my friend, we shall go home, and discuss your proposal."

"Awesome," said Duke.

Next day Tom laid a large box file in front of Duke, and said, "Read this as it explains it all." While Duke reached for the box file, Tom left the room. Duke opened the large box file with the words 'Operation Blackstone' written on the front. Inside were various newspaper clippings, and a few sheets with Tom's spidery handwriting. As Duke read the handwritten notes, he started to understand Tom more and more. Tom had laid out his life after being married into the Sharapovas, his family and his rise to chief enforcer in the family, the reasons he was doing what he was doing. Duke read the newspaper articles, and afterwards read about the death of Tom's wife and daughter which made Duke weep for Tom's loss.

When Tom returned, Duke was staring out into space with tears in his eyes. He turned to Tom and said, "My dear chap, I had no idea. You don't know how sorry I am."

Tom waved it off and said, "It's who I am and the way I am."

Duke nodded and said, "I totally understand."

Duke asked Tom, "So what happened after you left Odessa?"

Tom said, "The hunt for those involved started here, so Uncle Ivor was shipping out to here; so I tagged along, and found this place. The rest, as they say, is history."

Duke asked, "What happened to S&T Imports?"

"Well, technically it's still trading," said Tom. "We registered it under Russian law, so it's still a viable company."

"Good, good," said Duke.

Tom looked at Duke, and Duke could see by Tom's puzzled expression that he was confused. "Don't worry," said Duke, "I have a brilliant plan, just need to work out some details."

Over the next few months Duke and Tom worked on the plan. As the pieces fell into place Tom was impressed with Duke's enthusiasm and flair; Tom in a million years would never had thought of half the things Duke was suggesting. Then again, he had known one other person like that many years ago; this brought a smile to his face.

"So," said Duke finally to Tom, "first things first. You need to find all the relevant paperwork on S&T Imports."

"I am sure they are in the back somewhere."

"Good," said Duke. "Once I am back in the UK, I will re-activate S&T Imports, as you have signed me as the new Chairman. I will then register it in the UK as a private company. Then I will re-open the company bank accounts and start to transfer money around the world, and find decent offices where we can trade from. The money in the safe is easy to move, but the other stuff like the diamonds, gold and other trinkets you have acquired over the years will be more difficult; it will take me some time to finally shift it all, and convert it into cash." This brought a smile to Tom's face.

Duke went on, "You need to speak to Uncle Ivor and ask him when he is next planning a trip to the UK. I am sure we can make a run to the UK worth it."

"I'm sure we can," said Tom smiling, "What has uncle Ivor got to do with this?"

"He, my dear chap, is going to smuggle all the diamond and gold into the UK for us."

"Trinkets."

"Sorry?"

"And trinkets," said Tom, laughing.

"Yes of course, trinkets," replied Duke seriously. "Once I have established the company on a sound footing, you can draw on funds and start to move more freely about the world, as I start tracking down people. You won't need to scrimp and scrape for information anymore, plus any extra valuables you encounter on the way can be passed onto uncle Ivor who can deliver it to me for further distribution." This brought a smile to Tom's face.

"Under the S&T logo we will create a world class import and export business, delivering worldwide, above the radar or under the radar, depending what the client wants. We will become the name to be trusted to deliver anything anytime anywhere, and as we build we will expand. In the shadows I will create a clandestine operation, to rival any top government intelligence agencies. I will employ the very best programmers and analysts, none will know the whole picture, or what they are doing; as far as they know it will all be working towards the import and export business, but only you and I will know the real reason for S&T Imports. As you pass me a name, I can find them, check them and pass on their history within months possibly weeks, and 'hey presto', we are in business. What you think then, Tom?"

"Duke, to say I am impressed is an understatement," said

Tom grinning. "But one thing, Duke, that is bothering me."

"What's that, Tom?" asked Duke.

"On paper the plan looks excellent and well thought through, but are you not worried by the fact it's not technically legal?"

Duke laughed. "My dear Tom, you have given me something to dedicate my life to, sink my teeth into. Before I went home I was worried and wondered what life held for me, now I know. You have your quest, I have my new quest," said Duke, looking Tom directly in the eyes.

"OK then, put it there, partner," said Tom as he held out his hand. Duke took the offered hand, then they both hugged and started to laugh.

Next morning, Duke told Tom that he needed to go to the British Embassy to get a new passport and sort some things out. Tom looked confused. "What about the one you have already?"

"I need an excuse to get into the embassy. Once they realise who I am, they will be falling over to help me, and I need their help to get my large holdalls through customs via the diplomatic route."

"Sneaky," said Tom.

"Practical," said Duke. "If there is one thing I have learnt from you after all this time, it is always have a plan."

Tom dropped Duke at the British Embassy gates, and went to the docks to see if the Red Star was in, or if she was likely to return soon. Luckily for Tom, the Red Star was due in later that day, and would depart within hours, as she was only stopping for fuel, so Tom did not have a lot of time to prepare. Tom drove to a café for some lunch to wait for the Red Star to dock.

Later that afternoon, Tom drove back into the port and drove up to the gang plank, ran up it and shouted, "Permission to come aboard."

Two big arms encircled him from behind. "Always trying to

sneak onto my ship," said a friendly voice.

Tom turned and hugged Ivor. "How's it going, uncle Ivor?"

"Good, good. To what do I owe this pleasure?"

"I need a favour, Ivor."

"You always do, if you were not family I would throw you over the side for the sharks." This brought a belly laugh from Ivor, and a smile from Tom. Ivor held Tom and arm's length and said, "You look different," said Ivor.

Tom said, "For the first time in years I feel I am moving in the right direction." Tom asked, "How's the family back home?"

"All doing well, missing you of course. Will let them know I have bumped into you again, I know Vlad will be pleased."

"Give him my love, won't you," said Tom.

"Of course," said a smiling Ivor. "OK, so to what do I owe the pleasure of you trying to sneak onto my ship again?" said Ivor, laughing.

Tom explained, "I need three crates taking to the UK, my friend Duke will be there to pick them up from you."

"And of course," said Ivor, "no one needs to know. I sail on the next tide, so you better go hurry up and fetch your crates." Tom returned before the Red Star sailed and loaded the three crates. A last farewell from Ivor, before they left.

Tom and Ivor had worked out the password before Ivor would give up the cargo to Duke; Tom hoped Duke had a good memory, otherwise he would not only not see the crates but he would be surprised if he left the hold of the ship again. Watching the Red Star slip into the sea lane, Tom thought that Duke was right to carry on, he needed help. Tom thought Duke's plan was sound, and after a few years Duke should be up and operational, and then Tom could find and kill every-one who murdered his family; time was something they had on their side.

Tom drove to the British Embassy, where Duke was wait-ing. "Everything OK?" asked Tom.

"Super," said Duke, smiling. Back at the warehouse, Duke

explained to Tom, "Once I arrived at the Embassy I was shown into a waiting room, and after ten minutes a bored lower member of staff came and spoke to me. Well, I soon put him in the picture who I was, well he nearly had a seizure, I don't think I have ever seen someone bow that low," said Duke, laughing. "Anyway, I was immediately taken to the ambassador who turned out knew father, old school friends or something. So when I explained I needed a new passport and two large bags taken via the diplomatic pouch, he was most accommodating. Even got to speak to the parents to let them know I was safe and homeward bound. In two days' time I will be on a flight home with my new passport and goods stowed in the hull with a red diplomatic sticker on them."

"Two days," said Tom.

"Yes, old bean. Tomorrow is our last day together."

Tom slapped Duke on the back and said, "Well, we better make it a good one," to which Duke agreed.

Tom and Duke finalised the plan, and the way to contact each other. Duke said, "The old PO Box is a bit outdated and long winded and time consuming, we need something modern," at which Duke produced a small compact laptop and placed it in front of Tom. Duke opened the laptop and turned it on. "Got this little beauty while I was at the embassy, asked to use a laptop to send a secure message to old Pa, bent over backwards to show me how it works. Top of the range encrypted laptop," said Duke.

"How's it work?" said Tom.

"Well, you enter your password here, and see the envelope icon? If that is flashing you have a message. Open the message and it will be all encrypted. To de-crypt so you can read it, select the hand like a hammer and it will ask for a password. Enter the password and it will open the message. All done by a biometric algorithm programme, or something technical. And same for the reverse: type your message, then encrypt it and then send it to the email address. I have set you up an email address already." Duke showed Tom. "Once I am back home,

I will get one of these little beauties and email you with my email address, so we can start communicating.

"Things to note is the passwords need to be changed every thirty days, the laptop password and the de-crypt password can never be the same, and for extra security, if you enter an incorrect password for either of the two passwords three times, the whole laptop will wipe."

"Amazing," said Tom.

"Technology, my dear friend. So we can communicate in minutes rather than days by post, and all from the comfort of your own home," said Duke, laughing. Duke gave Tom the two passwords for the laptop, and made sure he was conversant in its use before he let it rest.

Tom asked, "Will the embassy not miss it?"

"Well, it was in the office when I left, if I am asked," said Duke, "and I don't think they would ever consider or accuse a future Peer of the Realm to be a light fingered thief. Just not cricket, old boy, bad form," laughed Duke.

Tom went on to explain he had sent three crates homeward bound with uncle Ivor; he was expected to be in England in three months or so. Tom gave Duke the password he had agreed with Ivor, and made sure Duke realised the importance of remembering it; if not, their little endeavour would end before it got off the ground.

That night Tom and Duke stayed up until dawn, drinking and talking, both trying not to think about the next day when they would finally go their separate ways. During a silent period, Duke said, "I want to thank you, Tom."

"What for, Duke?" said Tom, smiling.

"You have given me your friendship and loyalty and since I have been here, your trust." Turning to Tom and looking sincere, Duke said, "I promise you Tom, I will never let you down, you can always count on me for anything. This I promise on my family name."

Tom knew what Duke had said was most probably the most sacred oath he could have made, and it was not given lightly.

Tom smiled at Duke. "I knew there was a reason I saved your upper class sorry arse," replied Tom, which set them both off laughing.

Next day Tom drove Duke to the embassy gates and parked up.

"Well," said Tom.

"I know," said Duke.

They both hugged and slapped each other on the back. "Be safe," said Tom.

"You too," said Duke. Duke lifted his two large duffle bags from the Jeep and walked towards the embassy entrance.

Tom shouted, "Thank you, Duke."

Duke turned with tears in his eyes and shouted back, "Check your emails, you pirate," before stepping through the gate. Tom waved back and watched him disappear into the embassy, with a smile and a new hope for the future.

A few years later Tom was lounging around the warehouse when he heard the buzz coming from the laptop. Tom opened the laptop and entered in the password. The 'you have new mail' icon was flashing. Smiling, Tom opened the email, and it was from Duke. Duke went on to give him a detailed report since they had last been in contact, but best of all Duke had traced the next name on the list. Simon Muscrat was head of section CIA Kiev, now retired and living in Miami.

Tom smiled; he could do with a holiday in Miami.

A few weeks later, flying into Miami International Airport, Tom took a taxi to the complex address supplied by Duke. After renting a room for two nights, Tom set about finding Simon Muscrat. Tom found him more easily than anticipated; apparently Simon Muscrat now owned and ran a successful deep sea fishing boat hire business where, according to the brochure, from the email Duke had sent him, he catered for private charter, 'where you can catch your dream catch'.

Making enquiries at the marina head office, and picking up a fresh brochure, the boat he was looking for was the 'Majestic

Wave'. Tom easily located the Majestic Wave: it was an impressive sixty foot motor yacht. Tom approached the boat, and a rather large portly man came up on deck, with a weather beaten dark tanned face.

"Mr Muscrat?" asked Tom, holding up the brochure.

As soon as Simon Muscrat saw the waving brochure he relaxed, and smiling, said, "Yes, that's me, come on board friend."

"Thank you," said Tom. Not sure how much he was still in the loop or if he had been warned about the British agent's death, Tom decided to push his luck, and said, "Tom Jones is the name, from England. Got told if I was ever in the neighbourhood to look you up and you would show me the best fishing places in Miami."

"Oh, and who was it that gave me such a recommendation?" asked Simon.

"Stuart Pendall. Used to cross swords with him now and again,"

Simon looked confused for a minute, then he said, "Stuart Pendall. Not heard that name for a few years, but if Stuart recommended me, then you've come to the right place. Fancy a beer?"

Tom smiled and nodded. After a few beers, Tom paid for a full day's fishing for the next day, and what impressed Simon with a smile was Tom paid in cash. Next day, Tom was standing on the jetty waiting for Simon to arrive. When he finally did, Simon smiled at Tom, and said, "Boy, you are keen."

"Early bird catches the worm," replied Tom.

"You Brits and your sayings," said a laughing Simon. Simon steered the large yacht out of the marine and onto the open sea. Tom stood in the prow looking at the vast open sea. Before leaving the marina, Simon asked Tom what he wanted to try and catch.

Tom said, "Shark if possible, a big great white."

Simon stared at the chart for a few minute, smiled, and said, "Customer is always right," and put the yacht in gear and motored out towards the ocean.

At about twenty miles out, Simon throttled back the yacht into idle. Taking one of the big rods from the side, Simon helped Tom sit in the catch chair, and told Tom to cast out, and he would drop some bait into the water to attract sharks. As Simon was leaning over, dropping large fresh bloody meat over the side, Tom whipped the rod, which caught Simon just above the knees, which made him lose his balance and fall head first into the water.

Simon was dazed and confused; his first thought was how he had managed to fall over board, and then he felt the sharp pain on his thighs. Simon looked up into the dark eyes of a smiling Tom.

Tom put out his hand towards Simon as Simon reached towards Tom; Tom slipped a thin rope over his wrist and pushed his head under the water. Surfacing, Simon was confused by what was going on. "What the fuck you playing at?" said Simon, with his left arm held high about his head by the rope Tom was holding. "Who the fuck are you, man?"

"I am Tom Sharapova, the man you sent your assassins to kill in Odessa. So tell me about Operation Blackstone," replied Tom.

Simon stared down the barrel of a silenced pistol. He went very still and tried to tread water. Simon started to panic; as he felt something brush his leg, looking down he saw the dark shape of something gliding beneath the yacht. "Look, I don't know what you mean, I never heard of Operation Blackstone," screamed Simon.

"But you've heard of Stuart Pendall," replied Tom.

"Yes, he was a British Agent same time as I was in Kiev."

"Stuart told me you were the CIA handler of the agent who failed to kill Vladimir Sharapova on Operation Blackstone. I want his name."

Simon was now getting tired treading water, he said, "OK, Colonel Jack Packer. Now pull me out."

"Good," said Tom. "One last question. Who was your boss

on the operation?"

Simon said, "No way, they will kill me."

"By the looks of it, they need to get in the queue," replied Tom.

"You are mad, you don't get close to people like him."

"Let me worry about that," said Tom.

Simon felt another brush against his legs, although he had stopped moving them. Eventually Simon said, "OK, OK. It was James Landcourt, he was head of CIA Kiev, he helped plan the operation with someone from the British intelligence agency."

"Well done Simon, knew you could do it," Tom said as he shot him twice in the arms and let go of the rope; the last thing Simon felt was his legs being bitten off by a dark black shape coming from the deep.

Tom steered the boat back to the marina, and cut the engines just as it entered the marina basin, he slipped over the side and let the yacht slowly drift into the jetty.

Back in Belize, Tom sent Duke an email with the two names he had. Tom thought he must be getting close to the top; he had the name of the man who tried to kill uncle Vlad and who possibly killed Max. Things were looking up since Duke took over the business. Duke replied within a few weeks. Tom had expressly asked Duke to find Colonel Jack Packer first; Tom had a few scores to settle with that gentleman.

Duke said it would take a bit of time to track him down, but not to get disheartened, he was on the case. It took Duke over a year to eventually find out where Colonel Jack Packer was. Tom read the email from Duke and finally smiled. Tom had not been idle during the years; he had made many a good business deals, and had passed quite a bit of merchandise back to Duke.

Duke said to give him a day or two, and he would send Tom a complete dossier on the colonel. Tom smiled; one thing he had was patience. As promised, Duke sent a complete dossier on the colonel. He was still operational and living in New

York.

Tom pondered on how to proceed. The colonel was going to be the most difficult to kill, as he was as highly trained as Tom was, and would not be taken as easily as the others had been.

Taking a flight to New York, Tom booked into a five star hotel in the centre of Manhattan. Tom thought, why not indulge and be comfortable. Reading his file, Tom realised that the colonel was a masochist and bully; he like to inflict pain and see people suffer. Tom thought back to his early life, to an incident with a bully, which he had overcome quite easily. Tom noticed the colonel liked to attend a gentleman's club here in Manhattan; Tom started to form a plan.

Tom walked to the club, and entered at the reception. Tom asked if they did day memberships; the receptionist smiled at Tom and said, "Yes daily, weekly, or monthly, or you can have a full yearly membership."

Tom asked for a brochure and said, "Time permitting I will come back, thank you." As Tom left, the receptionist looked at the retreating Tom and thought, Brits, so damn polite, and giggled to himself. Tom studied the brochure, and tried to second guess what the colonel would like to do. The gymnasium and swimming: he did not think so. Squash or tennis: definitely not. Boxing, wrestling or fencing all were possible. Then Tom spotted 'all forms martial arts catered for'; this made Tom smile. The colonel would definitely like to inflict some pain whist doing martial arts on some poor unsuspecting soul.

Next day Tom took a monthly membership, paying in cash. He was handed a locker key. The receptionist told Tom his new pass would be ready the next morning, and explained to Tom the club was open from 6am until 11pm daily. The restaurant and bar were located, down to the right, where the restaurant and bar timings are listed on the door, and the lockers rooms are located down on the left, and through the big double doors were the facilities. Tom asked, "Do I have to sign in each time I attend?" Smiling, the receptionist showed Tom the member register, where he was expected to sign in each time he attended.

Quickly glancing down the register, Tom noticed the colonel had not been in for days. Tom changed into a tracksuit and decided to wander and get his bearings around the club. Tom was very impressed; all the facilities were modern and up to date.

After a few days, Tom was beginning to wonder if the intelligence that Duke had supplied was up to date, and the colonel was still in New York or even a member of the club. Tom knew he could not start asking questions about him as he would bound to find out, and the last thing Tom wanted was a visit from the Central Intelligence Agency because he had been asking about one of their operatives. Max had made the same mistake and it had cost him his life.

After a week Tom was just about to give up. Tom knew the longer he waited, the easier his cover would be compromised. One morning Tom was getting changed; he had not been idle, he had actually used all of the facilities on offer, as he liked to keep himself in top condition.

Tom had become nodding terms with a few other members, when one casually asked him, "Hi, I am Steve, fancy a game of squash? My normal partner has let me down, and he had already booked the court."

"Hi. Tom," said Tom, holding out his hand. Steve shook the offered hand and Tom said, "And I would love to, but I do not have a racquet."

Steve said, "I have a spare, you can use that." Tom thanked him and followed him to the court. "Do you play?" asked Steve.

"Bit rusty, so be gentle with me," replied Tom.

Steve started to laugh. "Don't worry, I will be."

After an hour where Tom was trying hard not to win – Steve was not making it easy for Tom, as he was not in Tom's league of fitness – eventually Tom lost the final game. Steve stood covered in sweat and breathing heavily, staring at Tom, who had not even broken out into a heavy sweat, and was breathing normally.

"Boy, for someone that's rusty, you play well," said Steve.

"You played better," said Tom.

"I suspect being British, you were letting me win," said a laughing Steve. "Fancy a beer after that, my treat?"

"Why not," said Tom. Tom found a table while Steve grabbed them each a beer. Steve handed Tom a beer and said, "Cheers, to a gallant runner up."

Tom replied, "Beaten by the better man." They both started to laugh.

Steve asked Tom, "So apart from being British, what you in the Big Apple for, Tom?"

"I am in antiques over on a buying expedition," replied Tom, thinking of the most boring thing he could think of, so hopefully he would not be asked too many questions.

"I see," said Steve. Tom was right, Steve was not interest in antiques.

"What about you then, Steve?" asked Tom.

"I am in construction, always a booming business in New York," said a smiling Steve. "How long you here for, Tom?"

"Not sure, depends how long my boss will fund me," said Tom, laughing. Tom asked Steve, "So do you venture to try anything else in the club?"

"No, not really, then again heard there are some bad arses in the martial arts set," replied Steve.

"Oh really, like to do a bit myself," replied Tom.

"Speak to Larry who runs the gym, he sets up matches," said Steve. "In fact, there he is now. Larry, over here," said a waving Steve.

Larry came across and Steve introduced Tom to him. Tom noticed Larry was a big bull of a man still in the prime of life, with an arrogant attitude to go with it. Tom smiled.

Steve explained to Larry, "Tom here is from England, and is into his martial arts, any matches coming up?"

Larry stared at Tom, and said, "Sure, what you into?"

"Anything really, as long as it's contact," replied Tom.

"Got a few fellas who would love to take on a Brit," said a laughing Larry, "in fact, a good friend of mine will be in tomorrow, he don't like the British much, he is ex-military, we all call him the colonel. Had a run in with a Brit a few year back and apparently he cocked up a mission he was on, never forgave him, so he classes all Brits with the same brush."

"Well, let's see if I can change his mind," said a smiling Tom. Larry started to laugh. Steve looked concerned for Tom.

Next day, Tom was in the changing room when Steve came in and said, "So you are here, thought you would have not showed."

"Why would I not have showed?" said Tom.

"I have been asking about and this colonel bloke sounds pretty nasty to me," replied Steve.

"Don't worry, I will handle him," said Tom.

"So you think you are a safe bet?"

"Steve, if I was you, I would bet on me."

"Sounds good to me, I will lay a few dollars on you then."

"A safe bet, my friend, a safe bet," said a smiling Tom. Tom went into the martial arts room, and already in there were Larry and four other men. As soon as they spotted Tom, they came over.

"So you turned up," said Larry.

"Why are people here so surprised I showed up?" said a laughing Tom.

"No laughing matter," said one of the men.

"The colonel will be here in a minute if you want to get ready," said Larry.

"Who's running the book," asked Tom.

"The book?" said Larry.

"Yes, you know, taking the bets," said Tom.

"I am," said one of the men. "Fancy your chances, do you?" he said in a snarl.

Tom smiled at the man and said, "One hundred dollars on

me," holding out a crisp new one hundred dollar bill.

The man took the bill from Tom and said, "It's your money and funeral, friend."

Tom went into the far corner and sat on the mat and closed his eyes and started to deep breathe. Although he had his eyes closed, his other senses were on full alert; he could smell, feel and hear everything that was going on around him. Eventually Tim heard a commotion and knew the colonel had arrived. Like a returning gladiator in Rome, he entered the room. Tom opened his eyes and looked at the colonel for the first time. He was about six foot tall, built like a bull with a shaven head and a face that did not look friendly.

Tom stared at the colonel with pure hatred. This man had killed Max, had tried to kill him and Uncle Vlad, and indirectly wiped out his family. Tom was going to enjoy this. Tom closed his eyes again; he was aware of his presence long before he stood in front of him. Slowly, Tom opened his eyes and smiled into the cold hard face of the man he was going to enjoy killing.

"So you are the daft Brit that wants a beating," said a laughing colonel, looking about to the men who had followed him over, who also laughed with him. "You don't look much," he said.

Tom smiled and said, "Typical loud mouth Yank, never won a decent fight without someone holding your hand," looking from the colonel to the men who were with him.

"Why, you bastard," shouted the colonel, moving towards Tom. Hands grabbed him before he could get close.

"Save it for the match," one of the men told the colonel.

Tom smiled and said, "Go now, you are bothering me," and closed his eyes again. Tom heard them retreat, muttering to themselves, the colonel with the loudest profanities. The place was crowded; the word had gotten around about the match between the colonel and some small Brit. The man running the book was doing a trade.

Steve approached him and the man was surprised when

Steve placed two hundred dollars on Tom. One of Steve's friends asked, "What are you doing betting on him, you seen the size of the other guy?"

Steve replied, "Trust me, I have played squash with this guy and looks are deceiving. I won't be surprised if a few people in here are in for one hell of a shock." Taking their friend's advice, a few others placed small wagers on Tom. Even the man running the book was looking worried, and started to stare at Tom.

Larry stood in the centre of the mats, and had the colonel and Tom stand opposite him. Tom was smiling.

"What you got to smile about, punk?" said the colonel. Tom just stared at him and smiled.

Larry explained this was a no holds barred fight. "Loser is the one who submits first. Any questions?"

Tom shook his head, and the colonel said, "Get on with it, why don't you."

Larry said, "OK gentlemen, if you are ready," and walked back off the mat.

The colonel and Tom circled each other, both trying to see a weakness. Tom was on the balls of his toes, moving slowly; the colonel was flat footed and slowly crossing each leg as he moved. The colonel tried to make a grab for Tom, but Tom was too fast for him; Tom knew that if the colonel did manage to grab him, then his power and strength would crush him. Tom was smiling; he had noticed the colonel favoured his left side, so perhaps he had an old injury he was trying to conceal.

Tom smiled at the colonel, and the colonel said, "What the fuck you smiling about?"

"You, you dumb arse Yank bastard," replied Tom.

This made the colonel roar and rush Tom. Tom side-stepped the colonel and as he went past, Tom kicked him on the right knee. The colonel tried not to show pain, but Tom knew he had found the colonel's Achilles heel. Tom now knew the colonel relied on brute strength and power to overcome opponents, not totally using style or technique. Tom also realised that just like any bully who had not been beaten, he had an overwhelming trust in his own ability; not even for a minute would he consider he was facing a better man.

Tom said, "You broke the golden rule of warfare, colonel."

"And what's that, little man?" said a smiling colonel.

"You underestimated your opponent."

The colonel looked confused by the statement, but Tom moved so fast the colonel saw a blur and felt a searing pain in his knee just before he fell over. Tom had crouched and side swiped the colonel's legs, just catching the right knee with his foot as it went past.

The place had gone silent; after all the shouting and encouragement for the colonel, the onlookers realised their champion was down. The colonel slowly stood and glared at Tom.

"Lucky hit," said the colonel.

"Skill," replied Tom, which made the colonel get even more agitated. Tom knew once the colonel reached his blind rage point and the red mist descended, it would be his downfall; once his anger had reached a critical level all his training would disappear and he would be using pure animal instinct to crush Tom.

Tom was right. The colonel had started to breathe hard, and his movements were becoming erratic and Tom could read all his moves before he executed them. The colonel managed to get an arm swipe to Tom's shoulder, making Tom roll to the ground. The colonel then tried to stomp where Tom was supposed to be, but only managed to stomp the ground; Tom had rolled twice, and came up behind the colonel and punched him in the kidneys, knocking the air from his lungs so he went down in a howl. The colonel was on his feet quickly, and rushed Tom before he had stabilised his position. Tom moved quickly and once again was behind a stumbling colonel, and Tom raised his knee and, with his foot, brought it hard down on the colonel's knee.

The colonel's momentum left him sprawled on the mat, with a searing pain in his right knee; Tom stood staring at the colonel, not even breathing heavily. Larry rushed over, and said, "OK, he's had enough, you win."

The colonel from the floor said, "I am OK, I can carry on," through gritted teeth.

"Don't be daft, man, your knee is blown," said Larry.

Tom turned and walked over to the man who ran the book and said, "You owe me money," holding out his hand and smiling.

After a shower and getting changed, Tom was sitting in the bar with Steve and a few of his friends. "Boy, did you teach that colonel a lesson," said a laughing Steve, "here's to you, glad I had a bet now," holding up his beer bottle.

Tom sat and smiled, holding up his beer bottle in response. Tom was waiting for phase two of his plan to unfold. It did not take long before the colonel and his followers entered the bar, and took a table in the far corner. Tom smiled over at a growling colonel, and raised his beer.

"No hard feelings I hope, old man," Tom said. "Fancy another beer, Steve? On me, I just made a few extra bucks."

Steve looked from Tom to the other table, and said in a whisper, "Hey man, what you doing? Don't antagonise them."

"You worry too much," said Tom.

The atmosphere was electric. Steve said, "You better watch your back, I think they are going to start trouble outside."

"That, Steve, I am counting on," replied Tom.

Steve looked at Tom and said, "Sorry man, getting too heavy for me, I am going home. I wish you luck." With that, Steve and his friends stood and left.

Tom made a big show of finishing his beer and standing up. Turning to the colonel, Tom said, "We'll be seeing you, and thanks again for the work out."

The colonel replied, "Sooner than you think," in a menacing whisper that Tom could not hear, but the two men on the table nodded in response.

Tom left the club, and walked slowly back towards his hotel. He had already worked out the best place to offer himself up for an ambush, away from prying eyes. As Tom turned down an alley instead of keeping to the main street, he heard a voice behind him, "Hey punk, want a word with you." Tom turned and there were the two men from the club, but this time both carried baseball bats.

Tom smiled and said, "Where is your leader, scared in case I beat him again?"

"Here I am," said the colonel, stepping into view. Tom smiled; he loved a man with an ego.

One man charged at Tom with his bat held high. Tom used his forward momentum against him, grabbing the bat; he turned him around and slammed him into a dumpster, knocking him out cold. The other man, after seeing his friend go down so easily, was cautious, moving slowly toward Tom and swinging the bat in front of himself.

Tom waited until the man was five steps away, and the bat was at its furthest point from the man's body. Tom did something the man did not expect: he rushed into his arms and head butted him. The man dropped the bat, and staggered. Tom quickly chopped the man on the back of the neck, and he dropped like a stone, out cold next to his friend.

Tom looked up at the colonel and said, "Only me and you, Yank, if you are man enough."

The colonel stood and stared at Tom, trying to figure out who he was, before he worked it out. Tom said, "Tom Sharapova, the man you tried to kill with Vladimir Sharapova in Odessa."

The colonel's face lit with the realisation of who Tom was and smiled. "Tom Sharapova, so it you who has been looking for Simon. Had a punk in Belize asking questions about Simon Muscrat. Had to cut his throat. Never gave you up, before I killed him. Most impressed by his loyalty."

"He was my friend and family and his name was Max," said Tom. "You not interested how I got your name as the agent on Operation Blackstone?" asked Tom.

The colonel just snarled at Tom and said, "Don't give a

fuck."

"Simon gave you up rather quickly, I might add," said Tom.

"He always was a pussy. After the Odessa fiasco I was side-lined by that shit, like it was my fault, " said the colonel. "So here I am," said the colonel, "if you want me come get me," and he started to laugh.

Tom knew out in the street fighting was different from a contest on a mat in a gym. He was sure once again the colonel was over confident, as he thought this was his battle ground where he had never lost, supreme in his ability in warfare and tactical combat, with the ability to read the situation and react with extreme prejudices. Tom slowly moved towards the colonel, never taking his eyes from his. The colonel stood and waited for his next victim to come to him so he could kill him. As Tom approached, the colonel pulled out a seven inch bladed knife, and waved it at Tom, and started to laugh.

Tom was only a few paces from the colonel when he crouched and kicked him hard in the knee again. The colonel gave out a howl, but did not go down, but Tom knew he was in severe pain. The colonel had started to try and regain his balance, when Tom grabbed him by the wrist of the hand holding the knife, and twisted upwards; the colonel instinctively opened his hand and Tom took it, and in one flowing motion plunged it into the colonel's heart.

As the colonel lay on the street bleeding out, his face was trying to understand how this had happened so fast; he was puzzled as to how this small man had overcome his superior position. Tom bent over the dying colonel and said, "For Max," as he pushed the knife further in to the colonel's slowly fading heart. The colonel tried to speak, but only blood would come from his open mouth. Tom patted the colonel's face, stared into his clouding eyes, smiled and walked away.

Tom returned to the hotel and had a long hot shower before getting some sleep. He sent Duke an email on the demise of the colonel, and asked for the dossier on James Landcourt.

While waiting for Duke to reply, Tom decided to move hotels; he had been in this one for over a week, and he knew the American intelligence agencies could be closing in, and at this stage it would be foolish to become complacent or take risks. Next day, Tom was surprised to see the email icon flashing from Duke. Tom thought, that was quick.

Reading the email made Tom frown. Since leaving the CIA James Landcourt had become a senator for Washington, and was tipped to be the next Presidential candidate for the Democratic Party. Tom stared at the email, trying to work out a plan; this was definitely a complication, but not insurmountable. Tom knew that as he went up the chain of command on those who were responsible for his family's death, it would be hard to get to them and their security would be tighter. It just needed more planning.

While Tom waited for Duke's next email, he made his plans. It only took Duke two days to forward an up-to-date dossier on Senator James Landcourt. Tom noticed he had virtually gone into lockdown at his private town house in Washington; he had not been seen in public for several weeks. Tom surmised that someone in the American intelligence agencies, and possibly the Senator himself, had started to ask questions and link the recent deaths, so they had decided to protect their asset more closely.

Tom rang the airport and booked himself on a single flight to Washington. As Tom was sitting having a quiet meal later that evening, he noticed the two men at the bar; they screamed 'government agency' by their dress and manner. Tom realised he had been found. Tom slowly walked over to reception and quite loudly told the receptionist he was leaving tomorrow morning and please could he have an early call to wake him, as his flight to Washington was at seven am.

Standing at the reception, in the wall mirror Tom noticed one agent speak into his wrist while nodding; he turned to his partner, nodded, and they both left. Returning to his room,

Tom only picked up the laptop and a few items, placing them in a little hand held rucksack.

Tom used the back stairs to the hotel underground car park. Locating the hire car Duke had ordered him, Tom drove from the well-lit garage into a dark, lightly-raining New York City. Tom's instincts were right: he had been found, and knew it was a matter of time before they closed the net, but smiling as he steered the car through the traffic out of the city, he remembered his golden rule he had always told Duke: 'Always have a plan'.

After booking the flight, Tom decided on a backup plan. Quickly finding that the distance between New York and Washington was only two hundred and four miles give or take a mile, he decided to take a drive, and his instincts were right; the airport tomorrow morning would be crawling with government agents waiting for him to arrive, and after he failed to arrive they would of course check the hotel, and find out that Mr Jones, the nice polite Englishman from room thirteen forty three, had pre checked out yesterday morning. They would then realise once again Tom had vanished, and by the time they worked it all out he would be in Washington.

The drive down to Washington was without incident. Parking up in the rental garage, Tom deposited the keys back through the letter box of the office door, as the paperwork had instructed. Tom realised his time in Washington was very limited; it would not take the Americans long to work out his next destination was Washington. The only saving grace was he didn't think the agencies would have worked out the connection from Miami, New York and Washington yet, so he reckoned he had at least a twelve hour window of operation.

Tom quickly made his way to a rundown part of Washington named the Russian quarter. Tom quickly found the shop he was looking for and entered. Tom sat at a table and a pretty smiling waitress came over and Tom ordered a coffee. Before the waitress left, Tom asked, "Please can you let Boris know someone is here to speak to him."

"Sure, will do," said the smiling waitress.

A few minutes later a large man came and stood next to Tom and said, "You want to speak to Boris?"

"Yes I do," said Tom.

"Follow me, Boris is this way," he said in a not too friendly manner. Tom followed the man out the back down a small alley to a side door. The man knocked twice and it was quickly opened. Tom followed the man in.

Tom stood alone in the middle of the room surrounded by at least ten hard face men, some holding guns. "Who are you to seek out Boris?" asked a voice from the back of the room, Tom could not see the face behind the voice, as that part of the room was in darkness.

Tom smiled and said, "I am Tom Sharapova, chief enforcer of the Sharapova family in Odessa."

The room went quiet and the voice again said, "And you can prove your rash statement?"

Tom slowly placed his hand in his inside jacket pocket and pulled out the wallet with the Red Star, and held it aloft for all to see. As Tom was showing the Red Star around, Tom could sense the atmosphere in the room change from aggression to fear. "Satisfied?" said Tom. "Now, which one of you clowns is Boris? I am on a tight schedule."

Boris came forward and offered his hand to Tom; Tom accepted the offered hand and sat at the chair Boris offered him. As Tom looked about, no one in the room would make eye contact with Tom; his fearsome reputation was world famous amongst Russians. Boris sat and looked scared.

"How may we help you?"

Tom explained to Boris what he required; Boris said, "You need to give me a few hours, in the meantime why don't you go back into the restaurant and have a meal, on the house of course."

Tom took Boris up on his offer, and went and had a delicious Russian meal, which brought back sad memories of home, and what he had lost. After Tom had finished his meal and was sipping a fresh cup of coffee, Boris came and sat opposite Tom. "Good meal?" asked Boris.

"Just like home," replied Tom.

Boris smiled. "We try to please."

"Let's hope so," said Tom, staring at Boris. Boris tried a half-hearted smile but failed and just ended up looking worried. Boris placed the suitcase next to Tom and the items on the table Tom had requested. Tom studied them and nodded. "Thank you Boris, I will inform Uncle Vlad that you were most helpful and the family can still rely on its American part of the family." Boris sat up a bit straighter and had a beaming smile appear on his face.

Tom collected the items and placed them in his pockets. Taking the suitcase, Tom thanked Boris for his help, and left the shop. Tom took the parked car from the front and drove it to the Senator's address. On arriving at the townhouse, Tom drove around the block and noticed externally there was no security cordon, so Tom assumed that all the security was on the inside.

Tom drove up to the main gate and stopped. A man from a security box just inside the gate came out carrying a clipboard. "Good evening, Sir, how may I help you?" asked the gate guard.

"DNHAC," said Tom holding up his gold badge, "here to speak to the Senior Secret Service Agent in charge of guarding the Senator, my agency has credible information that might affect the Senator's future plans."

"Can you wait here please," asked the gate guard. A minute later the gate guard returned and said, "Go to the garage, someone will meet you there." As the barrier was being raised as Tom passed, he noticed the second gate guard still on the phone. Tom smiled to himself; now that was easy, Boris and his men had done well – the stolen government car he was driving was still on the database as being from the CIA carpool, and a genuine agency car.

Tom drove to the garage as instructed, and parked up. As

Tom parked, a heavily built man approached with a smile on his face; as he raised his hand in a greeting Tom shot him in the head. Tom placed his body in the boot of the car.

Knowing how the CIA worked, Tom knew that a maximum of seven agents guarded the Senator, two outside at all times, two on rest, two around the house and one in the actual room with him, all rotating every half an hour or so, to avoid complacency and boredom. Tom stood next to the car, and it was only a minute before the other outside agent came into view. Tom held his hand up, and the agent came towards Tom; when he was only a foot away Tom swiftly removed the silenced pistol from behind his back and shot him between the eyes. Tom also placed his body in the trunk.

Tom entered the house, and followed the sound of the television down the hall. The door was open and lucky for Tom, one agent stood with his back to the door, while two were sitting. All three were watching a live American football game, and by the sounds of their voices and language, their team was not winning. Tom shot the standing agent twice in the heart, holding onto him as he fell. Tom used him as a barrier. Before the other two knew Tom was there and what was happening, Tom shot them both in the head. Tom let the standing agent fall into the room and closed the door. Tom stood across from the door and waited.

Five minutes later, Tom heard a voice coming down the corridor. "Hell Sam, where do you get off leaving me to do all the work? You three better not be dicking around in there." As he placed his hand on the door handle, Tom shot him in the back of the head, and the momentum of the opening door let him fall forward on top of the other three agents. Tom closed the door behind him. One to go and he was with the Senator.

Tom had taken one of the radios from the dead agent; he knew one was called Sam, as he had heard one from the house use his name. Tom waited. The radio crackled and Tom heard in the ear piece, "Mike here, Senator wants a coffee, going to the kitchen, anyone else want one?"

Tom spoke quietly. "Sam here, sure, on my way."

When Tom reached the kitchen, the agent must have heard him approach and said over his shoulder, "You ask the other guys if they wanted one?"

"Sure did, but they were busy dying," said Tom softly.

The agent turned with a half drawn gun, but was too slow: Tom shot him in the side of the head. Tom closed the kitchen door, and at the Senator's study door, opened it and walked in. The Senator was sitting at his desk. He looked up in confusion and said, "Yes, can I help you?"

Tom smiled and said, "Senator, I really hope you can," as he pointed his silenced pistol at the Senator's head. Tom said, "Don't bother, they are all quite dead. Just me and you alone, now be a good Senator and come sit down on the couch." The Senator did what Tom had asked, and came and sat on a couch. Tom sat opposite and smiled.

"So what's this all about?" said the Senator confidently.

Tom said, "Senator, tell me about Operation Blackstone please."

The Senator went a pale shade of white, and said, "I don't know what you are talking about."

Tom smiled and said, "You know what, Senator, that's just what Simon Muscrat said."

The Senator turned a ghostly shade of white and started to sweat, "OK, so you seem to know all about Operation Blackstone. So what you after?"

"Was it a Washington sanctioned hit?" asked Tom.

"Hell no," said the Senator, "it was a British operation, we were just along for the ride, to give the operation some credibility."

"So it was not an American operation?"

"No, not at all, only in as far as we supplied one agent to assist in planning. The whole operation was devised, planned and executed and run by the British MI5, their head of Station, and I got the impression it was not sanctioned by their government either," said the Senator.

"And who was the British MI5 Head of Theatre?" asked

Tom.

"Some hard arse woman called Julie Somerville, a right royal bitch, ruled her department with a rod of iron. The MI5 boys called her 'iron balls' behind her back, a ruthless lady," replied the Senator. "Who are you anyway?" asked the Senator. "You've gone to a lot of trouble to have our little chat."

"I am Tom Sharapova," replied Tom.

The Senator smiled. "I see now your interest in Blackstone. People have been looking for you for a long time, quite a reputation you managed to secure yourself, young man, amongst the world's intelligence community," said the Senator.

Tom looked at his watch. "Well, thank you Senator," said Tom, as he shot him in the neck with a tranquiliser gun. The Senator slumped down across the couch, softly snoring. Tom took a small rubber hose and a syringe from his pocket. Rolling up the Senator's sleeve, Tom placed the rubble hose around his arm and tapped it to make the vein protrude; once Tom saw the vein he placed the syringe into his vein and pushed the plunger all the way in. The Senator snoring eventually stopped, and Tom left the syringe in the dead Senator's arm.

Tom walked back through the house back to the car. Tom stopped at the gate and said, "Not sure but I think the Steelers are losing, they are not happy down at the house," said a laughing Tom.

"Their own fault," said the gate guard, "for supporting a crap team," also laughing. "Have a nice day," said the gate guard.

"You too," replied Tom, as he put the car into gear and drove toward the Washington Dulles International Airport; for the first time in years, he thought about going home.

Home Coming

Tom returned to his hotel room after a pleasant stroll around London; collecting his key from reception he noticed the pretty receptionist's attitude was cooler than it was a few hours ago. This made Tom smile; so the intelligence agencies had been to the hotel. Tom noticed the two agents sitting in reception. Casually walking to the lift, Tom went up to his room. Before Tom placed his key in the lock, Tom glanced at the top left of the door; the thin invisible strip of tape, not bigger than a hair, had been broken, which meant someone had been in the room, despite the 'Do not Clean' sign Tom had placed on the door knob before he had departed earlier that morning. Tom entered his room, and closed the door. Leaning against the door for a second, Tom smiled. The room had been expertly searched, even Tom was impressed by the efficiency of it.

Tom walked over to the closet and casually looked in; Tom had placed the coat hangers exactly three and a half inches apart, on alternate facing hangers, plus he had placed all his arms on his clothing backwards, whereas some were now forward facing. The pillow had been moved on the bed, as Tom had placed the opening pointing towards the window, and one now pointed towards the wall. The shoe rack where Tom had placed his three pairs of shoes had been moved, and no doubt bugged; he knew as a light sprinkling of talc was on the carpet from the shoes.

The light fitting had been touched, as the bulb bayonet switch was facing the other way; the air vent had been opened as Tom had lightly oiled the screws, which were now dry. Tom had also left the window slightly open at two inches; it was now four inches. His suitcase Tom had left on its end at an acute angle, it was now sitting straight. The laptop had been opened; he had lightly greased the opening catch. The phone would obviously have been bugged. Tom moved into the bathroom, and the place had been alerted. To a casual observer it would not have been noticeable but to Tom it spoke volumes. Tom guessed there must be at least three microphones and two cameras installed about the two rooms. Tom lay on the bed and closed his eyes.

Tom woke with a start. Looking about the dark room, he realised he had been asleep for a good five hours. Feeling rather hungry, Tom decided to have some fun with the intelligence agencies, to see how good they were. Tom took a quick shower, and dressed quickly and left the room. On the way down in the lift, it stopped on floor twelve, and a young couple got in. From behind them, Tom smiled; so the operation room is on floor twelve, nice to know.

Tom handed his key into reception, and left the hotel. It had been raining and that fresh scent after rain filled the air; Tom breathed in deeply turned right and walked down the road. He spotted four agents trailing him, a car, and two trying to stay ahead.

Tom walked about a mile down the road, before spotting a nice little Italian restaurant. Crossing the road, he looked in the window and pretended to study the menu. The couple in front immediately back-tracked, and entered the restaurant before Tom. Tom smiled, still studying the menu, and Tom waited until the two agents were seated, before strolling back down the road. As he passed a burger shop, Tom immediately stopped and turned around. The two agents from the restaurant were not far behind him. They quickly crossed the road when they spotted Tom coming towards them. Tom strolled back towards the Italian restaurant and entered. Tom was smiling as he was seated in the restaurant, wondering if the two agents would have the nerve to re-enter and try for a fresh table without causing a scene. Eventually, a couple entered the restaurant and ordered a meal.

After a pleasant meal Tom paid the bill in cash, and spoke to the Italian waiter in fluent Italian, thanking her for a lovely meal. Leaving a nice tip, Tom left the restaurant and strolled back towards the hotel.

The director of MI5 was still at her desk. Even if the current crisis was not happening, she was always at her desk until well into the evening; being single again and going home to a dark empty flat did not really appeal to her. The five year loveless marriage had failed after a year of her being appointed Director of MI5; luckily the divorce was amicable and no children were involved. Quite a feat, as the first female director she had something to prove. She was proven to be one of the best directors the agency had ever had, always looking for way to continuously improve with a lean approach.

Julie Somerville had joined MI5 in its fledgling years, just after the Second World War, and just before the start of the Cold War. Julie quickly gained a reputation for having more balls than most male operatives in the field, moving up through the ranks until achieving the ultimate achievement: Director of MI5.

She was called 'iron balls' by other agents who knew her, and it was even rumoured that when Margaret Thatcher was elected Prime Minister, she modelled herself on Julie Somerville, admiring a woman who had made it to the top in a usually dominated man's world.

Her phone rang, which she picked up immediately. "Yes," she said.

"Director of MI6 in reception, wanting a word."

"Send him up." Julie was at the door as the Director of MI6 entered. "Laurence, to what do I owe this pleasure?"

"Had a very interesting meeting with Ralph Sanders, head of CIA London," said Laurence, sitting down opposite Julie's desk. "Senator James Landcourt, Presidential candidate for the Democratic Party, and forerunner and the dead cert to get the ticket to the White House," Laurence went on, "found dead in his Washington townhouse, looked like a drugs overdose. But the Americans are not so sure it was a self-administrated overdose. Of the seven agents assigned to protect him, two were found in the trunk of a car at Washington International long haul car park, in a stolen government car, the other five killed in the house alongside the Senator, all with either single or double kill shots. The Americans suspect Tom Sharapova, as the gate guard was sure it was him that drove in the place earlier that night, and left about an hour later."

"Impressive," said Julie.

"Goes to show how good he is," said Laurence.

Laurence looked at Julie and said, "But you knew James Landcourt, when you were station head of Kiev and he was the CIA station head of Kiev. Don't you think it's strange that twenty four hours after his body was found, Tom Sharapova turns up in the UK?"

"Yes, I knew him," said Julie. "Not sure how his death is connected to me."

Laurence looked her directly in the eyes and said, "So you know nothing about Operation Blackstone?"

Julie look shocked; how in the hell did MI6 find out about Operation Blackstone?

Julie closed her eyes for a brief minute. When she opened them, she stared into the Director of MI6's not too friendly eyes. "Operation Blackstone," Julia smiled, "Not heard that for a few years." Julie went on, "Operation Blackstone was a covert operation run jointly by MI5 and CIA in Odessa, in the early eighties. As you know, Ukraine were in the early stages trying to gain independence from Russia, and it was thought that Odessa could be a stumbling block for independence as by tradition Odessa Russians are very loyal to Mother Russia, especially as the Russian Red Sea Baltic Fleet is stationed there and has it as its home base. The Odessa Mafia family is loyal to Russia, and runs the majority of life in the region so we needed to lessen their influence in Odessa. We tried various methods, nothing really seemed to work; then we set up a think tank and they came up with a plan to lessen their hold over the region, so James Landcourt and myself devised Operation Blackstone and gave the kill order to take out Vladimir Sharapova, head of the biggest family in Odessa.

"We were hoping that his death would cause panic in the region and there would be a power vacuum for decades, long enough for the Ukraine to gain independence."

"And?" said Laurence.

"We of course missed the target," said Julie quietly.

"Was the operation sanctioned by Whitehall or Washington?" asked Laurence.

"Hell no," replied Julie, "it was totally my plan, backed up by the Americans to give it some credibility."

"So no one outside your team or the Americans' team knew anything about the operation?" asked Laurence.

"Not that I was aware, it was meant to be a straightforward covert operation. Need to know basis only," replied Julie. "One American agent, one British agent, both handpicked by James and myself, using a local driver, tried to assassinate Vladimir Sharapova at his place of work. They used an unmarked car to make it look like a rival gang drive-by shooting. Unfortunately, they did not reckon on Tom Sharapova being there; his top enforcer, who saved his life, returned fire, and injured one of the agents in the process."

"OK," said Laurence, "so can you let me have the file on Operation Blackstone and I will get my team to check it out, but I think we found the reason Tom Sharapova is in town, and it's all to do with Operation Blackstone."

A week later the Director of MI6 placed an urgent call into the MI5 building, and after confirming a few facts, drove to speak to the Director of MI5. Once again the Director of MI6 was shown directly to the Director of MI5's office. "Laurence," said Julie. "Another visit, this is becoming a habit," she said, smiling.

Laurence passed Julie a folder and while she read it, Laurence gave her the report. "According to local enquiries, after the attempted assassination on Vlad Sharapova, that same day two females were admitted to the local hospital after a car incident involving a speeding black Mercedes. The two females later that day died in hospital, they were Natasha Sharapova and Grace Sharapova, wife and daughter of Tom Sharapova.

"After some arm twisting the Americans gave up their names on Operation Blackstone. Comparing their names and your file, it seems that Tom Sharapova has been on a vengeance spree, killing anyone who was or had anything to do with Operation Blackstone, who he blames for the death of his family. And after my team checked the American names and our file, it seems you, Julie, are the last name who had anything to do with Operation Blackstone still alive. So we can assume the reason Tom Sharapova is in the UK is to kill you."

That morning Tom left the hotel after a casual light breakfast in the hotel restaurant. Handing in his key at reception, Tom left the hotel and turned left down the high street. After about an hour walking, Tom stopped at a phone box and rang the number handed to him by reception when he first arrived. The phone rang once, and the speaker said, "CC one two one," and the phone went dead. Tom left the phone box. The whole phone call had taken less than a minute, impossible to trace.

Tom now had a few hours to lose his tails. A plan formed in his head, and he smiled and started to walk down to the busy intersection, followed by six agents. Tom walked down to the underground and bought a ticket. Standing on the platform, Tom casually spotted all six agents. Tom casually boarded the next train in and rode it to the next stop, crossed the platform and got on another train going in the opposite direction. Tom did this seven times, and knew by now the six agents were becoming frustrated. As Tom got off the last train, he ran over to the other platform. The platform was busy; crouching, Tom went to the very end of the platform. As the train stopped, Tom jumped onto the tracks in front of the train and moved to a small alcove in the tunnel wall and waited. After the train had rattled past, Tom jogged towards the retreating train. Tom knew he had five minutes to reach his destination before another train was on the track, and the agent had worked out what he had done.

Tom emerged out into a large open part of the underground system, spotting the exit hatch he was looking for. Tom climbed the ladder up toward another tunnel; this one was not part of the train tracks but a maintenance tunnel. Tom emerged from a door marked 'Emergency Personnel only' onto a busy station concourse. Tom walked down a ramp where he spotted someone busking. Tom waited until he had finished his song, spoke to the man, dropped him a twenty pound note, and the man smiled and walked off toward the exit. Twenty minutes later, the lead agent on duty got a call over the radio: "Stop and detain Tom Sharapova by any means possible." Talking into his wrist, he said, "Who has eyes on the target?" When no one came back, the agent started to swear.

Eventually the radio crackled in his ear. "Pursuit car one, we have the target moving on Regent Street going west. All agents converge on Regent Street. Car one, can you confirm co-ordinates," asked the agent.

"Yes target still moving West on Regent Street."

"Has anyone got eyeball," asked the agent over his radio. The radio remained silent.

"Area secure and covered, we can move in and take him," the agent heard in his ear.

"Remember who this man is, he is highly trained and extremely dangerous, do not take any chances," said the agent. All the agents had converged on the area; the agent from the pursuit car had joined the other agents on foot holding the tracker, still tracking west on Regent Street.

"The target has stopped," said the agent holding the tracker, "The target is stationary."

All six armed agents moved into position. "Can anyone positively ID the target?"

"Negative," came the response.

The lead agent was getting frustrated; they should have him sighted by now. "Anyone, can we confirm we have him?" asked the agent.

"Can only see a man with a hoody holding a guitar," said one of the agents.

The lead agent said, "All agents converge on the hoody, he must be the target."

All seven armed agents rushed to surround the man, shouting to him to, "Get on the floor and spread." The hoody obliged the shouting armed agents. Passersby looked on in shock as seven armed men were pointing guns at one man and shouting for him to lay down and spread his arms and legs.

Just then, three police cars arrived with lights and sirens blazing to add to the confusion. One agent approached the hoody, grabbed his collar and lifted him to his feet. The agent with the tracker turned off the beeping tracker.

After debriefing the hoody, the lead agent passed on the details to headquarters. "The hoody was stopped at the underground by a man who gave him twenty pounds to walk away wearing his shoes, the hoody thought it strange but twenty quid is twenty quid, after all."

The lead agent spoke into his wrist. "Stand down the area, target lost, continue the search." The agent smiled. "Nice one Sharapova, nice one."

Tom decided to do a bit of shopping before joining Duke; after all, he could not turn up to his first visit to the world famous Carton Club dressed like a tramp. Walking down the road, no one noticed Tom had no shoes on, or his scruffy appearance; that's what he liked about big city life, everyone worrying about themselves, and not interested in anyone else.

Tom walked into an upmarket bespoke tailors. Tom smiled at the salesman as he entered; the salesman stared back at Tom in horror. Clearing his voice, the salesman said, "Can one be of help?"

Tom pulled a wad of twenty pound notes from his pocket, and said, "I need a complete make over, my dear chap."

Staring at the money, the salesman smiled and said, "Of course Sir, please step this way," pointing towards the back of the shop.

Thirty minutes later Tom looked into the full length mirror; he was now dressed in a three piece grey double breasted suit, white shirt and light grey tie, new black shoes, a cashmere light grey top coat and a fedora hat. Tom smiled and said, "Lovely."

"Very you, Sir," said the salesman. Tom paid the bill in cash, and placed the receipt in the inside pocket of his jacket.

"What shall I do with Sir's other belongings?" the salesman said, holding up a bag containing the clothes Tom had entered the shop in.

Passing across a folded twenty pound note, Tom said, "I am sure we can find the appropriate rubbish receptacle."

"Of course Sir, glad to be of service," said the smiling salesman. Tom left the shop, turned right, and headed towards his appointment with Duke.

Tom arrived at the Carton Club with fifteen minutes to spare. Casually walking up the step, as if he had been in the building a thousand times before, Tom nodded to the doorman. As he held the door open for Tom, Tom passed the doorman a folded twenty pound note, and said, "Thank you," as he entered. The doorman touched his cap and said, "Thank you, sir."

Tom went to the reception, removing his hat, said, "Wellington Room, please."

The man behind the reception desk said, "Yes sir, of course," and waved one of the stewards over. "Gentleman for the Wellington Room, Jones."

"Very good, Mr Jenkins," said Jones, "this way if you please, sir."

Tom followed Jones up the large staircase to the Wellington Room.

Just before the Wellington Room, Tom said, "Jones, my dear chap, can I use the facilities before I go in?"

"Of course sir, door on the right here."

Tom pulled out another crisp folded twenty pound note, and passed it to Jones and said, "I am sure I can find my way from here, Jones. Sure you got other duties to attend to rather than wait for me, and I can see the Wellington Room from here, I'm hardly going to get lost."

Jones took the note and smiled and said, "Of course sir, hope you enjoy your stay," turned, and went back down the corridor and down the large staircase to reception. Tom waited for Jones to disappear from sight and closed the bathroom door. Instead of entering the Wellington Room, Tom entered the Waterloo Room.

As Tom entered the Waterloo Room, Duke stood and nearly ran towards him. They embraced, and Duke held Tom at arm's length and said, "The years have been good to you, you old pirate."

Tom, smiling, said, "Being a Lord certainly agrees with you," tapping Duke's expanding waste line. Both men hugged again and burst out laughing.

"Come, sit down; tell me your news," said Duke as he poured Tom a large brandy. Tom started by telling Duke about Senator James Landcourt.

Duke said, "Was a bit worried by that one, I must admit, him being a Presidential candidate and all. Top notch security, I would have imagined."

Tom laughed. "Yes, was a bit tricky, but you know the golden rule."

"Always have a plan," they said in unison, and both burst out laughing.

"So how did you do it old boy, do tell," asked Duke.

"Well, quite simple," went on Tom, "you know the Yanks and their paranoia for security. Got myself a nice shiny gold badge, borrowed a CIA car, drove up to the main gate and told the gate guard I was from the DNHAC, and had to speak to the Senator's secret service detail about a new security threat. They spoke to a secret service agent, and they waved me through."

"DNHAC," said Duke, looking confused.

"Do Not Have A Clue."

"Oh, my dear boy," said Duke, throwing his head back and laughing.

"Once I parked in the garage, the secret service was easily despatched, only seven of them. I went and had a chat with the Senator, who I must admit was very calm and professional to the end, but he gave me everything I wanted to know plus the last name. Nice touch, I thought. Heroin overdose, nice and simple," said Tom, "and the icing on the cake, as I drove back out of the gate I told the gate guard the agents were getting annoyed as their football team were losing, and perhaps they should leave them be." By this time both Tom and Duke had tears in their eyes from laughing so much.

Finally Duke said, "I took the liberty to have already ordered lunch, hope that's OK old boy."

"Yes, fine," said Tom.

"Good, should arrive in about ten minutes, this place is always punctual."

"You weren't wrong," said Tom.

Duke looked puzzled.

"When you said 'not the Carton Club' when we were in that bar in Belize City."

"Oh, yes." The penny finally dropped and Duke said, "See, told you I would stand you lunch here one day."

"Never doubted you for a minute," said Tom, which brought another laugh from both men.

"Nice code, by the way, from the phone call. Took me a minute to work it out," said Tom.

Duke laughed. "Need to keep you on your toes, old fella," replied Duke.

"Lucky you only got two rooms for private functions at the club," said Tom, laughing.

"Made sure the website was up to date last week, added the floor plan myself. Some of the old and bold committee members were against it, but as I predicted, it became useful," replied a laughing Duke.

There was a light knock on the door and Duke said, "Enter." Two stewards entered with two trolleys. "Just leave them there please, we can serve ourselves."

"Very good, my lord. Can you sign this for me, my lord."

"Of course," said Duke, "there you go."

"Thank you my lord, and if you require any further assistance, please ring." The men bowed and left the room. The whole operation had taken the stewards less than three minutes.

While the stewards were in the room Tom had lowered his head, and studied the folder Duke had passed to him, with S&T Imports emblazoned on the front. Tom was always impressed how the company had grown from strength to strength over the years; still a private company, with offices in over thirty countries, last year it boasted profits of over one billion US dollars.

Duke said, "Shall I be mother?" and served them both. The meal consisted of:

> *Starter: – Warm mousse of lobster with spinach, lobster butter sauce.*
> *Main Course: – Roast tranche of plaice, braised peas, onions and lettuce.*
> *Dessert: – Strawberries marinated with mint and vanilla, strawberry sorbet, pink champagne.*
> *Topped off with a bottle of Dehesa Del Carrizal Cabernet*

Tom admitted the food in the Carton Club was excellent, better than even Duke had said; no wonder his waistline was growing if he was dining out like this every day. After the meal, Tom sat back and said, "Duke, I don't think I have had a better meal in years."

Duke smiled. "Glad it met with your approval, old man."

After lunch, Duke said, "Let's sit on the comfy chairs. Down to business," as he pulled out a white piece of paper and passed it to Tom. Tom studied the piece of paper for a few minutes, then passed it back to Duke, who by this stage had taken a cigar from his pockets and had begun to light it. As he did so, he also casually lit the piece of paper and dropped it into the ashtray and, with his cigar, made sure the paper ash looked like cigar ash. Tom smiled; he had taught Duke well.

Duke raised his eyes to Tom. "Last name on the list." Tom nodded, and Duke went on. "Ironic really, last name and it happened to be a UK national. Please be careful though, Tom," Duke warned, "they will be well protected and by now will know you are coming for them."

"O ye of little faith."

"Not at all, I kind of like having you around," which made them both laugh again.

"Thanks for the new laptop and all the emails about mother," said Tom.

"My pleasure, old man. She is a delight and when I contacted her and told her I had news about you, she was beside herself, and I know she is proud of the man you have become. She is so proud of her Tom."

"Is she ok though?"

"Oh yes, I see her once a month and the new nursing home is top class."

"One of my assistants, Alice Mitchell, particularly has taken a shine to Grace. She is not the easiest woman in the world to please. A few of my assistants have been sent packing, but Grace seems to like Alice, they get on like a house on fire. Alice takes her regularly to visit and lay flowers on her husband's grave."

Tom smiled and was pleased his mother was in good hands.

"Duke I don't know how I can ever repay you," said Tom in a whisper.

"Don't be daft, old man," said Duke, laughing, "you made me a near billionaire and head of a successful private, import/export business. It should be me thanking you," which made Tom laugh as well. Duke went silent then said quietly, "I have the friendship of the greatest man I have ever known. You can take everything else away from me, but that I cherish that more than life itself." Tom leaned over and they both embraced again.

Just as Tom and Duke were embracing, the net was closing in.

"Last confirmed sighting near the Carton Club," crackled the radio.

"Damn," said the lead agent. He spoke into his wrist and said, "OK, all agents spread out and get the photograph circulated, he is around here somewhere."

An agent approached the Carton Club doorman and showed him the photograph. The doorman looked and said, "Yes, nice polite man, arrived this morning."

"You sure?"

"Definitely, gave me a twenty pound note for opening the door, only gents do that," said the doorman, smiling.

The agent said, "How long?"

"Not sure, two/three hours ago."

"Still inside?"

"Well, not seen him come out yet, and I've been here since nine this morning."

The agent quickly spoke into his wrist; the lead agent said, "All agents converge on the Carton Club, confirmed sighting." Minutes later, a car screeched to a halt outside the Carton Club and three men climbed out, all three were section chiefs sent by the MI5 director personally. One spoke to the lead agent and told him to cover the back and the front and to cover all access and not to let anyone enter or leave this building unless they had personally been identified. The lead agent nodded and spoke again into his wrist, to give him team their orders.

All three men walked up the steps but the doorman blocked their way. "Private members club, gentlemen."

The man in front pulled out a wallet, and flashed his badge. "Out of my way, national security."

The doorman pulled the door open and said, "Gentleman," while touching his hat.

The three men walked up to reception. Mr Jenkins behind the reception said, "Yes gentlemen, can I help?"

Thrusting the photograph in his face, he said, "This man."

Mr Jenkins gently took the photo from the man's hand and made a show of putting on glasses, which made the agent more impatient. "Come on, this is a matter of national security. Is he here?"

Mr Jenkins waved over Jones. "Jones, is this the man you escorted to the Wellington Room earlier today?"

Taking the photo from Mr Jenkins, Jones said, "Yes it is, sir."

"Please escort these gentlemen to the Wellington Room."

"Don't bother," said the man, "just tell us where it is."

"Up the main staircase, corridor to the right, bottom door."

The three men turned and rushed up the main staircase. Stopping short of the Wellington Room, the three men drew their side arms and were just about to enter when Duke opened the door of the Waterloo Room, and said, "Gentlemen, can I help you?"

"National security," said the agent, flashing his badge at Duke, "please go back inside, sir."

"How exciting," said Duke, "but I don't care what security agency you are from young man, this is the Carton Club and never in all its two hundred year history has a fire arm been brought past the statue of Lord Carton, the founding father of this club, which currently sits in the main lobby. It is one of the Club's founding rules."

The men stared at Duke.

"I am the twelfth Duke of Hampshire and a committee member."

Just then, the doors to the Wellington Room opened and none other than the current Home Secretary came out. There seated behind him were two Generals in full dress uniform. "What the bloody hell is going on out here?" said the Home Secretary.

"Looking for a fugitive, sir," said the lead man, showing the Home Secretary his badge.

"What, in the Carton Club? Ridiculous you idiot, you've been had."

"But we have sound intelligence, he was in the Wellington Room," said the lead man who was by now starting to feel uneasy.

"So you think I am having lunch with your fugitive? I shall speak to your Director personally, this is outrageous," said the Home Secretary.

"Outrageous," said Duke behind them all, "now get out."

As the men were leaving, the Home Secretary spotted Duke standing in the hall. "All in hand, your Grace," he said, smiling.

Duke said, "Not good, Fairfax. Men with guns. Shall have to report it to the committee."

"Whatever you feel is best, your Grace," said the Home Secretary, bowing deeply.

The three men put away their firearms, and as they passed Duke he said, "Not good, gentlemen, not good."

The men all nodded and said, "your Grace," as they retreated back the way they came.

Duke turned on his heels and with a spring in his step and a smile on his face said, "Another brandy, I think." Sitting back down, he pressed the buzzer beside him, and a few minutes later there was a gentle knock on the door. Turning, Duke said, "Stephen, another brandy if you please, and can you get someone to close that open window? It's turning rather chilly in here."

"Of course my lord," came the reply. "Straight away."

"Vanished? What do you mean, vanished?" said the MI5 director, getting to her feet.

"We had good intelligence he went into the Carton Club," said the department head.

"And?" said the director, getting more irate. Everyone had their heads down and no one dared look up. The director said, "OK, so who did he meet in the Carton Club?"

"We are not really sure."

"Well bloody well find out," screamed the director.

"Not that simple, we have interviewed and background-checked all the staff, most are ex-military types. As for the members, there were thirty two members and guests in the club: two Dukes, three Earls, four Government Ministers, ten MPs, three judges, and out of them, three are personal friends of the Prime Minster. The rest were leading businessmen who mostly happen to have close connection to the Government in one way or another, and as for their guests they ranged from a sprinkling of foreign dignitaries to family friends, so checking each one is going to be near impossible."

"This is a monumental cock up," said the director. The director looked at Smith and said, "Your department was in charge of surveillance, how did he get past you to the bloody Carton Club without you knowing about it?"

Smith looked up at the director, and said, "We had the place covered, I had six agents tailing him, but he managed to slip past us."

"Slip past us," said the Director in a low voice. "Well, Smith," said the director, shouting at him, "I suggest you get you team and bloody well find him," then she slapped the table. Smith stood and rushed out of the room, feeling rather pleased he had left.

After leaving the Carton Club, Tom turned left; he spotted the two agents straight away. Crossing the road, he went into a corner shop and brought a paper and some mints, and asked the shop keeper if he could have them in a bag. Leaving the shop, Tom pulled the collar of his coat up and his hat down, then turned towards the agents. He walked straight past them and down the road, after all they were not looking for a limping man carrying a white shopping bag, they were looking at the large white building on the other side of the road.

Tom knew the hotel was a bust, he could not go back there, but he never planned to once he had met Duke. Although it had been paid for for the next two weeks, the intelligence agencies would still have to sit on the place for at least that long, expecting him to return. He had not left anything of importance there; the laptop he had wiped, the passport was only good for one use, suitcase, clothes could all be replaced, so the hotel room still looked occupied waiting for him to return.

It started to rain, and Tom smiled. He loved the British weather; rain was an equaliser, everyone looked down, so CCTV cameras found it harder to pick up faces, especially if they were covered by an umbrella. Tom took the direction that Duke had given him to the safe house, which was the opposite end of London from the hotel. Tom thought, nicely done Duke my old fruit, still smiling. One thing Tom loved to do was walk; it always gave him time to think and let him see clearly for a problem. Then again he was not in a rush, and walking helps you blend in more.

At the safe house, Duke had prepared everything Tom could have possibly needed. Tom kicked off his wet shoes, and took off his wet clothes and placed them all in a large laundry hamper. After taking a long hot shower, Tom lay on the bed, closed his eyes and went to sleep.

For the next three days, Tom would stay put and wait. Tom thought about the last name on the list. After all these years, he had been driven by a quenching thirst for vengeance for his family; even now when he thought about Natasha and Grace, which he sadly admitted was getting less and less as time went on, at least his memories of them were happy ones, years before every little sound or picture reminded him of his loss, and gave him the drive to go on, but lately the enthusiasm was waning, and Tom was pleased it was going to finally be over.

The last name. He never once considered stopping until it was over, and he certainly had not even thought what he would do afterwards; he could not see himself settling down or retiring to a mundane existence.

After three days of just lazing around the flat, watching television and reading, Tom was getting bored. Tom knew the intelligence agencies would be in near meltdown, not knowing where he was. But during the time spent in the flat, he made a decision, which probably was going to be a mistake, but was a risk he was prepared to take.

Tom took the brochure of his mother's retirement home, and noticed it was more a villa complex than a single house, each resident having their own self-contained small bungalow. This made Tom smile; open grounds were far easier to navigate than one large roomed house.

Tom was deciding how to get to see his mother, when he noticed an envelope with 'car keys' printed on it. Opening the envelope, it contained a single key, and the instructions that the car was in the underground car park beneath the flat, full and ready to use, just in case.

Tom smiled once again. "Duke, sometimes you are a star," he said; he now could not think of any more obstacles to stop him going to finally meet his mother after all these years.

Locking the flat and taking the back stairs to the underground car park, Tom strolled to the parked BMW and opened it, driving up to the barrier which opened with the automated registration number software; impressive, thought Tom. Driving up the ramp into the sunlight, Tom noticed the car windows were tinted so no one could look in unless standing directly against the car. "Nice," said Tom as he put the car in gear and drove away from London.

Using the SATNAV, Tom drove carefully to the residential home. Not wanting to be stopped by doing something stupid, Tom never exceeded the speed limit and always stayed behind a car.

When the SATNAV told Tom he was about a mile from the

home, he looked for and then pulled into a layby, which had several other cars already parked. This one looked popular as it had a burger van parked at the end, so would always look busy; a single car parked sometimes can, to a bored traffic copper, give them an excuse to be nosy.

Tom took a map out of the glove compartment and studied the map for a few minutes, getting his bearings of the area. He locked the car, jumped the fence and followed the line of trees across to the other side of the field; once there, he followed a dirt track for about a mile, until he came to the outskirts of the nursing home complex.

Tom stood in the shadows of some trees and scanned the area. He noticed the place was quite sedate, not a lot of cars driving about, and people were less conspicuous, which made him smile. Tom located Grace's bungalow and took a deep breath and moved off.

Alice had just finished her visit with Grace, and was about to get in her car and leave, when she noticed a man loitering near the trees near Grace's bungalow. The man could not see the car park, or Alice. Slowly and quietly Alice closed her car door again, and slowly pulling the small Beretta pistol from her hand bag, Alice moved slowly along the wall towards the man.

Alice Mitchell had worked for S&T Imports for nearly two years now. Alice had a first class honours degree from Oxford. Alice was the only child of two doctors, but after spending her childhood being brought up in a medical environment, she decided a medical career was not for her, but it was still a surprise to her parents when she went for a degree in economics.

Alice was bright and intelligent and had many admirers. Alice's last relationship did not end well; the man was an obsessive type, opposite to her carefree attitude to life, and after a few months the physical attraction that had drawn them close finally ended. The man took it hard; Alice only felt relief.

One night while working alone in the legal department, Alice had come across an old dog eared folder, with only one sheet of paper. She did not recognise the writing, but thought it must be Russian or Eastern European. Alice loved a puzzle so she decided to translate the document, so when she had any spare time over the next few months she spent them on the strange document. Alice discovered the writing was Russian, so armed with a Russian dictionary she translated the single piece of paper. Finally, Alice studied the text, but it was confusing:

To whom it may Concern

I, Tom Backer, being of sound mind and body, give full power of attorney over the running of my company S&T Imports, to Grenville St Louis Hampton, Earl of Eastleigh and the future Duke of Hampshire. I give permission for him to govern the company in all aspects of investments, recruitment and market-ing. Furthermore I empower him to make all decisions on my behalf in respect of my company S&T Imports.
Signed this day Twenty Eighth day of March in the year nine-teen hundred and eighty three.

Signed By: Tom Backer
Tom Backer
Witnessed by: James McLeish
James McLeish, Ambassador for Her Majesty's government, Belize.

Alice sat and looked at the piece of paper, deciding what to do next. Alice picked up the phone and after it was answered said, "Alice Mitchell here from legal, please can I make an appoint-ment to see the Chairman."

"The reason you wish to see him," asked the other end of the phone.

"It's about a document I found regarding a Tom Backer."

"What is your extension, I will call back once I have arranged an appointment."

Alice gave her extension, said, "Thank you," and hung up. Alice was still not sure she had done the right thing.

While Alice was wondering if she had done the right thing, the telephone on her desk rang. Alice picked it up after the second ring, and said, "Alice Mitchell, legal department."

"This is the Chairman's personal secretary. The Chairman would like to see you about your enquiry, and he asks if you could bring your finding with you."

"What, now?" asked Alice.

"The Chairman is waiting for you now," came the reply.

Alice replaced the handset and thought to herself, that was fast. Now feeling apprehensive, she went to see the Chairman. Alice spoke to the secretary, and informed her who she was; the secretary smiled and told her to take a seat, the Chairman would not be long. Alice had only met the Chairman once; that was at a new contract celebrations party, and as Alice had worked so closely on the legal documentation for the contract, she was introduced to the Chairman.

Finally the secretary looked at Alice and said, still smiling, "You go in now; the Chairman is ready for you." Alice went to the large oak double doors, took a deep breath and gently knocked.

"Come," said a muffled voice.

Alice opened the door and stepped inside. Alice was surprised to see her boss, Stewart Gould, sitting opposite the Chairman. Both men stood as Alice approached the desk.

"Please take a seat, Alice. You don't mind me calling you Alice, do you?" said the Chairman, pointing to the vacant chair next to Stewart.

Alice said, "Thank you and no, not at all, Alice is fine." Alice sat and smiled at Stewart.

"Now," said the Chairman, "You found some paperwork on Mr Tom Backer, is that right."

"Yes Chairman," said Alice, passing over the folder to the Chairman. After studying the documents for some time, Alice was sure the Chairman was smiling to himself, as if he were remembering a long ago event.

Finally, he looked up, and passed the folder to Stewart. Turning to Alice, Stewart asked, "Where did you find this, Alice?"

"It was in one of the old cabinets, I was asked to go through them before they were replaced. I knew the document was not English, but my curiously was piqued so I decided to translate the document."

"And you now have both the original and the translation. Did you make any other copies apart from these?" asked the Chairman.

"No, Chairman, you have both the original and the English transcript," Alice replied.

"Good," said the Chairman. "Stewart you know what to do with that folder," said the Chairman.

"Yes, Chairman," said Stewart, standing. As Stewart moved towards the door, the Chairman said, "Stewart, let's try and keep it more secure this time." Stewart did not look back, but Alice thought it sounded like a reprimand and a warning.

After Stewart had left, the Chairman smiled at Alice and said, "I guess I better explain who Tom Backer was before you go poking about some more." Alice felt the Chairman's words were chilling and she wondered what can of worms she had opened up translating the document.

"Where to begin," said the Chairman. "Tom Backer was my oldest and dearest friend, he started our great company with a friend whilst he was living in Russia. Before he died, he made out that document you found, passing the company into my safe hands.

"Tom came from the East End of London, a child prodigy, if you like, before he was forced to flee London. Tom died in Russia, years ago." Alice listened to the Chairman, but had a thousand questions going through her mind. Holding up his hands, the Chairman said, "I know, Alice, you have hundreds of questions." Alice thought the Chairman had read her mind. "But please can I beg a favour of you, to forget the documents and Tom Backer and let sleeping dogs lie, on this occasion. But every cloud has a silver lining," said the Chairman, smiling at Alice. "I think I may have a new job for you, if you are prepared to take it, plus it might answer a few questions you have."

Alice now looked confused; had the Chairman not just asked her to forget about the document she had found, and everything she had learned about this Tom Backer? Now he was offering her a job. Going on, the Chairman said, "Tom's mother is still alive and kicking, she is a spry old lady, very independent and quite a handful if her last assistant is anything to go by," this brought a laugh from the Chairman. The Chairman went on, "Grace Backer lives in a residential self-contained nursing home just near Epping. In Tom's memory, I look after Grace Backer, make sure she has all the comforts of home, and generally make sure she is happy."

Before Alice spoke, the Chairman said, "Don't think it's going to be a picnic: the last assistant to Grace lasted a week before Grace had her running in tears."

Alice smiled and said, "Sounds like a lady after my own heart."

The Chairman smiled. He knew as soon as Alice walked in she was the right person for the job, and he was always been a good judge of character; Tom had taught him that. "Before you accept, let me explain your duties," said the Chairman. "Grace will be your number one priority, you are to visit her each day, make sure she needs for nothing, take her where she needs to go, arrange her appointments and general make sure Grace is happy. Of course you will have to give up your old job in legal. We will of course give you a suitable pay rise, and as a matter of course give you a company car; you will also control a company credit card to use for any expenses that Grace may encounter, and of course any time night or day if you need to contact me about Grace, you can, without consequence."

The Chairman went on, "During working hours, contact my personal secretary and she will put you through straight away, or out of work hours," he passed Alice a card over the desk, "these are my personal numbers.

"So what you think Alice, you game and up for a new challenge?" said the chairman smiling.

"Of course, I will not expect you to agree until you have first met Grace."

Alice smiling said, "Of course I will meet with Mrs Backer. One thing has crossed my mind, Chairman," said Alice, "is this offer because I found the document or my sparkling personality?"

The Chairman put his head back and laughed, "My dear Alice, I can see you and Grace will get on like a house on fire, she has the same cynical outlook."

Next day Alice drove down to introduce herself to Grace. As she was driving, Alice was thinking about the job offer, still unsure if she had been silenced with a terrific job opportunity or she had actually been headhunted because of her diligence. Arriving at the residential complex, Alice parked in the 'Residents Only' car park. The Chairman said he would phone ahead to Mrs Backer to let her know Alice was on her way down. Alice knocked on the door and waited, and after a few minutes, the door was opened by a silver haired lady, about her own height and build.

"Hi I am Alice, you are expecting me, Mrs Backer," said Alice smiling.

Grace looked at Alice and nodded, and said, "Yes, my dear, please come in." Grace said, "Sit down my dear, and let me look at you." Alice sat opposite Grace and smiled. "You are very pretty my dear," said Grace.

"Thank you, Mrs Backer," said Alice. "You look very well for your age, I must say, I notice the sparkle in your eyes," said Alice.

Grace smiled and said, "I think Grenville was right, we are going to get on very well, fancy a cup of tea? And please call me Grace."

After Alice had left, Grace rang the Chairman and said, "Grenville she is perfect, a spirit after my own heart."

"Knew you would approve, Grace," said Duke.

A few days later, Alice knew she had made the right choice; Grace, despite her age and the 'little old lady' routine, was as sharp as a razor, and nobody's fool. Alice knew they were about to become close friends. One day, Grace asked Alice if she could drive her to the churchyard to lay some flowers. On the way Alice brought Grace some flowers, and once at the church, Alice asked Grace if she wanted her to stay in the car.

"No dear, come with me, I know you are drying to ask me about Tom," said Grace, smiling.

Alice looked at Grace with a shocked look. "How did you know that?" said Alice.

Taking Alice's arm, Grace said, "We are so much alike, you and I, it would burn me up as well."

At the grave, Grace changed the flowers and then sat on the small bench across from the gravestone; Alice sat next to her and read the inscription:

Ruth Gloria Backer
Loving daughter of Grace and Tom Backer
Taken before her time, now with the angels
Tom Backer Loving Husband and father

Grace explained to Alice that Ruth was her daughter, who had died during the war, and Tom was her husband who also died in the war. "Both taken from me because of a silly war," said Grace softly.

Alice took Grace's hand. Grace went on, "Of course, Tom is not here, he died in Burma, and is buried over there, but I had his name added to the stone, so I can feel close when I come and visit," smiled Grace.

"But I thought the Chairman said he and Tom were best friends," said Alice.

Grace laughed. "Not my husband Tom, my son Tom." After a silence Grace said, "This was the last place I saw my boy before he left." Grace went on to explain the reasons and departure of Tom.

After an hour, Alice took Grace by the hand and said, "Thank you for sharing that with me, Grace."

"Of course, my boy Tom is not buried here either," which made Alice wonder, as Grace did not seem bothered by it.

Alice quietly said, "That has not really cleared up the mystery of Tom Backer." Grace sat and smiled.

Tom stopped outside the bungalow, and felt more nervous that he had done in years; will she recognise me, he thought, will she want to speak to me? All these questions were buzzing around his head; should he knock or just go in and surprise her? No, don't want to give her an heart attack, or a stroke with the shock of seeing him standing there. Just as he was deciding what to do for the best, he heard behind him, "If you are going to rob this old lady, you picked the wrong one."

Turning, Tom saw he was staring down the front of a pistol, held by a very attractive young woman. Tom said, "You must be Alice Mitchell; Duke said you often pop by and see my mother."

Alice was now confused, this man knew her name, but was speaking in riddles, so she lowered the gun and said, "And who the hell are you?"

Tom held his hands up, and said, "Tom, Tom Sharapova."

Just then the door opened and Grace emerged to see what the fuss was about. Looking from Tom to Alice, Grace said, "Tom, you always did have a way with the girls. Come here and give your old mother a hug."

Tom hugged Grace and did not hold back the tears; for so long he had needed to be with her, to feel emotionally attached again to the one person in this world who truly loved him for who he was. Grace was in floods of tears as well, and could only say, "My Tom, my boy," as she clung onto his neck. Alice was quite caught up in the moment and had tears in her eyes; she knew this was no ordinary reunion.

Alice shepherded them both into the bungalow and closed the door. Tom and Grace sat down and still holding each other, began to talk. Alice said "I will make some tea," and disappeared into the kitchen, not wanting to intrude on a very private and emotional time for them both.

When Alice emerged from the kitchen, Tom and Grace were sitting, holding hands, with their heads close and laughing. Alice thought she had never seen Grace look as bright as she did now. Alice placed the tray on the table and said, "I shall be off then, leave you two to catch up."

"No, please stay," said Tom, smiling.

"Yes, stay, Alice, I owe you an explanation," said Grace.

"OK, shall I be mother?" said Alice, picking up the teapot.

After a time, Grace said, "Sorry Alice, but let me explain." Still holding Tom's hand, she said, "This is Tom Sharapova, or Tom Backer as he was."

Alice stared at both Grace and Tom and looked dumbfounded.

"Don't worry," said Tom, "Let us explain."

Over the next few hours Tom and Grace explained to Alice the circumstances of the transformation from Tom Backer to Tom Sharapova. Alice sat nodding her head, completely blown away by their revelations.

When the evening light started to fade, Alice said, "Tom, you better go soon, the home's security guards will be starting to prowl." Tom nodded.

Grace squeezed his hand and said, "Promise me you will come back and see me again." Tom looked into Grace's eyes and could see the plea in them.

"Of course, mother, I promise," said Tom.

Alice asked, "Where are you parked?"

"About a mile away, in a layby," said Tom.

"I will give you a lift, if you like," said Alice.

"No it's OK, but you can do me a favour. Tell Duke, or the Chairman, I would like to see him at the flat."

"Of course," said Alice with a smile. Tom and Alice both

said their goodbyes to Grace and left, Alice to her car, and Tom across the grounds. On the drive home, Alice tried to get Tom from her mind, but all she could do was think about him.

Next morning Alice made an appointment with the chairman's personal secretary for ten am. The chairman's secretary had a list of immediate appointment people, and Alice was near the top.

At precisely ten am, Alice was sitting on the large comfy sofa outside the chairman's office, when the buzzer went on the secretary's desk. She picked up the receiver, smiled at Alice and said, "The chairman is ready for you now." Alice smiled back, and gently knocked on the large wooden doors.

On opening the door, Duke was sat at a large desk on the far side of the office. Standing, Duke came around the desk and with stretched out hands, said, "Alice my dear, what bring you to my door this early?"

Alice said, "Went to see Grace yesterday."

"Oh yes," said Duke, and seeing the tension in her eyes, Duke said, "how is the old dear?"

"She had a visitor," said Alice.

Duke put a finger to his lips. Alice immediately understood the room was not safe to talk in, so she just said, "Very well, asked after you of course."

"How kind, she is a dear," Duke replied. After a few minutes of bland idle chit chat, Duke said, "Well, my dear, thank you for the update on Grace, but I am afraid I have got a very important meeting in conference room three. I will walk you out, my dear."

Alice followed Duke from the room. He stopped at his secretary's desk and said, "Michelle, going to the meeting in conference room three," before striding off with Alice. Michelle looked puzzled and scanned the diary; she could not see any meeting in conference room three scheduled, but shrugged, and after all these years working for the chairman she was not surprised it was not in the diary.

Once in conference room three, Duke went to a hidden side

panel and pressed a green button. A whirring noise was followed by part of the ceiling opening and a glass cube ascended
which, eventually, joined another smaller one emerging from
the floor. Duke smiled at Alice, and waved for her to follow.
The glass cube had fitted neatly over the small conference table
and chairs.

Once Duke and Alice had stepped into the cube, Duke
pressed a button, and the door was merged into the glass cube,
with a hydraulic hiss.

"Impressive," said Alice.

"An evil requirement, in this day and age." Duke went on,
"State of the art soundproof room both ways, with air temperature monitors and enough oxygen for 10 hours of use,
totally secure."

"Do you not worry about being trapped in here if you forget
the time?" said Alice.

Duke laughed. "Not at all, my dear. The room also monitors your body vital functions, and if anyone present shows
signs of stress the room will automatically unseal.

"Look," said Duke, and he showed Alice a heads up display
on the wall of the cube, monitoring both of their vitals stat,
plus the room temperature and the amount of air remaining,
and a countdown clock to unseal.

Once again, Alice said, "Impressive, very James Bond."

Duke and Alice sat at the conference table, and Duke said,
"Shall we start?" with a smile.

Alice said, "I met Tom yesterday and I have a message from
him."

Duke said, "Thought you might, what did you think of our
Tom?"

"Nearly blew his head off, when I caught him snooping
around Grace's bungalow," said Alice. This made Duke put
his head back and roar with laughter. Alice looked at Duke
with a puzzled look.

"Oh my dear, I bet you made his day pointing a gun at
him."

"Don't understand," said Alice.

"My dear, let me explain the enigma that is Tom Sharapova." For the next two hours Duke explained everything to Alice about Tom, his life story, where he, Duke, fitted into the story and the reason for the company.

Alice just sat and stared at Duke and what he was telling her, nodding and shaking her head at times, other times with tears in her eyes, and other times laughing out loud with Duke; in fact, before Duke had finished his tale, she had covered the entire spectrum of human emotion.

After Duke finished, all Alice could say was, "What a man," and realised she was perhaps falling a bit in love with him. This thought made her blush, and Duke picked up on it immediately.

"No, my dear, you don't have feelings for people like Tom Sharapova, he is on a mission of vengeance and he has given his life and soul over to it, you will never be able to deviate him from that path, you will only end up getting hurt, if you get in his way."

Alice was silent for a bit then said, "After he has killed the last name on his list, what then for Tom Sharapova?"

Duke smiled. "Never thought of that one, my dear. Perhaps between us we can come up with a plan."

Alice smiled at Duke and said, "No doubt we can," which made them both laugh.

Next day Duke and Alice had agreed to meet in the underground car park to Tom's flat. Tom let them both in; he was surprised to see her, Alice was carrying a large brown bag which had the most amazing smell of freshly cooked pastries. While Alice went into the kitchen to make some coffee, Tom whispered to Duke, "What is she doing here?"

Duke held up his hand and said, "Tom, sometimes you got to trust me."

Tom, said, "Always will, Duke," before hugging him.

A few minutes later, Alice came from the kitchen with a pot of coffee and a plate of sweet smelling pastries.

While all three sat munching pastries and drinking coffee, Duke casually said to Tom, "Tom, I have explained everything to Alice here."

"What, everything?" said Tom, going tense.

"Yes, everything, and she is now totally on our side and part of the cause."

Tom looked at Alice and saw her smiling at him; all Tom could do was smile back. When Alice took the tray back to the kitchen, leaving them alone, Tom took Duke's arms and said in a whisper, "You told her everything?"

Whispering too, Duke said, "Yes, my dear chap, everything, warts and all."

"Blimey," said Tom.

"I know," said Duke, "and she still wants to know you, amazed me as well." He laughed as he patted Tom's face.

Tom said, "Let's all meet at mother's in two day time, I will meet you there, and see if we can come up with a suitable plan of action." The other two agreed and left.

In bed that night, Tom's thoughts turned to Alice; she was a very attractive young woman, about fifteen years his junior he thought, well proportioned, and smiled with her eyes. Duke and mother must trust her implicitly if they told her the whole story, they would not tell just anyone, they were both too shrewd for that. Tom was trying to work out Alice when he drifted off to sleep and for the first time in years, did not have a nightmare.

Tom once again made his way down to his mother's residential complex, parking in the same busy layby. He covered the last mile by foot. When Tom arrived, he noticed Duke's and Alice's cars already parked. Tom knocked on his mother's door, which was immediately opened by a smiling Alice; Tom smiled back as he entered. Duke stood and they embraced, then Tom went to Grace and embraced her as well.

"I shall make some tea," said Grace, leaving the three of them alone to chat.

"So," said Alice, "where do we start?"

Tom said, "I need to get close to this bloody woman."

"Close enough to kill her?" asked Alice.

"Yes," said Tom, "she is the last one on the list, the one that gave the orders to try and kill me and Uncle Vlad, but ended up killing my family. I need to look her in the eyes and tell her why she is going to die." Duke and Alice were both nodded their heads; strangely, they both understood Tom's obsession.

"So," said Duke, "How do we get Tom close enough to Julie Somerville, Director of MI5?"

"I can," said Grace, standing in the kitchen doorway holding a tray of tea.

"Sorry," said Tom, "what did you say, mother?"

"I said, I can get you close to her." All three looked at Grace with astonishment.

Taking the tray from her, Alice helped her sit in her high back chair. Before anyone else spoke, Grace said, "Be a dear, Alice, can you get me that brown box next to my bed, and bring it to me?"

"Of course," smiled Alice. When Alice returned and placed the box on Grace's knee, she sat back down; all three looked at Grace.

Opening the box, Grace looked at Tom and said, "What I am about to tell you might alter your perception on all of this, my son." Tom looked confused. Grace handed him a faded envelope, which Tom took, and extracting the letter, Tom read it; still looking confused, he passed it to Duke and over his shoulder Alice read it as well.

Grace said, "Julie Somerville is your birth mother, Tom." The room went so quiet that you could hear the ticking of the clock on the wall. Tom sat and stared into space as Grace went on to explain Tom's birth. "Perhaps I should have told you when you were growing up; I always thought in my heart she would eventually return and claim you, and take you away from me. That was always my biggest fear, while you were growing up. At first I tried to stay distant from you but after a few years I loved you so much I considered you my own child, and knew I could never give you up, so as time went on, and you grew into a wonderful young boy, I never had the courage to tell you."

Grace had tears streaming down her eyes. Tom went and kneeled down in front of her and hugged her. Duke stood and with his hands on his head, said, "Well, this is a game changer."

"Sit down, Grenville," said Grace, "you are making the place look untidy." Grace lifted Tom's head up and taking his face in her hands, said, "Can you ever forgive me, my boy?"

Tom stood and looked at all three and said in a quiet voice, "This changes nothing, mother. You were and always will be the woman who brought me up, were there for me, loved me and nurtured me and set me on the path to the man I am today, and you will always be my mother. This Julie Somerville may have given birth to me but I do not now, or ever will have any emotional affection for her. Plus it does not distract from the fact she gave the order to try and kill me, which lead to the death of my family. She is responsible and must still die."

Grace wiped her eyes and said, "That's settled it then, you better hear my plan."

An hour later, all three sat and stared at Grace. Eventually Duke said, "You devious old bird," to which the other two could only nod and confirm his sentiments.

Three days later Tom, Duke and Alice were sitting in the flat, and Duke said, "Well, I admit I cannot find any fault with her plan." The other two agreed.

Alice said, "How long have we got to set it all up?"

"Three days, four tops," said Tom. "I think I am on borrowed time. The intelligence agencies are not stupid, and will be closing in fast."

They all agreed for the plan to start in three days. Alice stood, turned to Tom, smiled and said, "See you soon." Tom smiled back, as Alice left.

Duke said, "Lovely girl, that, and so loyal."

"Stop it, Duke," said Tom smiling. "I know what you are doing."

"What, old man? I was only saying you could do far worse."

Tom punched Duke on the arm, and said, "Behave. Seriously, can you get your end done in the time frame?"

"How do you ever doubt me, my dear chap?"

"Never," said Tom.

Next day Tom answered the door and was surprised to see Duke standing there. "Hello," said Tom looking surprised.

"I know, broke protocol," said Duke, "but I had to see you one last time before you left, who knows when we meet again. These last few weeks have brought back so many memories of our time together, it's made me feel positively young again."

"You getting soppy on me, old man?" said Tom, smiling at Duke.

"Properly am," said Duke. "Listen, Tom, be safe and take care, and remember I am always here for you."

"I know Duke, you were one of the reasons I had the fortitude to carry on all these years."

"Now who is getting soppy." Both laughing, they hugged and both with tears in their eyes, Duke left.

Next day, Alice was sitting with Grace, and said, "Everything OK, Grace?"

"Perfect my dear, now can you pull that emergency cord? I can feel a mini stroke coming on."

"Of course," said Alice smiling.

Julie Somerville, Director of MI5, looked worried; although her security had been tightened around her, she was still feeling agitated. Tom Sharapova had totally vanished despite all the best efforts of every intelligence agency in the UK to find him; they still could not track him down. Perhaps he had decided to give up on her. After all, she was Director of MI5; he might have thought her as a target was too difficult, even for the great Tom Sharapova. No, that was foolish. After all, he had tracked down and killed every member who ever had or was connected with Operation Blackstone. She was the last one left. He would not give up now when he was so close. She wished sometimes she had someone she could lean on, and confide in, but you don't get to be director of MI5 by being soft.

While Julie was thinking, her phone rang. She picked it up straight away, and said, "Yes Smith?"

"A Doctor Randall from St Thomas' Hospital."

"What does he want?" said Julie, sounding tired.

"Something about a dying old friend of yours, a Grace Backer."

Julie was shocked; she had not heard that name in over forty years. "OK, put him through." There was a slight click, and Julie said, "Doctor Randall how, may I help you?"

Doctor Randall went on to explain they had had an elderly lady called Grace Backer admitted to St Thomas' Hospital. She had had a major stroke, but was not expected to live long; but she was still conscious and commanded the power of speech. "She does not have any relatives, but she asked me – sorry, this will seem a bit strange."

"Get on with it, doctor," said Julie, getting impatient.

"Sorry," said the doctor. "Had to write this bit down. 'Can you contact a Julie Somerville at MI5 and tell her before I die, I want to see her and tell her about her son'. Sorry, don't know if it makes any sense, but that's the message."

"No, makes perfect sense, thank you for ringing, Doctor." Julie replaced the handset and placed her head in her hands. As the phone went dead, Duke replaced the handset his end and said, "You are most welcome, Director Somerville."

Julie's mind was in turmoil. After all these years, Grace Backer, and the child she had given up and abandoned all those years ago. Of course, over the years she had justified and come to terms with her actions then, but she never told anyone she had given birth to a child, not even her ex-husband or family. She had often wondered what had happened to the child she had given birth to. She had even once or twice thought about tracking them both down, but something always stopped her from carrying out her plans.

"After all this time," she said out loud, wondering what type of man he had become, if he was still alive of course. That was a possibility. The Doctor did say Grace wanted to tell her about her son. 'Her son'. The notion made little or no sense to her; she had never had any maternal instinct towards the child.

Lifting the telephone, Smith immediately said, "Yes, Director."

"Smith, get me a car at the front and a security detail ready in ten minutes, and we are off to St Thomas' Hospital, to see an old colleague of mine."

"Of course, Director."

Ten minutes later Julie, emerged from the MI5 headquarters, and quickly climbed into a black Jaguar car, which had a Black Range Rover in front and one behind. Before the motorcade moved off, Julie explained to the driver and the two other men in the car they were going to St Thomas' Hospital near the Thames to see an old colleague; one man in the car spoke into his wrist to brief the two Range Rovers. As the motorcade moved off towards St Thomas' Hospital no one noticed the black BMW merge into the traffic behind them.

En route, the man sitting opposite Julie asked, "Have you got your bullet proof vest on, Director?"

"Of course Davis, bloody hot and uncomfortable as well."

"Cannot take chances Director, not with Sharapova on the prowl, and his favourite shot is two into the heart," said Davis, smiling at the Director.

As they neared the hospital, Davis said, "This is going to be a nightmare, general hospital, hundreds of people coming and going, security nightmare." The motorcade pulled up in front, and David said, "Stay here, we will do a quick sweep of the place before you go in." The director just nodded. Outside, Davis instructed the lead Range Rover to go cover the back of the hospital, while the rear Range Rover stay put and protect the Director.

Davis walked up to the general reception desk and said to the nurse behind the counter, "Come to see a Grace Backer, patient of Doctor Randall."

The nurse checked the computer in front and smiled. "Grace Backer, second floor, room twelve," but before she had chance to say, "but she not under a Doctor Randall's care," the men had left; in fact, she had never heard of a Doctor Randall at St Thomas'.

Davis and the two agents with him swept as they went; one took the stairs and Davis one lift and the other agent the other lift, all arriving on the second floor within minutes of each other. Davis and the two agents went to the second floor nurses' station, and said to the duty nurse, "Grace Backer."

"Sure, follow me," said the nurse. All three followed the nurse to room twelve, and there laying on the bed hooked up with three different monitors lay a comatose Grace Backer.

Davis told the two agents to go cover either end of the corridor stair wells, he would wait by the lift for the director. When Davis got to the lift, he spoke in his wrist: "Coast clear, bring her up."

Tom was standing in room thirteen, his ear piece crackled and he heard the familiar sound of Alice's voice saying, "Package arrived," then it went dead; Tom took the small ear piece out and threw it in the yellow 'contaminated waste' bin. Tom watched the agent go past checking the rooms as he went, casually looking in on the doctor in room thirteen, talking to the elderly man and taking his pulse in there, not giving it a second look; the agent moved on. Tom smiled at the confused man in room thirteen. Tom said, "Sorry, thought you were Mr Carmichael, ready for his knee operation."

"No," said the man, "I am in for gall stones."

Once again Tom smiled and said, "Typical administration, always getting it wrong."

"Tell me about it," said the man, "you are the third doctor I have seen today, and not one of them have a bloody clue." Tom patted the man's hand, and smiling Tom left the room.

Slipping into room twelve, Tom stood behind the door and waited. After receiving the go ahead, Julie left the car and with three agents, proceeded into the hospital, and at the lift all four got in and went to the second floor. Davis met the director as the lift doors opened. "Floor clear, Grace Backer is in room twelve just there on the left."

"Good," said Julie, as she started to walk towards room twelve. David and the agent started to follow. "Wait here," said Julie.

"But Director," said Dave.

"This is private," said Julie.

Davis shrugged. "Keep alert, men," said Davis, as all four stood by the lifts trying to blend in.

As Julie walked into the room, she closed the door behind her, then the strong arms of a man in a white coat held her close; she then felt a sharp pain in her neck. She turned and looked into eyes so familiar. She wondered where she had seen them before. Then the man helped her into the arm chair next to Grace's bed. Julie sat and tried to move and shout, but nothing worked; she was totally paralysed.

Julie stared into the eyes of the man in the white coat; the eyes looked so familiar. Finally she realised that she was looking at an image of her father.

Julie slowly turned and looked at Grace, who by now had sat up in bed and did no longer look like an elderly woman on her dead bed. Grace said, "Hello Julie, so good to see you after all these years." All Julie could do was nod her head. Grace went on, "Let me introduce you to someone," placing her hand on the shoulder of the man sitting on the bed. "This, Julie," said Grace, "is your son. I called him Tom. Tom Backer, or you might know him by another name: Tom Sharapova."

Julie went white as a sheet and she started to slaver from the mouth.

Tom said, "Hello mother," and smiled.

Tom leaned over and said, "After all these years of track-ing down everyone connected to Operation Blackstone, and before they died letting them know why they had to die – but of course you know the reason by now, don't you? And the irony of it all is the last name on the list is my own mother. Don't you think, mother, that fate has finally made us meet on life's own terms?

"Mother, I want you of all people to know my reasons. I had a wonderful life in Russia, the most beautiful perfect wife and daughter. Oh yes, mother, you were a grandmother; how do you feel, knowing you sent your assassins to kill your own granddaughter?" Julie just sat and stared, a small tear trickling down her cheek. "I was going to kill you as well, mother, to end my quest of vengeance, but over the years life has taught me so much, so I have decided as my birth mother I should give you some respect. I want to finally close the chapter on this part of my life, so I have decided to leave you in a world where only you exist, so for the rest of your life the only thing you can do is think about what you have done to your son and his family."

Julie sat shaking her head, and trying to speak; nothing came out and eventually she started to shake. Tom tipped her forward and she fell to the ground. Tom stood behind the door again, and nodded to Grace, who took the emergency cord and pulled hard.

Two nurses and a doctor were the first to react to the alarm going off from room twelve; as they rushed into the room, they looked at Grace still prone on the bed, then looked at the women on the floor who was having some sort of a fit. The doctor placed his head out of the door and screamed, "Trolley, cardiac arrest patient." Davis and the other agents stood and looked confused for a moment, then ran towards room twelve. All they could see was the Director of MI5 prone on the floor violently shaking, having some sort of a fit, with two doctors and a nurse trying to calm her down. The trolley arrived and they placed the director on to it, they then rushed her down to resuscitation, followed by one nurse, one doctor, and seven agents.

Before leaving room twelve Tom kissed Grace, and hugged her. Tom sat on her bed and held her hand. "You could do worse, you know," said Grace.

"Not with you, mother," said a puzzled looking Tom.

"Alice, she loves you, and I know you love her as well. Take a chance on life my son, you have been so long without happiness, you deserve happiness," said Grace, squeezing Tom's hand. "Not too long next time between visits," said Grace.

"Promise," said Tom, smiling, and then he was gone.

Tom walked in the opposite direction from the disappearing trolley; he walked down the stairs and casually out of the hospital, joining a group of doctors and nurses, and blending in, towards the hospital gates. At the gates, Tom crossed the road and took off the white coat, rolled it up in a ball, and threw the white coat in a street bin.

Walking down towards the Thames, Tom pondered on what Grace had just said to him; casually Tom walked towards the pier where a high powered motor boat was waiting. Tom jumped aboard and Alice said, "All OK?"

"Like clockwork," said Tom, "Grace's plan went like a dream."

Alice started to laugh as she pushed the throttle forward and as the boat picked up speed, she steered it towards the middle of the river and out towards the open sea. "Let's hope Duke has managed to complete his task," said Alice to a smiling Tom.

"Never doubt old Duke," said Tom.

A few miles out, she throttled back as she caught up with the slow plodding Red Star; she spotted the side ladder being lowered, and Alice steered towards it. Alice put the boat into idle as she steered it to the step platform, and tied off the boat. Tom immediately jumped from the boat onto the landing; Alice passed Tom the two large duffle bags that Duke had given her previously. "What are these?" asked Tom.

"Duke gave them to me before I left, said you would need two of them."

"Strange," said Tom.

Alice looked at Tom and tried to speak, but her eyes were full of tears. Tom looked into her eyes and felt a pain, in his stomach, he realised he would miss her so much and realised since Natasha, he was ready to love again. Tom held out his hand and said, "Please come with me, Alice."

Alice did not hesitate and took Tom's outstretched hand, and jumped onto the platform where they embraced and kissed for the first time. Alice said, "Hang on," jumped back onto the motor boat and opened all the sea cocks so the boat would slowly sink to the bottom of the sea, and untied the boat so it slowly drifted away from the ship. Both Alice and Tom went up the side ladder of the Red Star.

Halfway up, Tom stopped. Alice said, "Everything OK?"

"These two duffle bags. The old bastard, he knew, he knew I would ask you to come with me."

"As you said, never underestimate old Duke," said a smiling Alice. Hand in hand, they went up the rest of the ladder to a new life and a new future full of hope, love and happiness.

Next morning, one consultant, one doctor and five trainee doctors stood standing beside the bed in room twelve and there, sitting up, was Grace. The consultant checked Grace over and said, "This patient can be discharged, I cannot find anything wrong with her. In fact, for a lady of her age she is in rather good condition," said the consultant, smiling at Grace.

"But she was comatose," said the doctor.

"Well, not now she's not," said the consultant strolling from the room followed by the five trainee doctors. The doctor stood and stared at Grace in disbelief.

"Can you ring this number please, as it's my ride home," said Grace, holding out a piece of paper and smiling.

Epilogue

The new director of MI5 sat opposite the director of MI6 and said, "Is there anything we missed, any loose ends?"

"No, don't think so. Your predecessor is still in a vegetable state after her fit at the hospital, not said a thing, just lays there staring into space. Tom Sharapova has vanished so we presume he has left the UK, no doubt after hearing about Somerville, thought there was no point killing a vegetable."

"The only bit I don't understand," said the new Director of MI5, "is where did this Grace Backer fit into all of this?"

"Not sure, that's the mystery," said the Director of MI6.

"Julie Somerville briefed her team she was going to St Thomas' Hospital to see an old colleague, but Grace Backer had never been in the intelligence services, so we presume Julie Somerville must have got the wrong room but as fate happens, she decided to have her fit at that precise time, and Operation Blackstone, I think we can safely say, is now closed," said the new Director of MI5.

Duke took the offered cup of tea from Grace, and smiled. Duke said, "Thank you my dear. How's the new girl working out?"

"Oh, Sara is fine, not as good as the last one, but she will do," said Grace.

"So pleased," said Duke, sipping his tea.

"Got a postcard from my son the other day."

"Me too."

"Seems to be enjoying life with his new bride."

"Yes," said Duke, "and that reminds me, I could do with a holiday, and I always fancied Belize."

"That's nice, dear," said Grace, closing her eyes and smiling.

Next Book – "The Second Son"